MARKED BY THE DARK LORD

The Twisted Court (Book One)

Riley Storm

COPYRIGHT

©2023
Marked by the Dark Lord
Riley Storm

All Rights Reserved. No part of this book may be reproduced in any form or by any electronic means, without written permission from the author. The sole exception is for the use of brief quotations in a book review. The unauthorized reproduction or distribution of this copyrighted work is illegal.

This book is a work of fiction. Names, characters, places, and incidents are products of the writer's imagination or have been used fictitiously and are not to be construed as real.

All sexual activities depicted occur between consenting characters 18 years or older who are not blood related.

Edited by Olivia Kalb – https://www.oliviakalbediting.com/

Cover Designs by Jacqueline Sweet Covers

CHAPTER ONE

Mila

Twelve years earlier ...
I clutched the well-worn book tightly to my chest as I hurried down the steps and out the library door as fast as my short little legs could carry me. I was careful not to let the loose-hanging flap of rubber on the front of my shoe catch on the steps. The week before, I'd fallen, adding another rip to my pants and earning myself a lashing from Mrs. Johnson's hateful mouth.

I could handle that and the beatings. Those I was used to. I carefully hid a smile as I remembered I was a big girl now. I'd learned how to roll my body to ensure the blows went everywhere instead of just in one place. I was pretty proud of myself for that. It meant I healed even faster than I used to, as long as I pretended as if I was hurt worse than I was.

Yep, I was growing up! Soon, maybe, I would make Mrs. Johnson proud of me. If I kept up my reading, got a job, and brought money home, maybe she wouldn't beat me.

Anyways, it wasn't her words or blows that hurt me. It was when she took away my books. If I was late or spoke out of turn or didn't do something she figured I should've done, then Mrs. Johnson would take away my books.

My stomach growled big time as I scurried down the worn sidewalk, a reminder that I hadn't eaten since yesterday. Punishment for mixing sections of her TV dinner when I'd gotten on my tippy-toes to pull it from the microwave and burned my fingers on the hot plastic, letting it tip too far to one side.

And maybe I'll be able to buy some of my own food, so I can grow up big and strong like the other girls.

The lights turned red, and I paused as cars zoomed down the double road, the lanes separated by large concrete boxes full of half-dead plants. I could remember several years ago when they were full of flowers and fresh greenery, though I didn't know the names of any of the plants.

Now, like me, nobody seemed to care about them.

Just as the little hand started to flash, meaning the light would change soon, a noise I knew all too well made my ten-year-old body go tight.

Girls laughing. Giggling, really, because they were too good to laugh. I turned my head slightly to the side, staring in horror as four of them emerged from the corner store on the other side of the street, heading in the same direction as me. I knew them all by sight and name for a good reason.

No, please, not today. My book!

I clutched the copy of the next Nancy Drew book to my chest as I turned away, hoping to avoid their notice. I'd been looking forward to it for two weeks, ever since I discovered the first book way in the back. What a time I'd had, reading about Nancy and the Tophams, the Turners, and the case of the missing will. What a read! I was hooked.

Now I had the next book, which the library had needed to order, hence my wait. If the girls took it or broke it, I might never be able to repay the fine! And that would mean no more books at all!

Why do they have to be here now? I moaned, a bead of sweat trickling down the back of my neck as the light began to change. I could still make it. They were holding slushies and sipping them gently instead of enjoying them before the heat melted the ice too much. They weren't very smart.

The light turned yellow, and I got ready to

cross quickly. Maybe I would have to take a different way home. If only I could just get going.

"Hello, *Mila*," sneered Sarabeth, the leader of the group, as they crossed to my side just ahead of the light changing.

"Hi," I said, staring straight forward, trying not to draw their attention to the book.

"Nice pants," Margo snickered. "Another hole in them? Are you trying to start a new trend?"

The light *finally* changed, and I hurried forward across the street.

But the girls, with their longer legs, kept up with me, forming a half-circle, trying to force me to cross the street and onto the grounds of the Catholic school they attended. I didn't let them. If I went, they could beat me up without being seen. By staying on the street, maybe someone would stop and help.

Maybe.

"What's this?" Courtney hissed, yanking the book from my stubby arms. I tried to resist, but the blonde was the biggest of them all, and she easily pulled it free of my fingers. "A *book*?"

"Don't act too surprised," I said angrily, still reaching for it. "Not everyone is still learning their ABCs like you."

"Hey, shut up!" Courtney screeched, shoving me while holding the book, bending its precious pages.

I stumbled into the brick wall of a store that sold adult drinks, scraping my elbow off its rough surface with a pained hiss.

All four girls smiled at the sign of weakness, advancing on me.

"Come on, please," I said, backing away. "Not today."

"Why not?" Sarabeth asked. "It's a beautiful day!"

She was right. The sun was up, the birds were singing, not a cloud in the sky. It was a lovely summer day.

For everyone except me.

They hauled me out behind the store and started kicking me and pulling at my clothing. I tried to evade as best I could, but they tore at my shirt, laughing the entire time.

"Hey!" a voice shouted. "What are you doing?"

The second the bullies paused, I took off across the street. They came after me, though, their longer legs meaning catching up to me. I ducked behind some of the buildings into a parking lot, looking for a way out.

Book Shop.

The brightly lit sign on the back of an old converted house called to me. I didn't know there was a bookstore there, or else I would have gone in before. I ran for the entrance, making it inside just before they reached me, but the lock was up high. I jumped for it, trying to slide it shut to stop them. They'd already stolen my library book, but I didn't want them to do anything more.

"Here," a gentle voice said, reaching up and sliding the latch closed just as Sarabeth yanked on the handle. "Let me help you with that."

The door shook as Sarabeth pulled on it in frustration.

"*Go away!*" the lady who'd locked the door shouted, her face against the door as she slapped her hands against it with a *bang*.

Sarabeth and Margo screamed, and the four of them ran away, leaving me alone in my favorite type of place. A bookstore. Not just that—a *used* bookstore.

"Now, how can I help you, little girl?" the woman asked, looking down at me.

She was old, with thin white hair and watery brown eyes that made it look like she was going to cry at any second. Her skin was lumpy and filled with all sorts of big freckles and things I didn't know the name of.

But she had a kind smile, which put me at ease.

"You did by locking them out," I said. "Thank you."

"You're welcome. What brings you in?"

I frowned. Hadn't I just told her? Wasn't it obvious?

"I was running from those girls." I sighed.

Maybe she was too old to notice.

"I saw that. What can I help you with?" she asked again.

"I don't think you can. Unless you have any books on dealing with bullies?"

The woman looked me up and down. "I just might. Come, come along!" she said, stumping urgently toward the interior of her shop and then down a set of stairs. I followed as the hairs on my neck lifted, sending a shiver down my spine with each squeaky step.

What was that place? How had I never seen it before? And why did it seem so ... *old*?

"Come in, come in," the lady laughed as I hesitated outside a thick wooden door with weird symbols carved into it.

I did as I was told. The feeling intensified.

"Wow, these books are so old," I whispered, staring around the room.

"My special collection," she said, watching me closely.

The tingle grew stronger as my eyes landed on one particular book.

"Ah, very good," the old woman whispered. "You feel it, don't you? It calls to you?"

I nodded slowly.

"Then here. Have it."

"I don't have any money," I said, shaking my

head.

"You don't need it. Not from me." The woman suddenly seemed much older but also much younger. "Never from me, daughter. Here."

Before I could ask her what she meant, she shoved the book into my hands, the thick leather cover and bound pages almost more than I could carry. A curious clasp held it shut. I reached up, fiddling with it, but it wouldn't open.

"Is there a key?" I asked.

"Yes," the woman said, smiling.

A wave of sleepiness came over me, and I yawned, closing my eyes …

CHAPTER TWO

Mila

The present ...
I shook my head, clearing away the memory of the weird bookstore as I ran by the building where it had once been, my shoulders hunched against the rain. The old house stood abandoned and empty, boarded up since the very next day. Nobody had ever returned to it. I knew. I'd returned every day for weeks until I realized nobody was coming.

I wanted to ask how I'd gotten home after touching the book, but I couldn't remember. I must have been too excited over the free book and all but ran home in a daze. There was no other explanation.

Now there I was a second time, wishing the shop still existed so that I could run inside to escape my tormentors.

"Get back here, bitch!"

Some people changed as they grew up.

Sarabeth, Margo, Courtney, and Nicole did not. They still hung around in the same neighborhood, still picking on the same helpless little girl when they had a chance. Only now, I was a homeless girl, and they were all either sporting babies on their hips or black eyes over split lips.

I just stank and was cold all the time. I'd take that trade every day. Today, however, I would be the one with a black eye and a split lip. For a little bit, at least, until they healed. I never seemed to suffer for as long as anyone else. My wounds just … healed fast.

Turning down an alley between two buildings, I made a run for it, legs churning as I splashed through puddles on the gravel roadway.

I misjudged one, however, and cried out as I rolled my ankle and fell, hitting the ground hard and scraping my face and arm as I bounced off the stony ground.

"Got you!" Margo cried as she delivered a vicious kick to my midsection.

I gasped and coughed as the air was driven from my lungs, just in time for another foot to hit me in the back.

"Hah! Take that, you stupid bitch," Sarabeth spat from between her busted lips, courtesy of her husband. "That'll teach you to make fun of us."

"Y-you deserve it," I managed to get out as the kicks rained down hard and fast. "Too s-stupid, *urk*, too stupid to leave a man who hits you!"

"You cunt!" the ringleader shrieked, kicking harder.

"My shoes are getting dirty just from kicking her," Courtney said. "When was the last time you showered?"

"What do you think I was doing in the rain just now?" I countered, my arms now over my midsection.

A boot hit my forehead, splitting some skin and rocketing my head back. That one hurt. Warm blood mixed with the cold rain as the women continued to attack me. I went numb, my mind withdrawing from the pain.

There was no point in staying there. My insults fell on deaf ears, and nothing would change. The women would continue to take out the frustrations of their unfulfilling lives on me whenever they could. I didn't need to suffer with them any longer.

Someone yanked my hair back, and a hand slapped my face, but I saw it coming from a mile away and rolled with it, easing the sting. Those women wouldn't faze me.

Courtney kicked me hard in the stomach. I rolled over—just as Margo jumped on me with both feet.

Ribs cracked, and I screamed in pain, suddenly sucked back into reality.

"That got her good," Sarabeth snickered wickedly.

"What's going on down there?" a voice called from the mouth of the alley.

"Shit," Margo hissed.

"Run!" Nicole yelped, bolting down the alley, followed swiftly by the others, except Sarabeth.

"You think you're so much better than us," she sneered, staring down at me.

"I live on the streets. A cardboard box is a pleasant surprise for me," I said through gritted teeth against the pain in my side. "How on earth am I better than you?"

"Exactly," she said, hauling back with her foot. "You're not."

I tried to roll with it, but I was too slow. The boot hit my head, and I saw nothing but darkness.

When I came to, the rain was still coming down, but it was cold now. I was lying in a puddle, soaked to the bone, shivering. I stared up at the black sky, droplets washing my forehead clean of dried blood.

My side still ached, and I would be a mess of bruises everywhere for a day or two. But I would be fine in the end. I always was. Some days I wished I wasn't. Then I wouldn't have to put up with the frequent beatings when they came upon me.

So, leave, a voice whispered in my head.

But I couldn't. Niagara Falls was my home. It had always been my home, and it was still my home. Something about the city called to me. I didn't know how or why because it shouldn't, but it did. I belonged there. Somehow. Some way.

Fighting down shivers, which awoke all sorts of new pain and agony, I got to my feet and struggled my way to the back of the alley. It took me a solid five minutes, but I made it—out of breath and in pain but in one piece.

From there, it took another ten minutes to make it over a few buildings to where I'd lived for several years behind the bakery. There was a little opening in the brick that had once been coal storage or something similar for the ovens. Now it was home, with a curtain for a door and a ten-year-old sleeping bag for a floor.

I'd just finished hauling my battered body inside when someone pulled open the curtain. I placed a hand under the corner of the sleeping blanket, gently caressing the corner of that old book, the one with the leather clasp I'd never been able to open. I still had it all these years later. I couldn't bear to get rid of it. I touched it now, closing my eyes, preparing for the next beating.

Please make it quick. I'm not sure I can handle another one.

"There you are. I was worrying about you."

I looked up to see a young woman with a homely face, thick brown hair, and the kindest set of yellow-brown eyes I had ever seen.

"Lily," I whispered, relieved at the sight of the baker's daughter. "Thank goodness, it's you."

"I don't have anything for you today. I'm sorry. You're late, and Dada is pissed."

"Late?" I frowned, staring at the brick ceiling as if that would tell me the time. "What time is it?"

"Almost ten after four in the morning."

"Damn it." I was late.

The only reason Victor let me stay out behind his bakery was that I cleaned it for him every morning, free of charge. To him, that was worth a few loaves of bread or muffins that weren't good enough to sell to the public.

Lily snuck me a few other items, usually some pastries. It wasn't much, but it was enough that, combined with my begging and trashcan-diving, I could survive. Barely.

"Come on, hurry up," Lily said, helping me to my feet. "If you work fast, you might still be able to stop him."

"Let me go," I said once I was on my feet. "I'll be fine. Don't let him see you helping me. He'll just beat you, too."

"He doesn't …"

I gave her a long look. Lily fell silent, glancing away.

"Just go inside. I'll handle this," I said. "I can take it."

Lily looked ready to protest again, but then she turned and went back inside. I went after her, moving slowly. My sprained ankle was swollen to hell and back and not responding properly. Maybe I'd broken it, too? I wasn't sure. I would have thought the swelling would be on the way down by then from a simple sprain.

"Finally," Victor huffed as I went inside and got my broom, sweeping the detritus from the day before. "You're late."

"Sorry," I muttered. "I'm beat."

Victor didn't understand or appreciate my humor. Then again, I wasn't sure he knew what humor was. The baker was the grumpiest, most unsatisfied person I'd ever met. Nothing was ever good enough for him unless he did it his way. Any suggestions were met with yelling and shouts.

Or beatings.

I swept as fast as I could without missing anything. Victor would notice. As I moved, I felt lightheaded. Whether from the blood loss or something else, I wasn't sure. It probably didn't matter. I swayed on my feet, reaching out to steady myself on the side of an oven that was, thankfully, off.

The first drop slid down the inside of my nose and dripped free before I even realized what was happening. Then another. And another.

"Shit," I cursed, holding a hand against my nose as it began to bleed.

Victor heard my curse and spun to look from where he was preparing whatever it was that baker's prepared.

"You bleeding on my floor? In my bakery?" he shouted, instantly furious as he advanced on me. "You *dare*?"

"I'm sorry! I'll clean it!" I said, backing away. "I promise."

"Outside. Now," Victory snarled, holding up his rolling pin.

I ran for the door, dropping the broom. Victor kicked it, and it bounced off an oven leg before slamming back against his shin. He howled in irritation and followed me outside.

Crying out, I fell as he swung the rolling pin into my backside.

"Useless bitch!" he snarled. "You're done. Don't you dare set foot in my place again. I'll kill you!"

He kicked me for good measure, then spat at me. If it hit, I didn't notice.

A moment later, the door slammed behind me

and locked.

Overhead, thunder rumbled, and the rain, which had stopped at some point, started up again. Weak and feeling defeated, I crawled back into my hovel.

A hovel I would have to leave behind. As I had so many others over the years since I'd run away from Mrs. Johnson's "Home for Hurting Youth." Nobody ever asked if the name was meant to be ironic.

"Fuck them," I moaned as images of my tormentors flashed through my mind. "Fuck them all. I hate them! I hate them *all*. I wish they could live as I do. See what it's like to be me. I wish they could *suffer*."

A red glow filled the inside of my hovel. As I poured my hate, anger, frustration, and more into the interior, the red brightened and began to swirl.

Open me.

I looked around wildly for the source of the voice filling my mind.

Use me.

It was coming from under my sleeping bag.

Open me. Use me.

I pulled the sleeping bag out of the way.

Free me.

The room exploded with red light emanating

from the old book.

Open me. Use me. Open me. Use me.

The words were coming faster now. Repeating their message.

Free me.

The latch holding the thick leather binding closed shook and trembled.

Open me. Use me. Open me. Use me.

Gain your revenge!

Eyes wide, I reached for the book, the simple action igniting pain all over my body from my injuries. But there was no hesitation in my mind.

Fuck everyone who had ever hurt me.

CHAPTER THREE

Mila

The instant my palm touched the leather around the buckle, an image seared into my brain.

It was a man. He was older, though how I knew that I couldn't tell. His face could have been twenty-five or fifty, yet it was neither at the same time. Perhaps it was his eyes. They held a bluish glow, but that could have just been a trick from the book itself. What stood out the most, however, was that his eyes were slanted upward. That, and his pointed ears. His skin was blacker than any human I'd ever seen, like midnight painted onto his body.

The image was only there for a second, but the imprint it left on my mind would allow me to conjure it up with perfect clarity any time I wanted.

What followed was a surge of malevolence the

likes of which I'd never experienced. My skin crawled with the desire to hurt others, to inflict punishment and revenge, all in the name of some twisted form of *justice*.

That, I realized, came from the book itself. As if it were possessed by some entity.

Now I hesitated. Would I unleash that unknown being by using the book? Who was he? Why did I see him now when the book had been unchanged all these years?

If that's all it was, you would have tossed it the day the store disappeared. Yet you kept it. Something compelled you to.

And now it was compelling me to let it free. The voice was rising in my mind.

Use me. Free me. Use me. Free me.

With trembling fingers, I fumbled with the latch. I was tired of always being someone else's punching bag. Of never getting the break that would help me lift myself free of my squalid circumstances. Why couldn't I be the one to change my life? Why not me?

The light from the book pulsed, lighting my tiny hovel with a wicked glow before fading just as swiftly. On. Off. On. Off.

What should I do?

Revenge will be yours!

That was new. The thing knew what I wanted. It knew what I longed for. The scenarios I'd plotted out in my mind, the violence I'd dreamed against Sarabeth and the others.

Revenge.

The book flew open to a page, the letters on the thick paper foreign to my eyes. They were like nothing I'd ever seen before. Flowing and beautiful yet utterly alien.

As I stared at the page, my mouth started moving, and harsh sounds emerged without my consent. I looked at the words in shock and a tiny bit of horror. Could I somehow *read* the language? How was that possible? I'd never even learned more than *bonjour* in French, and it was the second official language of my country! There was no way I could know it.

I tried to back away from the book, to yank my eyes from the pages, but I was held fast, bonds of red *something* circling my wrists, keeping my hands glued to the corners of the book.

Pages turned on their own, and I continued to speak. Chant, really. The words rose and fell with a strange rhythm. The red grew more intense, filling every corner of the little brick alcove until I could see *through* my hands it was so bright. I tried to cry out, but words continued to tumble forth.

Malice and delight danced in my blood, circulating through my arteries and veins, filling my entire body with their eagerness to *hurt.*

An image of Victor, the baker, came to mind unbidden. Then Margo. Nicole. Courtney. And finally, last of all, their ringleader, the one who'd instigated most of my torment since we were young schoolgirls, Sarabeth.

Whatever I was in contact with, it chuckled, the sound a mixture of excitement and promise. They would suffer tonight. All of them. They would suffer my punishments. The things I'd thought about in the back of my mind, that part where humans accepted just how evil they were while knowing they could never actually commit such heinous acts.

Most couldn't, at least.

Whatever I was unleashing, it took those despicable acts of revenge and, with a shriek of excitement, tore itself *free* from the book as I shouted the final word. It hovered in front of me, a ball of swirling, sickening red energy. I stared, and for just a moment, I saw a mysterious face in its depths. It was different from the first image, and it was smiling, revealing a slightly lopsided grin.

Then the thing shot out of my so-called home. Abruptly freed of the book's trance, I turned and poked my head past the ratty sheet just in time to see the mass of red enter the bakery.

A second later, the noises began. Lily's high-pitched shriek and then a deeper, more masculine shout that quickly became a terrified scream.

I flung myself back behind the sheet, pulling my knees to my chest in terror as the screams continued. Rocking back and forth, I looked down at the book. It was dull now. Empty. Yet I still felt a pull to it. Like I couldn't quite let it go.

As I reached for it, the ends snapped upright to close, and the latch locked.

"What have I done?"

The first words in English I'd uttered since opening the book seemed to shake me from my catharsis. I grabbed the sheet and yanked it down to wrap the book so as not to touch the leather exterior. I had no idea if it would make a difference or not, but it seemed prudent.

Then I ditched my hovel and ran for the bakery's back door. The screams were ongoing, though only from Victor's throat. More panicked than terrified, they grew in volume as I flung the door open. Where was Lily? She'd only ever been nice to me. I didn't want to hurt her!

Just as I entered the bakery, the screams stopped.

I stared in shock. Standing in the middle of the bakery was a hovering red body of sorts. It lacked legs, and the arms moved in and out of existence, fading and returning in a wild pattern. I didn't recognize the face, it was different than the one I'd seen in my mind.

The kitchen was a baking disaster. Flour coated every surface, and some sort of liquid batter dripped from the counter. All manner of cooking implements, from rolling pins to cookie cutters, icing tubes, mixers, and more, were scattered around as well.

"You!" I shouted. "Stop!"

It whirled on me with a hiss. "*You wanted this!*" it cackled.

"Wanted *what*?"

The thing cackled and swiftly moved to one side, where it yanked open an oven that had been set to max.

I stared, horrified, as the scent of burning flesh filled the room. Inside the oven, cooked to golden-brown perfection, was Victor. He'd been … baked.

"What have you done?" I gasped.

"*You wanted this. You dreamed of it. Now you get it. Amateur. When I'm done, I will come for you. Then I will be free!*"

Then it was gone, diving straight through a wall. The lights went out at the same time.

I wanted that? I'd dreamed of it in the deepest, darkest corner of my mind, where revenge was sweet, but I'd never truly *wanted* it. It was just a dream to keep me warm on a cold night. Now it was coming true.

I tried not to shiver at its final statement. That

it was coming for me when it was done.

It was going after Sarabeth and the others. It had to be.

Alone in the dark, clutching the book to my chest, I nearly wept.

Except I wasn't alone.

The scuffle of a shoe on the concrete floor alerted me to the fact that someone else was still in there with me. I looked up, afraid it was the red thing coming back to finish me off.

Between two ovens, I saw a terrified little face.

Lily.

"Oh my god, Lily, you're alive!" I exclaimed, a strange wave of relief coming over me. That thing had left her alive.

Except she had to watch and listen to her father get turned into some sort of human pastry puff.

I took a step toward the scared little waif, for once feeling like the protector, but Lily shied back, her eyes wide with fear.

She was scared of me.

Of course she is. I was just talking to the thing that murdered her father. It said that I wanted this. She blames me.

"I'm so sorry," I whispered, guilt descending on me like a guillotine. "Lily, I'm sorry. I didn't mean this. I didn't mean for any of it."

She pushed herself farther back between the

ovens as if I would come for her, too. That bone-deep fear in the eyes of the only person who'd ever been kind to me broke something inside me.

I turned and fled out the back door, clutching the book tight while running across the slick pavement, past my hovel with all my meager belongings, and into the darkness of the night.

I had to get away. Somehow.

CHAPTER FOUR

Korr'ok

My boots clomped as I descended the concrete steps to the exterior basement door. A low jangle emerged from under my heavy cloak, muffled somewhat by the rain, which made the thick material slick and glistening in the muted light of the old bulb illuminating the entrance.

I didn't bother to approach in stealth. I wanted them to know I was coming, that death had reached their door. Pausing on the small landing, I rolled my neck as battle lust started to come over me. Tendons creaked and popped, my hood slipping back as two wickedly sharp horns emerged from the thick mane of black hair covering my head.

Lifting my fist, I banged it against the door in a slow, thunderous rhythm.

Boom.

Boom.

Boom.

"Open up," I growled loud enough that I knew the occupants could hear me.

I doubted they would answer, but if they were willing to oblige and make my life easier, who would I be to argue?

There was no response. I hammered on the solid wood again, the same three knocks. Each time I slammed my gloved hand against the door, it jumped in its frame. There was no way those inside could miss it.

There was still no answer.

"Fine," I said to nobody in particular, shrugging my shoulders to loosen them.

Then I punched the door with movements so swift most would only see a blur, precisely locating each blow near the hinges and lock. Splinters and chunks of wood flew around. The door stood still. Then I reached out and tapped my index finger on it.

With a slow *creeakk*, the door toppled inward.

"Hello," I said with a broad smile as I stepped onto the door and entered the dive bar. A wet mist followed me inside, courtesy of the fog billowing off nearby Niagara Falls during the rainstorm. It was inescapable in the town, a part of life, and I embraced it, feeling it wrap me in a second layer.

"Who the fuck are you?"

There were four of them seated around a table built specifically for poker. They appeared normal, like regular humans. But they weren't.

Even if I hadn't known that ahead of time, the fact that they didn't cower before me was evidence enough. I was near seven feet tall, with skin blacker than the darkest night, and had horns poking up through my hair. Oh, and my eyes always glowed with a red hue.

"I'm bored," I rumbled. "Let us just cut the bullshit, shall we? I would love to be done with this. So, hand over the girl."

"What girl?" it was the same speaker both times. He was thick, but of the type of thick with a layer of fat covering some serious muscle. His plaid button-up stretched tight around his biceps, revealing thick, hairy forearms. A long beard and unruly mop of dark brown hair gave him the air of a lumberjack, which I was sure was what he was going for.

The man next to him and opposite from me, the only one who refused to meet my gaze, wore a slick business suit clearly tailored to hide his rather frail body. No muscle at all.

To my right was a lithe, middle-aged male. He stared back at me, unblinking, while toying with a black bracelet around his right wrist. Blond hair was pulled back in a ponytail. He met my gaze without a quiver.

That one first, I decided mentally.

The one in front slowly turned in his chair. He wore tan pants and a red collared shirt with a lopsided grin that screamed *frat boy*. It was, all in all, a very odd grouping to be playing poker.

Although there were no cards or chips on the table. Clearly, they hadn't been doing that.

I listened to the room, every sound, then sighed as I pinned the leader in his seat with a gaze.

"The girl you have under the table, I can hear her heartbeat," I growled, sniffing the air. "Not to mention, I can smell her fear from here. Give her over, and I won't kill all of you."

Bracelet chuckled at that. "I don't think you realize where you are," he said calmly, snapping his fingers.

Three more people came in from another room, including a woman who glared at me with hatred, entirely out of proportion for what I'd done. I'd never met her before, so she must just be eager to prove herself, I decided.

The room was starting to take on a reddish haze, and I grinned eagerly at what I knew was to come. A fight. Blood would be spilled. Bones would crunch, and death would permeate it all. It was what I lived for. My pants grew tighter as I thought about it, blood boiling, arousing me.

I would need to fuck something once I got

home. Otherwise, I would never sleep. I hadn't had a fight like that in some time. Seven of them. One of me.

It wouldn't be fair, but I didn't care.

"Last chance," I said, reminding myself why I was there. It wasn't just to kill. "Give up the girl, or I'll rip the spine from each of you."

"You aren't welcome here, *Fae*," Bracelet spat. "Leave us."

I chuckled. "You underestimate me."

"Look, he's getting turned on by me," the female laughed.

"Not you," I said coldly, without emotion. "But for your deaths. For the fires of battle. *That* I look forward to. You're just a walking corpse already. I intend to finish the job."

"You're sick," she spat, clearly unnerved.

I threw my head back and laughed to cover my true feelings. "You have no idea, *ghoul*. Now, enough talk."

Having revealed that I knew their secret, the ghouls at the table shot to their feet, mouths unhinging as they revealed extra rows of teeth. Claws jutted from fingertips, and eyeballs grew larger, more haunted as their true forms were unveiled.

I already knew what they looked like, however, and I didn't wait for them to finish. I stepped to the side and, with a grunt, kicked the door across the room.

The three newcomers took the door in their chests, knocked backward, momentarily out of the fight. I went forward, fingers jutting forward. With a gasp and a wet *shlick*, I tore Frat-Boy's spine from his body. Whirling, I slammed the bloody thing into Bracelet's face, forcing him to parry. I then swept his legs out from under him and moved past as he fell.

Frail-Boy from the far side of the table came at me next, fearless in his hideous alternative form. All teeth and claws, he had no fear. Which was great because it made it easy for me to duck and slam my horns into his jaw. I bellowed in battle fury as blood dripped onto me. I flung my head sideways, sending Frail-Boy into Lumberjack.

They went down in a heap. I spun past them, reaching down and plucking the spine from Frail-Boy as I did. I reached Hate-Bitch next—I really needed to get better with naming my enemies, I decided—and grabbed her head in both hands just as she started to get up from under the door.

"Still not a hole worth fucking," I spat as I pulled her head from her body, blood fountaining from around her throat.

She died with a sigh. I turned and hurled her head at Bracelet as he recovered, then threw my hands up in a cheer as I hit him right in the face. "Now kiss!" I crowed as she left a bloody print on his lips.

The other two newcomers died swiftly. That tended to happen, even to ghouls, when you ripped out their spine. Which I did with prejudice.

Then it was just Lumberjack and Bracelet left against me.

"You should have just handed over the girl," I said, glancing at the poker table where the human victim was still hidden.

"Fuck you. Who are you?" Bracelet spat.

"It doesn't matter what my name is," I said, stalking forward, drawing a wickedly sharp dagger from under my cloak. "You should have listened."

Lumberjack came at me first, his jaw yawning wide open. I dodged to the side, dragging my blade through the corner of his mouth and then through his neck. He collapsed, gurgling in pain. Though the wound wasn't mortal to his kind, it was debilitating.

Bracelet came at me next, lunging with faster reflexes than I'd expected. Still nowhere near mine, however. I caught him by the throat, holding him mid-air as I sneered in contempt.

Then I sliced him in half and drove my dagger up through his chin. By then, Lumberjack was staggering back to his feet. He turned to run. Exposing his spine.

A few seconds later, I was standing up from his body, spine dangling from my fist. I breathed deeply, slowing my heart. My cock was practically tearing itself from my pants. I needed to fuck something. Anything. And soon.

I headed for the table, grabbing it and flinging it back. Maybe she would be grateful to her rescuer and—

All thoughts of that died at what I saw under the table. It wasn't a girl like the contract had stated. It was a fucking *child*. No more than seven or eight, not the young adult I'd been led to believe.

My arousal died out in a heartbeat, replaced by simmering anger that threatened to explode then and there.

"You're free now," I said, pulling my hood up quickly to cover my horns.

The young brunette cowered in place, trembling as she stared at me, her doe eyes filled with terror. I bit down a snarl as I realized she was wearing nothing but a nightie. How exposed and vulnerable she must feel.

"Did they hurt you?" I asked, noting a tear in the shoulder of the gown.

"N-no," she said, shaking her head.

I pointed at the ripped clothing. "What about that?"

She clutched at it with a hand, trying to hide

it. There was a hesitation. "I did that," she said finally, looking away.

The lie was obvious. What wasn't was *why* she would tell it.

"Come on," I growled, deciding it wasn't any of my business. "Let's get you home, where you'll be safe."

To my surprise, she recoiled at that suggestion, clutching at the torn shoulder as she did. My eyes narrowed.

"I don't want to go," she said in a tiny voice.

I frowned at the change. She was *more* afraid of the idea of going home than she was of me. I should be a monster to her. She was, after all, *human*. I should be foreign to her. Yet my glowing eyes and all the dead bodies were *less* frightening than going home.

Understanding started to fill me. Her father had been *very* eager to get her home.

"Let's get you back to your father," I said, testing my theory.

The girl cowered deeper into herself.

I nodded. "Did you get kidnapped?" I asked gently. "How did you end up here?"

"I ran away," she said in that tiny childlike voice, answering without hesitation. Too trusting for the world. Far too trusting.

"I thought so," I said gently, crouching down. "Why?"

The only response was a glance at her torn nightgown.

"I thought so," I said again, extending a hand after quickly wiping the blood off on my cloak. "Come with me."

"Where are we going?" she asked nervously.

"To pay your father a visit," I said darkly. "One I don't think he's going to enjoy. Will you be safe with your mother after?"

She girl thought about it, then nodded. I sighed. Far too typical of a story.

"Come, then, let's go."

She rose to her feet and took my hand, following me out of the bar. Sighing as raindrops started to soak her nightie, I pulled her up and under my cloak. There was a brief cry of surprise at the unexpected movement, but then she snuggled in tight.

I shuddered at her touch, ignoring the burning sensation in my chest, and strode up the stairs to the back of the building. We were just crossing a well-lit alley when a figure burst out of it at full speed and slammed into my side, rebounding away.

My entire body lit on fire as we touched, energy coursing through my veins as every hair stood straight up and every nerve ending flared to life.

Twin orbs of blue were briefly visible, the only

things I could see in the dark as they practically lit with their own energy.

I stared, stunned by my body's reaction to a simple touch. I wanted to reach out and grab her. Stop her. *She* would be the solution to the battle lust that was surging anew. Her body, under mine, her cries muffled by my lips or my hand. Moans smothered by my cock as she took it deep into her mouth, accompanied by my groans.

My fingers tightened as I pictured wrapping my hands around her waist, pulling her hard against me as I slammed deep, taking her holes, making them mine. Making *her* mine.

"S-sorry!" she stammered in a voice that sank deep into my soul.

Then she was gone, darting off into the night.

CHAPTER FIVE

Mila

I ran on, through the barely lit parking lot and across the street, through the bus depot lot. I didn't see any of it. My mind was still focused on the baleful red stare of whatever thing had been under that hooded cloak.

It wasn't human. I knew that. It couldn't be. No human had eyes that glowed red like that. And the way the hood bulged at the top in two places. Did it have horns? I wasn't sure. Yet I couldn't stop thinking about it. About him.

The barest of glimpses, of skin darker than the night sky, of muscle and brawn, and two lips, thick and all but calling to me. Even now, the wind whispered to me, urging me to turn back. To give myself to him. His hands, so large against my tiny body, he would control me. Own me. *Make me his.*

I shook my head, trying to clear the insipid

thoughts. Tonight was too much. The book, which I still held to my chest, unable to throw away, and now that? I had to be dreaming. Or unconscious. Perhaps that kick had knocked me out, and it was all just some sort of ultra-realistic dream. That would make sense.

"Yeah. Just a dream," I told myself, splashing through puddles as the rain continued to drum down, soaking me as I darted across the next street and raced in front of a lone car.

The driver slammed on the brakes and thrust his fist at me, his mouth moving, shouting obscenities most likely, but I couldn't hear through the window. I didn't wait, running on, past the train station and gingerly dancing across the tracks. I made my way a few hundred feet before ducking through an opening in a chain link fence on the far side.

Wet, mushy grass and mud greeted me as I headed for the embankment and the wooded glen on the far side. The center of the ATV park was a common place for those of us who lived on the streets. I would find shelter there. Away from whatever had happened at the bakery. One of the regulars would take me in. They always did, even if I had to pay the price.

I slowed, both because of the treacherous footing and a feeling of safety. Logic started to weigh on me.

There's no way all of that actually happened. It

can't be real. Books don't give people power. Nor do huge people in cloaks have red eyes and horns. None of this is real, Mila. Get it together. You're losing your mind.

I reached the edge of the forested area and started climbing. The encampment was in the center of a bowl-like depression concealed from the outside. None of the ATV paths went through it, making it perfect for setting up tents and other makeshift shelters. The owners of the ATV park knew about it, but as long as we stayed in the center and out of the way without harassing the ATVers, they let us stay. For now, the mutual arrangement was working out well.

Halfway up the slope, a wave of insidious energy flowed up and over the lip of the bowl, racing down and over me, freezing me in place. I sank into a crouch, limbs shuddering, despite my best attempts to get them to stop. My hopes of a safe haven suddenly seemed futile.

In the dark at the top of the slope, a purple glow could be seen through the rain. *That* wasn't normal for the area. Maybe flickers of reddish orange from an oil-barrel fire, but not that. That wasn't right.

"Something's very, very wrong in the world tonight," I said to nobody.

A moment later, sounds reached my ears. Grunts so deep they were almost nonvocal, like a lion's rumble, and then shouts.

And screams.

"*Ahh!*" I clamped my hands over my ears, the book still pinned to my chest by my knees as I rocked back and forth. I was hearing Victor's shrieks all over again in my mind and seeing his perfectly baked body in the oven. The scent ...

Motion up ahead caught my attention. Someone was running down the slope within feet of me. I grabbed the book with one arm and lunged for them as they passed, trying to stop them.

The person spun around with a yelp, and for a moment, the purple light let me see their features.

"Ricky?" I hissed, recognizing the bearded former biker. "What the fuck is going on?"

He looked at me but didn't seem to truly *see* me, his gaze going through me.

"M-monsters," he stammered, still backing away down the slope.

"Monsters?" I echoed. "The police? Are they raiding?"

Ricky's eyes were wide, letting me see the whites even in the dark night. "Monsters. Real monsters, Mila. Run. Come on, run. They're coming. Horns. Tusks. Swords. Monsters!"

I stared at him. Tusks? Swords?

"What do they want?" I asked, shifting the book to my other arm as I glanced up the hill.

Ricky trembled as he stared at my chest. I frowned angrily. Now was not the time for that sort of leering. Not that I had tits large enough to ogle anyway, but still. Men. Always a one-track mind.

My thoughts changed as he lifted a hand to point at me.

"T-t-that," he stuttered. "They wanted the book. The book that glowed red."

I looked down to see that the previously unseen red runes on the back cover of the book were glowing a dull red.

"This?" I asked, but Ricky was already running again, heading back the way I'd come.

Looking back at the book, I, too, started down the hill. The noises were getting louder, the grunts more intimidating. Whatever was in there, I wanted no part of it, real monsters or not. I turned and ran, but not back the way I came. If they wanted the book, then I needed to get rid of it fast. Send them far away from me and anyone else.

The river at the base of the falls was just the place. If I hurled it down there, the surging waters would carry it far, far away. Then the nightmare would be over.

Mud splashed everywhere as I ran across the ATV park and its trails. The cold sank into my bones, but I didn't let it stop me. Being cold was better than dealing with whatever sword-wielding tusked monster was behind me, that was for sure!

Eventually, I reached the far side, crawled under another cut section of fence, and into the back of the municipal building lot. The Bridge Offices building was off to my right as I padded past the abandoned maintenance garage and crossed the street. I was close, so close. A short stumble down the embankment, and I would be free of my burden at long last.

I cleared the building, only to see a purple glow in the trees that covered the slope down to the river.

"Shit," I cursed, changing directions, going back the way I'd come, and then heading south to the tracks for a hundred feet. The train bridge was empty at that time of night, and since I wasn't planning on crossing into the United States, I would be just fine.

I hoped.

Heavy footsteps became audible behind me. I didn't even look. I just burst into a sprint, heading onto the bridge where I could safely throw the book away.

Bright light on the far side of the bridge stopped me.

"Of all the—are you fucking kidding me!" I howled as the train worked its way across the bridge from the other side. If I kept running down the tracks, it would hit me.

I didn't stop. Maybe I could use the train to discourage my pursuers. Perhaps I could lose them among the bridge's spans. There was space for me to avoid the oncoming train. It would be risky, but the alternative seemed much worse.

We were out over the embankment but not the river when my pursuer caught me.

A gauntleted hand grabbed my shoulder and spun me around. I stumbled backward, staring up at the horrific beastly visage. Thick horns jutted from the top of the bovine-looking face, while two eyes glowed purple from underneath a leather-looking mask. Big, flat nostrils snorted hot air into the rapidly cooling night. Two tusks jutted upward from the thing's mouth.

Below the neck, the creature was decidedly human. Thick muscles like a bodybuilder covered its frame. Armored and spiked gauntlets wrapped around the hands all the way up to the elbows. More leather covered the rest of the torso. Both hands were currently empty, but a giant sword strapped across its back poked out from behind one shoulder.

"What are you?" I gasped as one of the thick hands wrapped itself around my slim neck and hauled me from my feet.

"We're the Gray Knights," it rumbled in guttural tones as two others like it appeared out of the dark. "And you're coming with us."

CHAPTER SIX

Mila

"Please," I whimpered, "I didn't do anything. Let me go. I don't want to die."

The bull-headed human thing snorted. "That's what they all say. You're not going to die. Though once the Court decides your fate, you might wish you had."

All three of the things chuckled nastily, sending a fresh burst of terror down my spine. It was a miracle I hadn't pissed myself. There was still time, though.

"Hand it over," one of the other Gray Knights growled, extending a hand.

I didn't move.

"The book!" it barked as we walked back down the tracks and into the ATV park, away from the oncoming train. "Now!"

I tried to extend it to him. Maybe I could just

give him the book, and it would all be okay. That was what Ricky said they were after, didn't he? But my arms refused to obey. They clutched the spine so tight my knuckles turned white.

"Drop it!" my original captor ordered, shoving me forward, ripping the shoulder of my shirt as it caught on his hand, nearly leaving me shirtless.

In my desperate attempt to maintain my modesty, I dropped the book. It hit the ground, the clasp popping open as it landed on a particular page. I stared as it glowed red again. Words came to me from the symbols on the page, just as all three of the Gray Knights charged.

I shouted the final word, and with wet *thwumps,* the three beings were suddenly gone. The red glow faded, and I was left alone with half a shirt and no idea what was going on. Without thinking, I grabbed the book and ran toward the embankment down to the Niagara River. I *had* to get rid of that thing. It was evil. It had to be.

More of those things—or maybe the same ones?— charged out of the ATV park and toward me, ordering me to stop. I didn't, of course. That would be silly. Instead, I hopped over the guardrail, lost my footing, and started tumbling down the embankment, curling my body around the book to protect it.

Why I did that when I was going to get rid of it, I didn't know. I just did it. I hit a tree halfway down and saw stars as the air was driven from my lungs. I gasped helplessly, trying to suck down air that refused to come. Dimly, I was aware that the bull-man things were coming after me.

Get up. You have to get up. You can't stay here. If you do, you're dead.

They'd said they wouldn't kill me, but that was before the book had opened and I'd attacked three of them. I had no idea what would happen next, and I didn't want to find out. Get rid of the book, then run away. Make them choose which to go after. It was a shit plan, but it was all I could come up with.

Trying to push aside the agony in my body and the terror of not being able to breathe, I got to my feet and continued down the slope. My lungs slowly recovered, allowing precious oxygen to flood my brain, giving me a slight endorphin rush of relief.

"Halt!"

I looked back, the nearest Gray Knight far closer than I'd hoped as it charged down the slope with a surefootedness that was infuriating. With its size and the rain, it should have been unwieldy as all hell. Not so, apparently.

I kept going, the trees stopping me from picking up too much speed as I slammed into them. I would be covered in bruises, but those would fade quickly. They always did. Ever since

I was a child, I'd healed from beatings with uncharacteristic swiftness.

It should have been a blessing. Unfortunately, it just meant I got beaten twice as often. Ah, the irony.

Clearing the last of the trees, the raging waters of the Niagara River greeted me. Though they were normally much calmer and more tepid that far from the Falls, the rain was giving them extra energy.

My plan suddenly changed. I could lose the Knights *in* the river. Then I wouldn't have to give up the book. Maybe I could learn what it was and what it could do. How to use its powers to do some good. Maybe.

All I had to do was survive the rapids-like conditions of the water. At least it was the middle of summer, and despite the cool rains, the water wouldn't be instantly deadly.

Probably.

I started toward the edge of the water, a new plan formed and set in my mind. But halfway there, I stumbled to a halt as soft purple light shone in front of me in an oval shape. Gray Knights emerged from within, fanning out to either side of me as more emerged from the slope behind me.

I was trapped.

"What the fuck is going on?" I all but whined,

frustration and fear swirling around inside me, vying for dominance.

"Mila Florence."

I stiffened at the new voice. It came from the throat of a human. A regular human with a normal head and an average-sized body. None of the ridiculous super-inflated muscles of the Gray Knights. He strode toward me, carrying a staff and dressed all in loose gray clothing.

"It's just Mila," I said through clenched teeth, trying to keep them from chattering in fear. How the hell did they know my name?

"Very well, *Mila*," the man said as he approached.

Somewhere between an old thirty and a young fifty, he sported a bald head and no facial hair. Yellow-tinged eyes stared back at me, unafraid of my gaze. Why should he be afraid anyway, given all the hired help he'd sent after me?

"Who are you?" I asked. "I've never seen you around."

The man sniffed with a disdain that seemed to come easily to him. "I prefer not to sully myself by leaving The Place Behind. The mortal realm is not suitable for someone of my … stature."

My eyebrows rose. "You're speaking words but not making any sense."

"Yes, I get that a lot from your kind."

"I don't know if you know what a mirror is or

not, but you and I, we're the same. Well, other than the fact that you both *have* a dick and *are* a dick. But let's not get too pedantic, shall we?"

"My, my, such big words for a gutter rat," he spat with aristocratic arrogance.

"The library is free," I said calmly. "Public resources and all. You should try it. Might bring you down a notch or two."

The man's narrow, axe-like face tightened in anger.

"You are under arrest," he said stiffly. "For the unauthorized use of magic and by an unlicensed practitioner at that. Two very serious charges. You are to come with us to The Place Behind for trial at the Court."

I stared at him, then the bull-thing next to him. "Can you tell him to speak plainly, please?"

The man sighed. "You used magic. Without permission. That makes you naughty. We catch and punish naughty people. Is that simple enough for your pathetic human brain?"

I glared at him, then looked down at the book.

Come on, baby, help me one more time.

The book started to glow red, and I reached for the clasp.

"Ha," I hissed softly, eager to use *more* magic on the egotistical twatwaffle.

Something shuffled behind me, and the world went black.

***

When I came around, I was being carried by four of the Gray Knights, each holding a limb. My clothing was ripped and torn.

"Let's go," the gray-clad man ordered, and we stepped toward the river's edge and the portal.

Clearly, I hadn't been out long. Perhaps the jolt of being picked up had brought me around.

I started to speak but then fell silent as my eyes landed on the gray man's right hand. It was curled around the book. *My* book. I wanted to reach for it, to grab it and take it from him.

Then we went through the purple oval and emerged on the other side.

"Hey," I said in sudden recognition. "I know where we are. We're behind the Falls!"

I'd taken the tour many times over the years. Niagara Falls had always held a special fascination for me. I could watch water tumble over its edge for hours on end and had done so frequently. But it was *behind* the Falls that had always called to me for some reason. Being back there, I felt almost at peace, in a weird way. Like I was close to where I belonged.

Now I was scared shitless.

"Hush," the gray man said, waving his hand at one of the walls.

I gasped as the solid rock wall wavered, then disappeared, illuminating a tunnel. "No *way*."

The gray man glared at me. I gave it right back, but it slid off him with ease.

We entered the tunnel and followed it around a corner. Behind us, the fake wall shimmered back into place once the last of the Gray Knights was through.

But my attention didn't last long on that fact. Because, moments later, we emerged from the tunnel onto a platform high above a yellow-tan landscape.

Below us was a city of stone.

"Where the fuck am I?"

The gray man just chuckled ominously.

CHAPTER SEVEN

Korr'ok

It was nearing five in the morning by the time we reached the girl's home. I didn't know her name. I didn't want to. Names held a certain sort of power in my world. I preferred to stay anonymous. Very few knew my true name. Most only knew the alias I'd adopted since leaving my home.

"You should be happier to be home," I remarked as we walked up the driveway, my fingers wrapped firmly around her tiny wrist. It would be so easy to break, but I held my strength in check. She wasn't my enemy. If anything, I pitied her.

"Why?"

"Because your mother loves you. They hired me to rescue you from those creatures." My voice was flat. I understood the concept of love. Of family. But only in an intellectual way.

"Goools," she said, not quite properly pronouncing them. "I know them."

"Do you now?" I rumbled, looking down at her.

Twin sparks of blue flame stared back up at me from a face of a woman, not a girl. They burned into me so brightly that I stumbled backward with a hiss.

"Are you okay?"

Blinking, I rid myself of the vision of the woman from the alleyway. Why was she in my mind? And why was my blood burning and rushing between my legs? I turned to look back out over the very modest estate toward the city beyond as if I could somehow see her out there. As if she would be waiting for me.

"Fine," I responded, snatching the girl's wrist before she could dart off. Again.

I'd made that mistake shortly after extracting her. She'd run off, wasting only a few minutes but proving that children were an irritant all the same. That was why they were one of my rules.

No Gods. No Innocents. And most of all: No. Children.

My rules, however, were about those I would not kill. In my world of magic and malice, children were few and far between. They rarely survived the appetites of creatures such as ghouls long enough to be rescued. Let alone any of the stronger beings that lurked in the shadows. It was a miracle this one had been alive, let alone untouched.

Almost like she wasn't in danger ...

I looked down at her torn nightgown once again. The blood surged from my groin to my biceps. I wasn't on anyone's "good" list. Far from it. I was a cold-blooded killer. Enough money and I would kill anyone as long as it didn't violate my rules.

But the idea of a father and his daughter ...

With a snarl, I started marching us up to the house again, putting thoughts of the blue-eyed woman and good intentions out of my head. I had a payday waiting, and I intended to secure it.

My thick, meaty fist hammered on the door, shaking the house to its foundations.

Too many distractions tonight. I needed to return to The Place Behind and clear my mind. A good fight with Dachor would probably do the trick. Then a steak and some rest. Being on Earth, with all its scents and busyness, was always taxing. It intrigued me to no end, but prolonged periods could be overwhelming.

The door opened.

I reared in surprise as a pair of bright blue eyes poked out from the darkness within, too bright and round to be natural.

Surging forward, I wrapped a fist around their neck, hoisting them from their feet.

"What is this sorcery?" I snarled, easily lifting the large human until they were at my eye level.

"That will be enough, Rokk," another voice said from within the shadowy interiors.

My eyes focused on the speaker. It was my employer, Abhed. His short, rotund body was hidden under a plush red robe, the type worn at night, not by a mage, though I knew he had some dabblings in magic. His house was positively infested with magical residue, though it was more like layers of very thin varnish instead of a thick coat of primer.

"Please put my majordomo down," Abhed repeated, then frowned when I simply opened my hand and did as requested. "What has gotten into you, Rokk? You were so professional upon first meeting. Now you come, nearly break my door in, and almost kill one of my best servants?"

"I brought your daughter back," I said, dragging the girl into the house to present her. "Alive and unharmed."

My lips curled upward at that. I always negotiated a large bonus for "unharmed" when it came to ghouls. It was unlikely, but in the event I got to them fast enough, I deserved to get paid. It was one of those times.

"Yes, I can see that, thank you," Abhed said, smiling at his daughter.

She leaned slightly away, putting part of my

bulk between him and her. I didn't shift away, nor did I move to intervene. Theirs was not my business to be involved in. But I did note it *very* odd that Abhed did not make any move toward her, nor did he seem overly happy. Simply satisfied, like a businessman making a deal.

"*Darla!*"

I stiffened as a shape rushed out of a side passage, past the unconscious majordomo—who, I'd noticed, had green eyes. Not blue.

Why am I seeing this woman everywhere? Who is she to me? Have I met her before?

Someone with eyes that bright seemed like an easy face to remember, but I had lived for a long time, so it was hard to be sure.

The mother embraced the daughter, then, with a nervous glance up at me, scurried them both off to the side, out of my way. I noted that they also specifically did not go toward Abhed.

I pushed that thought away. It wasn't my business.

"There is the matter of payment," I said, extending a hand.

Abhed seemed flustered, and for a moment, I thought he would try to renege. I almost wanted him to. That would give me an excuse to ... cut loose. But he reached into the folds of his robe and removed a little sack. I snatched it from his sausage-like fingers, so short and stumpy, and examined the contents.

The gold coins jingled pleasantly to my ear as I weighed them in my hand. It felt appropriate, though I would count it once I got home.

"Tell me," I said, pocketing the payment. "How did the ghouls get her?"

"What?" Abhed looked past me at the door, his point obvious.

"The girl. Your daughter," I said. "How did they get her? They didn't harm her, which is uncommon. She should have been little more than body parts by the time I arrived."

"She was out of the home," Abhed said slowly.

"School?"

The two women were looking nervously back and forth between Abhed and me now. I could tell I was treading close to an uncomfortable subject.

"Yes," Abhed said. "She was on her way home from school."

"Interesting," I mused. "You sent her to school in a nightgown? A nightgown that was ripped before she got there?"

"It is time you should leave," Abhed said angrily, pointing at the door. "Our deal is concluded. You are no longer welcome here."

I felt his magic wash over me as he said that. I snorted, reaching out to catch the spell in a palm, toying with it. Abhed's eyes went wide at the casual display of power.

"I am not some vampire to obey your welcome into your home," I snarled, stepping closer to him. "Nor am I some underling who you are free to use your pathetic magic on without consequence."

Abhed gulped.

"You are a bad man, Abhed," I said in a calm conversational voice as I advanced on him. "Little girls? That's despicable."

"I don't have to suffer this," the seedy man snapped, reaching into his robe, the red cloth rumpling. "Not in my own house."

In the blink of an eye, I was in front of him, my hand closing over his wrist, keeping it pinned inside his robe.

"I don't think you're the one suffering," I said, glancing at the wife and daughter.

The wife was shielding the daughter, but her eyes knew what doing that would get her.

"Hitting your wife?" I sighed.

Don't do this. Don't get involved.

It was too late for that. I generally didn't care what people did to one another. But that was adult to adult. This ... this was different.

"You!" I barked at the wife.

"Y-yes?" she stammered, clearly terrified.

"Do you have access to his money, or some

money, anything? Are you in his will?"

"Yes," she said quietly.

"Good. You're in charge now. This is all yours. I suggest you sell it and move far away."

Abhed stiffened, trying uselessly to break my grip on him so he could escape. "What about me?"

I hauled him from the ground and used his back as a battering ram to blow open the front door as I stepped over the still-unconscious majordomo.

"You," I said, grinning and baring my teeth, "are going to spend some time with others just like you. You're coming with me to The Place Behind. The Court will judge you for your crimes."

Abhed's screams echoed into the night.

CHAPTER EIGHT

Mila

I stared down at the city of stone, speechless. We were behind the Falls. That should mean underground. Instead, a sun that was far too yellow to be normal shone down upon us. The day was bright and clear, and the light blazed, but it was actually rather cool. Everything had a mild sepia look, like a cheap movie trying to convince you it was filmed in Mexico. Except it was real and not a filter.

"Let's get moving," the man in gray ordered the brutes carrying me.

We started walking again, my body swaying in their grip as I hung upside down. My head was free, however, and I craned it around, trying to figure out what was happening.

The city of stone below us was busy. Figures moved through it as we walked down the ramp from the cliffs that lined the side of it. It was through those cliffs that we'd emerged.

I gaped as I saw all manner of creatures moving around. From short creatures that had to be dwarves to things of glitter and tentacle that were pure mystery, they came in all shapes and sizes. I saw a centaur trot by at one point.

"You're minotaurs!" I gasped, staring back at my captors and their bull heads on human bodies, understanding starting to sink in.

As I looked at them—none responded—my eyes were drawn back up the ramp as someone else came out of the crack in the cliffs. They had to duck slightly to fit, and as they stood up, a black cloak slid free of their head.

I gasped. Those eyes! They glowed red, just like the thing I'd slammed into earlier in the night. He shrugged back the entire cloak, seeming to revel in the yellow light as it caressed his inky black skin and caused his onyx hair to shimmer.

Pearly white teeth revealed themselves as he stared down at me, and our eyes locked. He dragged someone after him, but I had no time for that. My focus was on the monster. Horns jutted up from his head, long and wickedly sharp looking, matching the malevolent glow of his eyes.

There was no doubt he wasn't human, not entirely, but he had the facial features of an extremely handsome man, and his pecs were thick and powerful, probably bigger than my tits. Shoulders as wide as a truck held the cloak back while one of his biceps flexed, dragging the other person along with him as he descended after us.

I was half-naked and being carried by four bull-men, but I couldn't shake the thrill of excitement that ran through my body upon seeing him again. The eerie red of his eyes under his hood had never fully left my mind during my flight. I'd written it off as a hallucination, something my panicked mind had come up with.

But there he was, in the light of day, such as it was, and I was still seeing him.

He seemed to be seeing me, too. My eyes traveled down his torso, noting how his shirt clung to his body. I also noted the tightness of his pants, particularly around his cock. Was that normal, or was his bulge growing as he watched me? I thought it was the latter, and my clit tingled slightly in response.

We halted at the bottom of the ramp, and I watched as he approached, dragging a short, round human behind him. At least, the man appeared human. After the past hour, I wasn't about to assume anything.

A tall, slim figure covered in fur with a giant sloped brow strode by, momentarily occluding my view.

Bigfoot?

When it passed, Red-Eyes was closer. I could practically see his cock against his pants now.

Knowing that I was making him hard had a reflexive action on me. I bit down as my nipples grew hard and warmth circled my clit, the blood swelling my mound against my desires. The man had *horns* and skin far darker than any human. It seemed to swallow the light.

He was evil. There were dark stains on parts of his outfit. Was that blood?

"Who is this?" he growled as he approached, addressing his question to the man in gray. "Why have you brought her here?"

"Lord Rokk," the man said with clear respect and perhaps a bit of fear as he turned to see the speaker. "She is under arrest for the unauthorized use of magic."

I barely heard the reply. *Lord* Rokk? The monster, the very *manly* monster, was a lord of this place? That meant he was in charge. Perhaps he could help me.

"Please," I begged. "Help me. Release me. I didn't know what I was doing. I didn't mean to. I don't even know where I am. I—"

My throat closed as Rokk leaned closer to me, his nostrils flaring wide, sucking all moisture from my mouth. Even breathing was hard. The hairs on my body stood on end as he ran his eyes up and down my body, his gaze lingering on certain intimate places as if he could see past the flimsy clothes that covered me.

"Lots of bruises," Lord Rokk remarked.

"Mostly self-inflicted."

Rokk's eyebrow rose.

"You don't care about things like bruises when you're running for your life," I said sullenly. "I fell down a hill. There were a lot of trees. Do the math."

"And this?" Rokk asked, suddenly grabbing my chin and wrenching my head to the side. "That looks like a boot."

"None of your business," I hissed in a mixture of pain and defiance, trying to ignore the surge of heat where his fingers touched my jaw. It felt good.

Too good.

I shook my head free. The monster withdrew his hand, but not before I caught him looking at his fingers briefly. Had he felt it, too? What was going on?

"I can smell the magic on you," he said disdainfully, suddenly standing up tall, any hint of a connection gone. Hatred turned his eyes baleful. "Despicable. Forbidden without permission. A scrawny thing like you would never get permission, either. It's the Court for you."

I shivered. Everyone kept talking about the Court. What was it? Why was it so bad?

"At least you'll have company," Lord Rokk

grunted as he stormed off. "Fitting company, too."

His captive's eyes went wide as he was dragged behind the giant monster with red eyes and a magnificent ass.

Stop it, Mila. Get yourself together. You're going to die here. Stop thinking about what his cock looks like!

The gray man gestured at the minotaurs holding me, and our little procession headed down a large boulevard toward a giant building of black stone that towered over everything around it.

"Let me guess," I said as my voice recovered from Rokk's close presence. "We're going to the evil tower thing, aren't we?"

"You can drop the act," the man in gray grunted. "It's getting annoying."

"What act? I have no idea where I am or why or who any of you are. If I was acting, then I should be in movies winning Oscars, don't you think?"

One of the minotaurs cuffed me across the side of the head at a gesture from the man in gray. I groaned, seeing stars for a brief second.

"*Ow*," I hissed.

Gray-Man sighed. "You are in The Place Behind. You are on your way to the Court to be judged for your crimes. What is not clear about that?"

"Oh, I don't know, everything?" I said, dripping sarcasm.

"If you knew nothing, then you wouldn't have been able to defeat three Gray Knights with your magic," he countered. "So, either you're lying and pretending you're dumb, hoping we'll go softer on you, or you somehow used stronger magic without knowing. What do *you* think I'm going to assume is the case?"

"I don't know what I was doing," I said softly. "It was the book."

I frowned as I mentioned the book, realizing that, ever since Rokk appeared, I hadn't longed for it to be back in my hands. Even now, I was still focused on the midnight monster too much to want it.

Had he somehow broken my hold on the thing? I'd kept it with me for twelve years. The only possession I'd never thrown away or tried to sell, including my own body. Was I free of it at last?

Too little, too late, though. The damage is already done.

"Enough of your excuses," the man said before whispering a word. His staff tip glowed purple for a moment.

Nothing happened. I opened my mouth to laugh and insult him.

No sound came out.

My eyes widened in horror as he chuckled and gestured for my captors to continue bringing me toward the black tower that rose above all buildings near it. A wall surrounded it, thick of stone, just as dark as the rest. Compared to the ivory-colored buildings everywhere else, it was impossible to avoid the ominous undertones.

Without warning, the *gong* of bells rolled out over the city, emanating from the heart of the tower complex.

"Ah," Gray-Man said. "How fitting."

I stared at him, frowning, trying to ask what he meant. My mouth worked, but no sound came out at all. He must have been able to read my lips, however.

"You've arrived at the perfect time," he said. "Court is in session."

The minotaurs carried me through the gate. All the while, I screamed in silence.

CHAPTER NINE

Korr'ok

I shouldered my way through the thick cloth and into the nearest building the moment I was out of sight of the human woman. Abhed yelped as he came along unwillingly, the cry only magnifying when he hit the stone wall that I tossed him up against.

My breathing came in deep, ragged breaths as I tried to regain my composure. The surge of heat and insatiable lust that consumed me like a raging inferno refused to die. It was only fanned by the blue flames I saw deep in her eyes, a vision I could not deny, could not cast aside.

"A-are you okay?" Abhed squeaked.

With a snarl that shook the dust from the ceiling, I snatched him up in one giant hand, his bones rattling as I thrust my face inches from his. "I am *fine*," I growled. "And if you speak up again, I will squeeze my hand until your head pops off. Is that understood?"

Abhed opened his mouth, thought better of it, and closed it, then nodded quickly.

"Hnngh," I grunted, dropping him unceremoniously to the ground.

In the distance, deep gongs sounded as the bells of the Court rang, signaling to any who resided in The Place Behind that the Court was soon to be in session.

Which was where I had to be. Not there, in a building with a cock I couldn't get to deflate, all because of a rogue human woman.

"Useless," I snapped at the air, striding across the room. "She's nothing. Nobody. I would break her simply by breathing."

My breathing calmed somewhat but refused to settle fully. The anger that had burned as bright as the desire for the strange woman continued to rumble inside me, a volcanic temper ready to go off with the slightest provocation. How *dare* a human affect me like that? She had no right.

The gongs continued, reminding me of the duty I'd volunteered to uphold. I was no shirker. Regardless of what was happening inside me, I would take my place on the Jury as if it were any other day.

"Come on," I hissed, snatching Abhed and storming from the building.

At some point, the tenants who'd run

cowering when I'd entered would re-emerge, but they were the least of my worries. I was well-known in The Place Behind for a reason.

I stomped down the streets, various creatures taking care to move from my path. One hapless wood elf was a little too slow and took a hip to the shoulder for their troubles. They started to protest but quieted once they realized who it was that had hit them.

I snorted as they danced out of the way, long brown hair floating effortlessly behind them.

Damn Hippies.

Whether or not the creature heard my thought, something caused it to look back at me.

I reared back, nearly wrenching Abhed's arm from his body as the elf's blue eyes stared back at me.

It blinked and looked down in terror. When it glanced back up, the usual large amber cat eyes of the elves were all that I saw.

"Damn that woman," I snarled, continuing on, well aware that my cock was hard and pushing against my pants.

How dare she arouse me like this!

Yet the memory of her did. The way she'd been almost spread-eagled by the minotaurs as they carried her. Much of her body exposed through the ripped clothing. Vulnerable.

That must be it. She couldn't fight back. Not that

they ever do, anyway. They all come to me willingly. They want to experience it. She would, too.

Not that I would ever mate with a human. I would break them. I was a Sidhe, one of the Lords of the Fae, not that anyone knew my true heritage here, far from Faerie itself. But many women who came to me were already stronger than humans, and my touch was rough on them.

A human stood no chance, especially one as small as her. So tiny and frail. She would need protection from the likes of me. I wasn't her savior. I was her doom.

I was still thinking about her body when I entered the gates of the black tower. I didn't hurry. I never hurried.

Abhed scrambled to keep up as I walked the warren of hallways, forced to skip along almost sideways, given my bulk and my hold on his arm. I didn't care. The pedophile rapist deserved far more than some discomfort.

A smile split my lips as I thought of the punishment he was going to get.

"Put him in a cell," I barked as I reached the holding cell area.

"Of course, Lord Rokk!" cried the gnome sitting at the desk, gesturing with his pen at a pair of minotaurs standing around idly. "Charges?"

"Pedophilia. Rape."

The gnome paused, pen hovering over paper. "Is that all, Lord Rokk? We don't normally deal with …"

"You question me?" I growled, tilting my head downward.

"No, of course not! Just wanted to make sure I got it correct, My Lord. Wouldn't want an error, no, sir!"

"That's what I thought," I grunted. "He also lied to a member of the Jury and had me assassinate a group of ghouls who he said kidnapped his daughter. So, that's premeditated murder of a magical being, times four. Wait. Seven. There were seven in total. That ought to do."

The gnome grinned as he scribbled. "Oh, yes, the Court will judge him for sure."

I looked at Abhed as he was dragged down the corridor and basked in the sheer terror flowing off him.

Farther down the hallway, a small head poked out from between some bars. Blue eyes stared at me.

"Damn woman," I hissed, turning away, ignoring the curious look on the gnome's face as I stormed from the area and up to the courtroom.

"Jury Member Rokk," a deep voice echoed from everywhere and nowhere all at once as I entered the room from a side door, striding to a group of thirteen high-backed chairs carved from blackened bones. "How nice of you to join us."

I settled my ass onto the plush red velvet seat cushion and rested both forearms on the rests before looking up at the speaker. Yellow-orange eyes with vertical pupils the size of a sword stared back at me from the giant crimson dragon who sat curled on a perch at the front of the room.

Under his perch, in giant letters, was a sign that simply read "Judge."

"Hello, Dannorax," I said slowly, letting the dragon know I wasn't intimidated.

The huge, scaled lizard snorted, ten-foot-long jets of flame erupting from each nostril on the end of his massive snout. Magic abruptly pressed down on me, pinning me firmly to the seat.

I sighed but didn't fight back. Dannorax was the Judge of the Court in The Place Behind, and he made sure everyone knew it.

"*Judge* Dannorax," I said after several moments of magical pressure, again not reacting immediately. I hated playing his games, and while I wasn't outright afraid of him, there were a few creatures in the world I wouldn't tangle with willingly. Gods were first. The capricious beings were troublesomely powerful. Dragons were probably next on the list. Insanely strong, a straight-up fight against one was a death sentence most of the time. But they had weaknesses, including their arrogance, and Dannorax was a prime example of that.

The pressure lessened as I addressed him properly, and the dragon settled back onto his perch. Two other members of the Jury were not yet present, including Dachor, whom I hoped to arrange a sparring session with after we adjourned our current session.

I had far too much rage built up over the strange human woman to be able to relax without some bloodshed. Sitting on the Jury was fun, and I enjoyed the punishments meted out, especially when I got to be the one doing them, but it so rarely resulted in the type of straight-up fistfights that let me work out my rage on someone.

Dachor was perfect for that sort of thing.

"All present members are accounted for," Dannorax said without addressing me directly.

I stifled a frown. What was Dachor up to that he wouldn't be present? I wondered. And how would I blow off some steam now?

"The Court is now in session," Dannorax rumbled. "Bring forth the first defendant."

A grin spread across my face as Abhed was hauled out from behind a door on the other side of the room. His face was bruised, and one arm hung awkwardly.

Watching him suffer some more would be a

start to improving my mood, at least.

CHAPTER TEN

Mila

I stumbled forward through the opening in the bars, courtesy of a "gentle" push from my guards.

"Some red-carpet treatment *this* is," I huffed, the darkened room certainly no Ritz-Carlton. Not that I'd ever stayed in one, but the phrase seemed appropriate.

I froze, spinning back as the door *clanked* close in my face. "I can speak again!"

"How joyous," the jailor muttered in a harsh voice that did *not* sound like it should be coming from a bull's mouth. "For you."

"You know it," I said with a grin, having absolutely no idea why I was feeling defiant. My circumstances certainly did not warrant it. I was inside a jail cell, in some weird place that shouldn't exist. I had no idea how to get home or what future awaited me at this "court."

"Hey, come back!" I called as the guards moved on, back out of the prison block, leaving me alone. "I want my phone call."

There was no response. I watched, and once they left my field of view, I listened until I could no longer hear their footsteps. Silence reigned, and I abruptly felt every inch of my five-foot-three frame. Which was to say, small and scared.

The chill of the cell sank in through my ripped clothing and latched onto my bones. Its weight was oppressive, weighing me down, making every step feel like it took twice as much effort. I slumped forward against the bars, hands above my head, fingers wrapped around the vertical supports. The metal was cool to the touch.

"I take that as no phone call, then," I said to the air. "Telegram, maybe? How the hell do people communicate here? Wherever the hell 'here' is? Ugh. I'd like to wake up now. This dream officially sucks."

"Ain't no dream, that's for sure."

I whirled, my heart thundering in my chest as a feminine voice spoke from somewhere behind me. Staring at the cell, I tried to find the speaker. But it was empty. Like it had been when I'd entered. The tiny bunk beds running along the left-hand wall were both devoid of occupants. As was the desk and the toilet. There was quite literally nowhere else to *be*.

"Are you spying on me?" I hissed, staring at the

ceiling, looking for cameras and a microphone or something. "Answer me!"

"Nobody spyin' on you, darling, trust me."

I stiffened as the voice again came from thin air, but that time, I could better locate the sound. It *seemed* to be coming from the bottom bed. Except there was no one—

Wait a second.

The longer I stared at the bed in the deep shadows of the cell, the more I could detect some oddities. For one, the pillow and bedcover —calling it a comforter or blanket would be far too generous—were indented as if someone were lying on it. Second, I could almost make out the outline of *something* on the bed. It was vague, more like one section seemed a tad too blurry compared to the rest, but it was hard to see.

"Who said that?" I called softly, staring hard at that spot, wishing there were lights in the cell, not just the crappy lights in the hallway outside. "Show yourself!"

A hefty sigh preceded twin dots of red appearing over the pillow as eyelids slid back. I stifled a gasp. Unlike Lord Rokk, whose eyes were big and glowing, hers were more like pinpricks of solid red.

The eyes moved as the owner sat up. I could sort of see it happening. The color-blending effect was slower than the movements.

"What the fuck?"

"What are you staring at?" the thing growled somewhat angrily, getting up from the bed and taking a step in my direction.

The bars rattled as I slammed back against them, forced to look upward as usual, though only by a few inches. At least she wasn't a giant ... whatever she was.

"Relax," the soft honeyed accent said, my eyes picking up a hint of a mouth moving as she spoke. "I ain't gonna hurt you."

"Hardly reassuring from a ghost," I said, shocked I managed to get it out without stammering.

"Ghost? I ain't a ghost. Sheesh."

"What are you then? 'Cause you're basically invisible. That makes you a ghost."

The eyes peered down at me, somehow able to do so condescendingly, even though I couldn't see the rest of their features.

"Ghosts are mindless things, and they most definitely are *not* invisible. Trust me, that ain't me."

"Oh. Sorry? What are you, then?"

"Me? A wraith. Come now. We're not *that* rare. How can you not know?"

I shook my head. A wraith? "Lady, wraith person, whoever, I don't know *anything*. I've never heard of any of this. I don't even know what 'this' is, dammit!"

The wraith stood still as I slumped to the floor, hope seeping out of my body and sinking into the stone below my backside as the weight of it all began to take hold.

"Oh, get up. You're just in jail. It's not like you're on the Tartarus Line or something."

I looked up. The confusion must have been fully evident because the wraith-thing sighed and sat on the edge of the bed near me.

"That would be where the people sentenced to death go. Tell me, what *do* you know, human?"

"Mila."

"What's that?"

"My name is Mila. I know that," I said. "That's about it, honestly."

"Hoo, dear. Tell me everything."

"There's not much to tell," I said. "There was a weird old book. I opened it, read some words, red light appeared, and then those minotaur things, the Gray Knights. They appeared from a huge purple egg in the middle of the air and came after me. Then I was brought here."

I purposefully left out Lord Rokk, though I wasn't sure why.

"I see. Did they tell you anything?"

"That I was under arrest for unauthorized use of magic as an unlicensed user," I quoted.

"Whatever *that* means. It's not like magic is real."

The wraith was quiet. "Do I look 'not real' to you, hun? What about this place? Is it not real, too? All this fake, just to prank you, hmm? Naw, I dun' think so."

"I ..."

"You'd better get used to it quick. You're gonna be going before the Court with that list of charges. You need your wits about you. A pretty thing like you ... that's a bad time."

"Why? What is this place? Where am I? Under Niagara Falls?"

The wraith started to lie back down. "You really are new. The whole thing is called 'The Place Behind', but most of us just call it The Crack."

"Huh?"

"Behind? Your behind is your ass? And you emerge from a crack in the cliffs? Aka, your asscra—"

"Okay, I get it now," I said, waving a hand.

"More specifically, you are currently in jail at the Northern Lakes Magical Enforcement Court."

"That's quite the mouthful," I observed.

"Yeah. Most of us just call it The Twisted Court."

The lights went out in the hallway, followed by a voice echoing down the hallway. *"Silence and sleep! No noise.*"

The wraith sighed as I fumbled for the rungs to the upper bed.

"The Twisted Court?" I whispered, hanging my head over the edge. "Why call it that?"

She rolled over, presenting her back to me. "With what you're in here for, you'll find out soon enough."

CHAPTER ELEVEN

Mila

I awoke with a start, yanked from a warm, cozy dream about a man with red eyes and a tender touch. I was covered in a thin layer of sweat and blood in places it shouldn't have been. It took several long breaths to get myself back under control.

Just a dream. It was just a dream.

From below came the sound of someone sniffing the air. "Someone been dreamin' the good dreams," my cellmate drawled with a low chuckle. "Mmm, tasty."

I fought back a retch. She could smell my arousal? Great. Just great.

"Come on," the wraith added, moving to stand in front of the cell door. "It's breakfast time."

That was the last bit of advice she gave me.

Once the doors opened, we walked out and formed a line with the other prisoners. There were all sorts in with us. I saw more wraiths, but also some small creatures like me, with goat-like legs and curled horns on their human heads. A couple of what looked like dwarves. Two huge flabby human-esque women. They were far too large and rotund to *be* humans, but I didn't know what else to call them. The tusks jutting from their lower jaws confirmed that they were something else.

There were more, including what looked like an elf to my untrained eyes. Numerous human-looking beings as well, but I was beginning to know better than to judge only by what parts I could see.

We filed forward into a mess hall, where we waited our turn, slowly shuffling ahead as the people in front of us were served what looked like a piece of bread, some scrambled eggs, and slop. I didn't hold out hope that it was oatmeal. Nobody in there was that lucky.

"Hey!" I exclaimed as someone cut in line in front of me without a word. "Excuse me, but you just—"

The creature turned around with an angry hiss, and I gasped, stepping back from the feline face.

"You know what," I said, waving a hand. "Never mind."

The last thing I wanted to contend with was a literal catwoman. She had human proportions but was covered in fur from head to toe and sported a forward-facing cat ... well, face.

"You should deal with that smell if you want to survive."

I glanced over my shoulder at the woman who had spoken. Other than her eyes, which were far too bright a green to be normal, she looked perfectly human. Long black hair braided tightly down her back, and a long, diamond face with a sharp jaw and tiny pert lips that were incredibly mobile, practically dancing with emotion themselves.

"How am I supposed to do that without a shower?" I asked.

The woman laughed, silky and seductive. "You can't wash off the scent of fear, little human."

Fuck. First, I reeked of arousal, and now, fear? I looked around anew, realizing for the first time just what position I was in, and it wasn't good.

I was the newbie in jail, and more than a few people were looking at me with a mixture of hunger and hatred. Some threw covert glances my way as if watching, waiting to see what would happen to me, while the rest ignored me.

"Good luck," the green-eyed woman said dryly, then pushed past me to advance her own place in line.

Three more creatures did the same, shouldering me aside until I was out of line. I tried to ease my way back in, but the violence-laden glares I received from all manner and color of eyes were enough to send me slinking to the back.

Eventually, I got served, the dregs of everything making their way onto my plate.

"Yummy," I muttered, looking around and discovering my next challenge.

Where would I sit and eat?

All the tables were occupied, and those with open spots were guarded by types that glared me away.

"Here, if you aren't going to eat, I'll take that from you."

It was the same cat-lady from before. She unfolded herself from her seat like a flower and snatched the tray from my hands without jostling a thing on it.

"Hey!" I snapped. "That's mine."

"No. It's mine," she said, stabbing my bread with a claw and nibbling on a corner of it.

I went at her. "Give it back!" I was starving, and I had no idea when the next meal would be. I was going to have that food no matter what—

The catwoman backhanded me, casually spinning me around. I staggered backward, shocked by the sudden physical attack.

"You *bitch*!" I cried and launched myself at them without thinking.

Calling it a fight would have been generous. What really happened was I clung to her like a spider monkey for all of three seconds, punching her head. Then she dropped to the ground and rolled until somehow, she was behind me, her arm like a steel bar around my neck.

"If this were any other time, I would continue to show you how pathetic you are," she purred in my ear. "But now isn't the time. So, I'll see you tonight, little human. Be prepared to show how sorry you are."

I blanched at the overtly sexual undertones. She was a cat. How did that …?

She let me go and rose to her feet, licking the back of her paw and grooming her whiskers while staring down at me.

"Get out of my sight."

"Right," I said, crawling away before getting to my feet just as everyone else got up.

Oh, great …

But they started filing toward the nearby doors instead. I didn't try to get ahead of anyone that time, just sort of went with the flow.

We went outside. The same yellow sun was in the sky in the same place as before. I frowned. Did it ever rise and fall? Or just hang there permanently?

I saw a set of eyes glowing nearby as they looked at me and went over to it, thinking they looked familiar.

"Hey," I said.

"Fuck off," came the reply from a very male voice.

"Uh, sorry," I said, shaking my head and moving away as the wraith did the same, going to stand near a cluster of other red eyes.

People were grouping up all across the outdoor space, a bumpy but solid stone surface. Very few were on their own, and those who were looked like the type I didn't want to mess with. Even cat-lady was grouped with a trio of people similar to her. She saw me looking and grinned, extending her tongue to slowly lick her paw before she groomed herself some more.

Anger boiled, my temperature spiking. For most of my life, I had been bullied. Used and hurt by those who were bigger or meaner than me. And before that, it had been worse. I remembered little about my parents, but none of it was good. Now I was somewhere brand new, where nobody knew me, and still, they looked down on me.

I was tired of it. I didn't want them dead, like Victor, but hurt? Yes, I wouldn't mind if they were hurt. If they learned to *back off*. To leave me alone. That was a lesson I wouldn't mind teaching them. Could the magic, if that's what it truly was, do that? I wished I knew. I wished the words on the pages of the book would come back to me.

"You got a fuckin' problem?"

The cat-lady was up in my face now. I hadn't noticed her coming. She was fast.

"Yeah," I said. "With you."

I recalled the way I'd felt back in my hovel. The anger. The fury burning me from the inside. The words on my lips, the *power*. I closed my eyes, swearing I could feel it swelling.

"What the fuck are you doing?" the cat-lady hissed, backing away from me. "Are you insane, girl?!"

"What are you talki—"

I stopped talking as I lifted my hands in protest and saw the glowing red balls of energy.

"You're crazy!" the cat-lady said, backing away. "You can't do that!"

"Why not?" I snarled, stepping toward her. "It sure looks like I am."

"Stay away from me!"

"You deserve it," I said coldly, thrusting my hands forward.

Nothing happened. The red glowing stuff stayed in my hands as if stuck with glue.

"Uhh," I said, shaking my hands, trying to get rid of it. "What the ..."

Alarms began to scream, and guards in full

armor came storming into the yard. They had large silver shields, which they locked together as they advanced.

"Hey!" I said, lifting my hands. "I didn't mean it. I don't want to—"

Something hard hit me from behind. I fell forward just as the guards rushed for me, large truncheons descending with vicious force all over my body, beating me senseless. I screamed at first, but one of them clipped me across the jaw, stunning me into silence.

"Get her on her feet," one of the minotaurs barked, and I was hauled up roughly, my feet not responding, forcing them to drag me across the ground, blood dripping from several wounds.

"Where are you taking me?" I tried to ask, but it came out as "dfh fhhh uuu fngg eeeee." Or something like that. I was barely conscious. Their response, however, was crystal clear.

"Let's see how long you last in solitary before your mind breaks," one of them chuckled.

"Nah, she won't break," another said. "I saw the schedule. She's up for trial soon. And you know how the dragon likes to punish lawbreakers like her. Human. *Female.*"

The entire group chuckled nastily.

I started sweating with fear again.

CHAPTER TWELVE

Korr'ok

"I didn't touch her!" Abhed shouted as he pleaded his case, a miserable satyr sitting next to him, the latest person to be punished by having to defend those at trial. He hadn't done much, simply letting Abhed make his own plea.

"Jury Member Rokk?" the dragon rumbled.

"He's lying," I said. "The girl was terrified of him. He wanted her back to continue his nasty ways, so he enlisted me to deal with the ghouls who had supposedly 'taken' her. Seven of them died in the process of me rescuing his daughter."

"And was she truly in danger?" Dannorax pried.

"Unknown. She claimed no, but she's young, and they were ghouls, so it's entirely possible that they would have turned on her. But at that moment, I don't believe she was in mortal danger. I was able to return her with all digits attached and no flesh wounds, despite them having a six-hour head start. Everything points to the defendant being a liar."

"But I'm not lying!" Abhed shouted, sweat pouring down his temples.

The room was rife with fear, filling my nostrils in the most pleasant ways. It was my favorite stage. Terror. But before he soiled themselves, which was never fun. The fear was the best.

"Jury, please vote," Dannorax said, flicking a paw in our direction.

Abhed stared at us, his eyes pleading.

One by one, however, we all gave the vote he didn't want to hear.

"Guilty," I said with great pleasure, voting as the final member.

"That makes eleven guilty votes. A unanimous decision. How fun. Now, what punishment shall we give today?" the dragon asked the courtroom. "Anyone have any requests?"

"Castration. Then make him eat it," someone called.

I grinned as Abhed clutched at his groin.

"Staking," someone else said.

"Skin him!"

The comments went round the jury, and many

of those in the audience who came to experience the justice meted out.

"All very good ideas," Dannorax said, lifting a paw to stall further suggestions. "As Judge of this Court, I pronounce the sentence of one Abhed Miller to be ... *death by incineration.*"

He lifted a paw. Many of the jury and audience leaned forward eagerly as Abhed began to shake violently. He looked around for help but only found those interested in his suffering.

"Help me," he gasped, steam emerging from his mouth. "Please. I don't want to die."

We laughed.

The steam turned to smoke as Abhed screamed. His shoes burst into flames. The smell of burning fat filled the room as he was quite literally cooked from the inside out. Blackened ash poured from his mouth and ears, and then he was entirely engulfed in flame for several seconds, the intense heat contained by Dannorax's magic so that it didn't spread.

Less than half a minute later, there was nothing but a pile of ashes. A gnome with one working leg stumped in from outside, wheeling a cart, and brought out a dustpan to sweep up the debris. He dumped it into the bin attached to his cart, then left without a word.

"Excellent. We will break for lunch before returning for this afternoon's trial," Dannorax said, tapping a claw on some flint, the spark serving as his official pronouncement.

Everyone rose. I did so faster, heading for the door with only a cursory nod to the other jury members. Despite the fun of the sentence, I couldn't shake the image of the woman with blue eyes from my mind. Even as I'd watched the yellow-orange flame of Abhed's funeral pyre, her eyes had stared back at me from everyone in the audience.

It was infuriating. I needed to fight or fuck, and I couldn't decide which. I was unnerved, and that *never* happened to me. But the thought of her body, against mine ... under me ... her holes mine for the taking, her cries as I ravaged her body. The images circled endlessly inside my mind.

I left the courtroom and headed for the jail. I could summon her if I wanted. I had that power. There were rooms I could take her, throw her against the wall, and rip her clothes from her body. She would slowly slide down the wall, impaling herself on my cock until she begged me for more. I would toy with her clit, making her wetness coat me until I'd had my fill and emptied myself inside her.

A growl tore from my throat, sending people scattering out of my way as I walked the hallway, heading outside where the prisoners would be.

There was something about her. Something

different, and I needed to know *what*. Had she cast some sort of spell on me that I wasn't aware of?

When I got outside, there was a commotion in the prison courtyard. I watched as the guards surrounded and beat someone wielding red magic. With a flash of recognition, I realized it was the woman.

I reached out, touching the magic as it faded, the flavor of it tantalizingly familiar. Frowning, I tried to place it, but I couldn't. Angrily, I headed for the prison entrance.

"I'm here to see Warden Grolk," I snapped before the ginger-bearded dwarf at the front desk could ask a question.

I didn't wait for a response either, simply heading for the hallway that I knew led to his offices. Behind me came a flustered cry, followed by the stomping of heavy boots as the dwarf rushed after me.

"Lord Rokk, I'm sorry, but the Warden isn't taking visitors right now."

"Fine. Then you can show me where the human woman who came in yesterday is being held," I said.

"But, sir, I ..."

I gave him a withering glare. Dwarf folk were tough, hard people. I'd give them that. But I was tougher and harder. He looked away first.

"That's what I thought," I said, pushing open the door to the warden's office.

Warden Grolk was at his desk. The ogre was a beast of a man, matching my height but several times as wide in the stomach. His big, bulging eyes looked extra big and bulgy today. He squirmed as I entered, and when his eyes flicked downward for a split second, I understood.

"Harassing the prisoners again, Grolk?" I said with disgust, ignoring the soft sounds emanating from under the desk.

"What do you want, Lord Rokk?" Grolk asked sullenly. He used my full title—false as it may be, though he didn't know it—but there was no respect in the voice. As warden of the prison, he was only a step or so below me on the power scale, so he didn't feel the need to kowtow to the jury members as most others did.

"A human was brought in yesterday. Female. Very tiny. Blue eyes. Unlawful magic use. I need to see her."

"Why?"

I stared at him. He stared back at first, his black irises overtly hostile. But we both knew he would cave, and soon enough, he did. Too eager to get back to the prisoner under his desk, I was sure.

"Fine, whatever. She just got sent to solitary for more magic use," Grolk muttered, tossing me a key. "You know the way."

I grabbed it and left him to his own devices as I headed into solitary.

It was time I got some answers.

CHAPTER THIRTEEN

Mila

By the time I could think straight again, the magic was gone, and the guards were busy shoving me into a shoebox standing on its side. There was barely enough room in the solitary cell to turn around. Lying down was out of the question, even for someone as small as me. Thankfully, I could wedge myself down with my knees against my chest and sit on the cold hard floor. Anyone else would have had to resort to standing.

"I'd like a hot towel and tea, please!" I called to nobody in particular. "Maybe some painkillers, too."

My sides ached. Everything hurt, really, but I knew it would fade. It always did, the cuts scabbing over with astonishing rapidity and the bruises going through their healing cycle so fast that if I sat and watched for an hour, I could note the change happening.

But it still freaking hurt.

Body. Mind. Soul. I was run down. For the first time in a long time, the beatings were starting to get to me, affecting me mentally. But why? It wasn't like I was unused to them. My parents got me accustomed to that life when I was a child. My earliest memories were of being slapped for crying. I was four? Five?

Then they just never came back when I was around eight. I didn't really know how old I was. Birthdays were not a thing in my 'family.'

I stared at my hands, almost wishing my parents were still around so that I could at least ask them about the weirdness. Could they use magic? Did they know what was going on with me?

If they were alive, though, I knew who I would target next. I frowned. The magic I'd used last night and then nearly again in the courtyard had been controlled by *me*. Impossible as it should be, it was.

So, what was that thing that killed the baker? That was no spell. It was most definitely alive.

I resisted thinking about Sarabeth and the others. I didn't want to know if I was responsible for their deaths as well. Cowardly bullies they might have been, death wasn't what I wished upon them. More misery, sure. Getting hit by a truck? I wouldn't shed a tear. But I didn't want to be the one who killed them.

You already have. You know what that thing meant about going after the others. You can't deny it.

Maybe, maybe not. But there was nothing I could do about it in solitary confinement in a magical world I didn't know existed until the day before.

A key inserted itself into the lock and turned it with a heavy *thunk.* The door opened smoothly, admitting a wave of fresh air that carried a charcoal scent that burned pleasantly in my nostrils.

"Ah," I said without looking up. "Finally. I hope you steeped the bag for long enough."

"What are you talking about?"

I scrambled to my feet, all thoughts of towels and tea vanishing from my mind like snow before a warm sunny day.

"You," I said, mouth drying out until it was more parched than the Sahara.

"You."

It was him. The monster. He was there. At the door to my jail cell. There was nobody with him. We were alone, just the two of us.

He stepped forward, his shoulders so broad they pushed against the walls of my cell. There was no escaping it. I was at his mercy. Whatever he wanted from me, I couldn't deny.

I backed up the one step I could until my shoulders were pressed against the far wall. The monster-man lowered his head, stopping only inches from mine, his burning red eyes boring deep into my soul. I breathed heavily and deeply, chest arching up and back slightly, shoving toward him.

"Who are you?" he asked in a soft rumble that washed over me, puckering my skin and lifting tiny hairs on edge all over my body.

"My name is Mila," I answered robotically, eyes locked on his, hypnotized by the swirling flames at their core. "Who are you?"

"My name is Korr'ok." He frowned mightily after saying that and shook his head fiercely, pushing me flat against the wall. "But you must call me Lord Rokk."

"Okay, Lord Rokk. But I already knew that was your name. I asked *who* you are."

When he smiled, my knees gave out. I started slumping down the wall toward the floor. Korr'ok's, a.k.a. Lord Rokk's, arm clasped my waist.

I hissed, freezing him in place.

"Am I hurting you?"

"No," I said, trying to stifle the trembling of my arms and the hammering of my heart as it sought to burst through my chest. "Not hurting."

"Good." Korr'ok brought me out of the cell. "I don't need you fainting on me. There are questions that must be answered."

"That sounds nice," I replied as he placed me against the wall outside my cell, the cool metal sending a refreshing wave through my body, though it was held at bay by his lingering touch.

It felt *really* nice to have one of his giant arms around my waist. Very nice, indeed. So nice that my nipples were standing on edge, easily visible through my tattered clothes. Korr'ok's eyes flicked down, lingering on my breasts and the parts of them he could see through the tears.

I swallowed, the action forcing a lump out of my throat.

"I have a lot of questions," I said.

Korr'ok frowned. "You're a prisoner. You don't ask questions. You *answer* them, am I understood?"

A thrill of excitement raced through me as I nodded my obedience. What the fuck was going on with me? Why did I *like* doing as he said? The man was a monster. He had freaking *horns and red eyes!* I shouldn't want to kneel in front of him and do as he commanded. I was stronger than that.

Wasn't I?

"Do you ask me the questions before killing

me?" I murmured.

"I will not be the one to kill you," Korr'ok said.

"So, what, just here to interrogate and make fun of me?" Some of my backbone was returning as I learned how to resist the almost unnatural desire to fall to my knees for *other* reasons.

"That depends," Korr'ok growled, grabbing my chin and causing my clit to start throbbing. "Are you worth making fun of?"

"Probably not," I said dryly, which was the only dry part of me by then. "I have my own place that I don't have to share with roommates. In this market, how can you make fun of that?"

Korr'ok glanced past me at the tiny solitary cell, raising an eyebrow as if to question the validity of my statement.

"The rent is cheap?" I added helplessly.

There was no further reaction. Lame.

"What do you want with me?" I asked, looking up to lock eyes with him once more.

There was a long moment of nothing as he stared back. I thought I saw his body twitch once or twice, but I must have imagined it. The silence continued, and I grew tired of the standoff between us.

That vanished as Korr'ok leaned in closer and pressed his lips to mine. My eyes flew open as he pressed me against the wall and forced his tongue into my mouth. Hands gripped my waist and lifted me from the floor.

It felt so fucking *good*, the heat of his body, the strength in his arms easily moving me how he wanted. I was his to command, and my body exploded with its heat. My clit throbbed, eager for his touch. I squirmed in his grip, wishing he could do *more*, but just as quickly as he was there, he was gone.

He pulled away, turning his back on me. I saw his shoulders rise and fall, and the muscles along his neck and shoulders were locked rigid.

"Who are you really?" I asked. "Everywhere I've gone in the past day, it seems you're there. Are you following me? Why? Who are you to me?"

Korr'ok whirled on me, anger creasing his features.

"The magic you were using," he said sharply. "On the field earlier. Where did you learn it?"

I stared at him incredulously, stunned by the shift in demeanor. "*Learn it?*" I asked, not bothering to contain the peals of laughter that followed. "*Learn it?* Mister, I don't know the first thing about it. How many times do I have to tell you people this? I opened a book, started saying some words I don't remember or know how I knew, and then poof! It all happened."

"Book?" Korr'ok asked, his thick, bushy eyebrows knitting together with sudden intensity. "What book?"

"How would I know?"

"You will tell me," he commanded. "One way or another."

"I have nothing *to* tell you, don't you get it?" I snarled, pulling away from his grip and stepping back into my cell. "I've already told everyone everything I know, which is basically nothing. I was homeless. A nobody, okay? When I was younger, some crazy lady who ran a bookstore for what I'm pretty sure was a single day gave it to me. I couldn't even open the stupid thing until last night!"

Korr'ok didn't look convinced. "If you were a homeless, tiny witch, why did you keep the book for so long? Why not sell it? It's an odd possession to keep, don't you think?"

I thought about that, not for the first time. "I don't know," I admitted. "I don't have an answer to that other than it just felt 'wrong' to let it go."

The giant sexy monster man snorted in disbelief and stood to his full height. "You are a terrible liar."

Rolling my eyes, I stepped fully into the cell and crossed my arms. "If you don't like it, sue me."

The evil grin that came over his face sent me slinking to the floor, making me forget all about our kiss. "I'll see you in court very soon."

CHAPTER FOURTEEN

Korr'ok

I slammed the door to her cell angrily, nearly shearing the key in half as I twisted the lock closed.

"Temper, temper," Mila *tsk*ed from the inside.

Ignoring her jibe, I stormed back down the hallway, my fury all but palpable.

Damn that infuriating woman! I'd gone looking for answers but came away with more questions. Who was she to have such a pull on one like me? I bared my teeth as a guard on patrol rounded the corner. The minotaur took one look at me and slammed himself against the wall, trying to be as flat as a pancake.

I left the cell block behind, shouldering my way into an empty office. My jaw was clenched so tight that my muscles were spasming. Fixating on the pain didn't help. The desire to turn around, go back into Mila's cell, and finish what I'd started with that kiss was near unstoppable.

She was so small and frail that she wouldn't be able to resist, but I now knew she didn't want to. Her body had betrayed her, welcoming me in and begging for more. I could still taste her lips on mine, but what was worse was the scent lodged firmly in my nostrils. Her sex had been so thick I could have tasted it.

And I *wanted* to taste it. To spread her legs and run my tongue up their vulnerable insides to the peak, where she would first start to squirm and moan before she screamed as I stretched her tight little pussy with my hard cock. I wondered if she would even be able to take me.

There was one way to find out, of course, but I somehow resisted. I had no idea who she was, and the more I talked to her, the more confused I became. Until I could be sure she wasn't secretly out to harm me or worse, I had to be careful. It would be hard, given the lust she awoke in me, but I would have to.

To give in could mean harm to me or, worse, the discovery of my true persona. I liked the life I'd built for myself in The Place Behind, and I didn't want to lose it for what would probably be a lousy lay.

I snorted, knowing I was lying to myself. She would make me spill my seed over and over again, I was sure. In her, on her, I didn't care. Her entire body would be mine. It would not be lousy. Of that, I was positive.

Slowly, my breathing came under control, and with it, the urge to fight or fuck waned. My cock still twitched impatiently in my pants, but it would have to wait until I was back in my quarters to achieve relief.

For some reason, the thought of finding someone else to take care of it did not appeal to me.

"Answers," I told myself. "I need more answers."

Thinking back over my conversation with Mila, I cursed myself a second time. I'd given her my real name without thinking! In the decades since I'd left my home in Faerie, I had never *once* made that slip up. With her, I'd done so without hesitation. Why had I wanted her to know the truth about me? It wasn't like she would recognize the name anyway.

Angrily, I left the boardroom, making a beeline for the only place I could think of that would give me answers: the evidence locker. It was two floors below me, and the stairs provided another opportunity to release the energy still circulating through my veins. I needed to be calm, to think properly. No more mistakes.

The head of evidence, a crotchety middling demon, didn't look up from her book as I approached the wired cage blocking access to evidence. That was the wrong move. My temper immediately spiked anew.

"I need to see the effects of a woman brought in yesterday," I said. "She was human, to be punished for unauthorized magic use. She had a book with her."

The demon didn't immediately look up, instead finishing her page before slowly craning her neck back. The skin was stretched far too tight over the body, its reddish hue turning more to rust than the usual vibrant crimson. "I need more information than that."

Between the lack of respect, the initial ignorance, and now her sheer laziness, I'd had enough. With a snarl, I reached through the cage, grabbed her neck, and slammed her face on the desk. "*Now!*"

The demon rebounded off the desk, glaring at me with overt hostility.

"Try it," I dared, rolling my neck from side to side. I could use a good fight. A demon would be just the target to take my ire out on. Baring my teeth, I tried to goad the bitch into making a move.

She must have had at least one brain cell working, however, because she decided against a physical engagement.

"Very well, Lord Rokk," she said tartly. "But

this will be logged."

"Oh, trust me, I'll have a word with your superior about your conduct, too," I said with a sneer. As if her "log" mattered to me.

"Grolk appointed me to this position and trusts me to do it," she said.

I leaned in until my skin was pressed against the cage, my eyes as close as they could be.

"Not *that* superior," I said in a deathly quiet whisper.

The demon looked troubled, her throat bobbing up and down from a nervous swallow. I swear I could see beads of sweat forming on her red brow, though demons didn't actually emit sweat. But any time someone threatened to go have a casual conversation with one of the greater demons as if it was no big deal, that was a time to give pause.

"Tiny human woman. Blue eyes. Where is her stuff?" I repeated.

I was in no mood to fuck around or deal with any of the usual power-tripping bullshit that happened in the Black Tower. She must have finally realized that because, without another comment, the demon reached over and pressed a button to let me in.

The gate to my left popped open.

"Thank you," I said, flashing a smile that was anything but nice. "Where is it located?"

"Hasn't been filed yet," she said stiffly. "Sitting in a bag on the table at the back of Row C."

"Perfect." I strolled into evidence and down the indicated row.

As promised, the cloth bag was on the table, a tag with a scribble lazily attached to it. The book was inside. I removed it and set it on the table, staring, trying to identify it. But I couldn't.

There were untold books out there with magical characteristics. Spellbooks, diaries, relics, and more. I didn't know all of them, not even a fraction of them. But ones that let a human wield magic as strong as *that* were few and far between. Usually, one needed a basis of magical learning to get much out of an enchanted item.

Mila either knew absolutely nothing, or she was one of the greatest liars I'd ever met. I'd called her one to her face, but nothing about her story rang false to my ears. That didn't mean it was true, but *she* believed it to be true. Unless my desire to fuck her brains out was clouding my judgment.

And given that I had revealed my true identity to her, that idea was starting to hold more sway.

Perhaps I should head back to her cell and fuck her senseless to get it out of the way. Maybe *then* I could think clearly and solve the riddle of the magic that should be familiar but wasn't.

It was time to change that. Reaching out to the book, I cast a spell on it to try to identify any magical elements.

I frowned and cast the spell again. Then I opened it and sent my spell query a third time. Then a fourth near the back.

"What the fuck?" I turned the book over and over. The clasp was the only place my spell even returned a hint of faint magic.

Mila did say she couldn't even open the book until yesterday.

Frowning, I inspected the clasp very closely. On it, I could pick up three traces of magic. One I didn't recognize but was the least powerful. One had that same familiar energy.

And a third I knew very, *very* well.

Something very weird was going on. Very weird, indeed. My suspicions were growing.

If the book itself was no longer magical, however, then where had the magic gone?

The answer slammed into my forehead along with my palm. *Of course.* Mila had been without the book when she used the magic again in the courtyard. If it wasn't in the book, it had to be in her! And I had missed it.

I had no idea what was happening, but it was quickly becoming apparent that Mila was more important to me than I'd realized. Two things needed to happen. First, I needed to visit Dannorax and have Mila's trial moved up immediately.

Secondly, I would have to ensure that when it came time for her punishment, I was the one who Marked her.

CHAPTER FIFTEEN

Mila

My lips still burned the next morning where he'd kissed me. Running a finger over them as I lay in a ball on my side, I expected them to be puffy and tender. Instead, they were normal. Yet the tingling burn didn't go away.

I had barely slept, a mixture of the horrifically uncomfortable posture I was forced to assume within the tiny cell and the constant sexual slideshow that filled my brain. It had taken me hours to calm myself from a state of sexual delirium. No number of self-inflicted orgasms had been able to help either. Nothing had sated my need. Nothing could.

Except for Korr'ok.

"Who the hell are you?" I whispered to the empty box—calling it a "room" was far too generous. "And what are you doing to me?"

I pondered those questions for an unknown amount of time. There was no light, no way to tell what time of day it was or how long had passed. Five minutes? Three hours? A day? I didn't know. I tried to keep track but holding onto a single thought that wasn't about Korr'ok was infuriatingly difficult.

It always came back to him, to the pressure of his fingers on my waist, the searing, burning heat of his tongue as he ran it softly over the inside my mouth, exploring, touching, *taking*. I hadn't been myself. The real me would have stopped it. Turned my head aside. *Anything* but thrust my hips at him as I had, inviting him to fuck me in my prison cell where anyone could see or hear if they passed by.

Since when had I ever been *that* horny?

The answer was never. Nobody in my life had ever awoken such need between my legs as the horned monster. I suspected nobody ever would, either. There was something different about Korr'ok. And it wasn't just that he apparently went by two different names. Which was the real him?

Being on the ground, I felt more than heard the approaching footsteps. They paused outside and were followed by the metal ratcheting of a key. Slowly, aware that my body wouldn't like me after not moving for so long, I started to unfold my limbs as best I could to assume a crouch.

The door swung open.

"Time's up, tiny witch," the guard growled. "Let's go."

"Yeah. Give me a sec—*Aaiiii.*"

The scream tore from my throat as the guard hauled me out of the cell without delay, forcing muscles and tendons to assume positions they'd been locked out of for hours. Pain lanced through my skull, and I thrashed wildly, piercing shrieks filling the hallway.

A meaty fist backhanded me, and I fell to the ground, sobbing in agony.

"Dumb bitch," one of them grunted, grabbing me by the wrist and dragging me.

Another took the other side, and they hauled me off to a square room while I shuddered in pain.

"Hey!" I shouted as my meager clothing was ripped from my body. "What the fuck is that for?"

I stumbled in a circle—legs still only partially responding—only to be greeted by a blast of frigid ice water from a hose. I fell to the floor as tiny ice daggers stabbed across my skin. The guards stood and laughed while I bleated for them to stop. They didn't listen.

The water mercifully cut off. I started to recover, only for them to dump a bucket of soap over my head. It dripped down my naked body.

"Scrub," someone said. "You have thirty seconds."

Not sure when the next chance to "clean" myself would come, I did as instructed, trying to keep my back to the guards.

On what must have been precisely second thirty, the water blasted me again, removing all the soap. Then, finally, it stopped.

"Here, dry off," one of them grunted, tossing something at me.

I grabbed it, somehow managing to actually catch it. When I held it up, the piece of fabric unraveled to the size of a washcloth. I eyed it while the guards again laughed uproariously, leering at my nudity. The tears added fresh wetness to my cheeks as I patted myself dry as best I could, though I was unable to do anything for my hair.

Clutching my hands to my body, I waited to see what was next.

"Put this on," one said, and a piece of clothing landed over my head.

Turning away from the minotaurs, I hurriedly donned the boring beige one-piece outfit. It fell loosely around my ankles, and the arms extended past my wrists. I zipped it up, finally feeling somewhat modest.

"What is this all about?" I asked, wishing

like hell I knew how to use the magic. What I wouldn't have given at that moment to rip out the eyeballs of my tormentors.

"You looked and smelled like shit," one of the guards grunted. "You have to be somewhat presentable for the Court."

I stared at him. "You're joking, right? I thought that was just a fucking metaphor."

The guards looked at each other, then back at me. The soft, grunting laughter that followed was not very promising.

"No metaphor. It's trial day."

Despite their assurances, it didn't truly kick in that they were serious until I was chained up and ushered into a literal courtroom. But that wasn't the most surprising part.

"Holy fucking shit," I gasped, stumbling to a stop at the sight before me.

The literal *dragon* coiled at the front of the room stared at me with giant yellow-orange eyes that had vertical black slits as long as I was tall. Twin jets of flame burst from each nostril in contempt, and then it turned its attention away.

Under his perch, in giant lettering, was the word "Judge."

"You have got to be kidding me," I breathed in disbelief, the minotaurs shuffling me between the rows of seating to a box right up front.

Right next to the dragon, who bared his teeth

in some sort of demonic smile.

Most of us just call it The Twisted Court.

My cellmate's words echoed in my head, suddenly taking on a new meaning as the cruel malice of the room weighed heavily on my shoulders, pushing me into the hard wooden chair, all alone at the front of the room. Hope seemed to be sucked from me in the presence of the massive crimson beast.

Struggling, I turned my gaze to the left, where two rows of ornate, high-backed chairs sat empty, waiting for occupants. The ebony wood and blood-red cushioning did nothing to lift the mood of the oppressive room. If anything, it worsened as I contemplated what sorts of creatures would sit *there*.

Time and again, however, my attention returned to the dragon at the front. The judge of that ... place.

Despair settled in as all manner of monstrous and demonic creatures filed in to occupy the chairs.

I stiffened in my seat as a particularly large beast with two horns and skin darker than the wood of his chair appeared.

"You!" I shouted angrily, standing up.

The minotaur guards roughly shoved me back into my seat, easily overpowering me.

I sat, glowering at Lord Rokk. He ignored me,

instead exchanging pleasant greetings with the dragon, whose name I learned was Dannorax.

Everything was happening so fast. I looked up sharply as a hooved creature clopped up to stand next to me, his lower legs reversed at the knee and covered in fur.

"Who are you?" I asked.

"Your counsel," he spat, clearly unhappy about the fact.

A fire lit in me at his attitude. "Gee, you're so supportive. I really feel like I have a chance with you defending me."

The creature looked at me with deep brown eyes full of malice. "You can't be serious. You have no chance. The only thing left to be decided *here* is how you'll die. It's a waste of my time and effort is what it is. You should have just obeyed the damn rules."

"Well, that's easy for you to say," I fired back. "But when you have no idea what you're doing, let alone that there are *rules* about it, it's sort of hard now, isn't it?"

"Not my fault," he said stubbornly. "Now shut up."

"Court is now in session," the dragon rumbled, interrupting my response.

What happened next was almost a blur. The gray-clad man appeared out of nowhere across the aisle from me, announcing the charges against me. I was well aware of those by now.

My counsel didn't deny anything. He simply argued for the simplest, quickest death.

When I asked him why he wasn't trying to do something more productive, like find a way for me to live, he shook his head.

"It's all I can do," he said under his breath. "Trust me. It's better than the alternative."

"Alternative?" I mumbled, wondering what could be worse than death.

The entire thing was a sham. Nobody cared about me or what I was doing. The realization sank in slowly throughout the short trial. Everyone was convinced of my guilt. Nobody cared that I hadn't the foggiest notion of what I was doing, nor had I meant to hurt anyone.

They just wanted to see me suffer. One of the creatures, a mighty beast of a man nearly the size of Lord Rokk who was draped in furs and with hair braided down his back, actually leaned forward almost hungrily, watching me with golden eyes like he could feed off my hopelessness.

"Jury," Dannorax said eventually. "You have heard the evidence and charges. Please vote."

I stared, as, one by one, they voted.

"Guilty," Lord Rokk rumbled, the final voice to seal my fate.

You bastard, I mouthed at him.

"I do enjoy unanimity," the dragon said, his head rising as he uncoiled his neck. "And these are my favorite types of cases to hand out punishment, as you all know."

A low chuckle ran around the court, striking fear deep into my bones.

"Are there any here who would wish this woman as their charge to mete out 'punishment' as appropriate?" the dragon asked slyly, the hidden meanings behind his tone obvious.

To my utter shock, Lord Rokk was the first to rise from his chair, eyes blazing bright.

"She is mine," he snarled in a voice that brooked no arguments.

Dannorax laughed. "Very good. Are there any challengers?"

"She. Is. *Mine*," Lord Rokk growled defiantly, and the entire room *cracked* with energy.

No other member of the jury rose to challenge him. But I did notice the fur-covered giant of a man shifting in his chair as if he was considering speaking out. In the end, however, I was handed over to Lord Rokk for punishment.

"And here you said you wouldn't kill me," I muttered as the minotaurs removed my cuffs and shoved me at him.

One of his giant hands landed on my shoulder, grabbing at the edges of the jumpsuit.

"Trust me," he said, ripping the jumpsuit from

my body and exposing my body to his greedy eyes. "By the time we're done here, you might wish I had."

All around us, the crowd leaned in closer with anticipation, a low rumble of eager energy filling the room.

CHAPTER SIXTEEN

Mila

"W-w-what's going on?" I stammered, covering myself with my hands as best I could. "What are you doing to me?"

Korr'ok loomed above me, larger than ever, it seemed.

"Kneel," he commanded, reddish lines starting to glow across his body like his skin was parting.

Somehow, I stayed standing, shaking my head. "If I'm going to die," I said bitterly, "then I'm doing it on my feet."

Where my courage came from was anyone's guess. It certainly wasn't my usual tactic. That place, those people, were changing me, it seemed. Forcing me to think about life in different ways as I came to understand just how little I'd known of the world.

Now, it seemed, I would die without understanding *any* of it. How fitting.

"*Kneel*," Korr'ok repeated in a firmer tone, the weight of his voice a physical thing that slammed into my shoulders and buckled my knees, driving me to the ground.

I had to put my hands out, exposing myself, to balance and stop myself from being smashed flat to the floor. The cold tile sank its chill into my skin, racing up my arms like some sort of death grip. Around me, the courtroom faded as black clouds gathered above me and fog whirled in, surrounding Korr'ok and me in a sphere.

"What the fuck is going on?" I asked, staring up at the terrifying figure.

His horns were longer. Weren't they? Or did I imagine it? His features looked darker, less human, the cheeks starker as the skin grew gaunt. But that wasn't all I noticed. His muscles were thick and covered his entire body, taut with force as he flexed, drawing the shirt tight across his abs. Deep breaths stretched his core, drawing my eyes lower …

"What the fuck?" I yelped. "Why are you fucking hard?"

Korr'ok's cock was pushing against his pants, a thick bulging outline impossible to miss. He looked down at me and lifted one hand. Red energy coalesced in his upraised palm, a swirling mass that slowly resolved into a circular emblem.

I watched wide-eyed as he plucked it from mid-air with his other hand as if it were some sort of solid object.

"You will be bound to me," he intoned. "Mine to command. Mine to *punish*."

"I'm not going to be your slave," I hissed, shrinking away from him. "I would rather die first."

"The choice has been made for you," he spoke. "You will not be a slave, but a prisoner."

"A lot of people would fail to see the difference," I shot back, glancing around us at the black smoke that had occluded the rest of the courtroom.

What was everyone else seeing? Were we alone in there, or was it like a one-way mirror?

"You lost the right to choose when you committed your crimes," Korr'ok said with finality, gesturing with his right hand.

I cried out as his magic seized my body and lifted me into the air, pulling me close to him until we touched. My head arched back uncomfortably while his pecs pressed against my cheek. His abs against my chest.

His cock against my lower stomach.

Hissing at the feeling, I closed my eyes, fighting back the rising sensation, the answering lust to his obvious arousal. I would *not* let him have control of me. I would *not*.

Lightning flickered in the black clouds. Red lightning. That couldn't be a good sign.

Korr'ok's magic lifted me higher until I was face to face with him.

"Put. Me. Down." I said each word slowly and firmly, offering my best glare.

He clenched his fist in response and kissed me as I was yanked in even closer to him. His lips burned against mine, awakening a fresh ache between my legs that I couldn't stop from rising like a tsunami into my mind, battering aside weaker urges and desires, such as morals and modesty.

I wanted *more* of this touch, of the liquid fires that were his lips. I wanted them on mine. On my neck, suckling at my breasts and trailing their inferno between my legs. I needed to be bent over and ridden, taken and used like I was meant for it. My pussy was instantly warm, and the heat grew with every passing second as the cloud of blackness and lightning grew tighter around us, like a cocoon sealing us in.

"Please." The world tumbled from my lips like a moan.

Korr'ok's eyes glowed like miniature twin suns in the darkness, peeling back the darkness as they devoured my naked, exposed body. They paused at my breasts, glowing brighter as he moved his gaze between my legs. His nostrils flared wide as he drank in my scent, feeding off my desires.

I could barely breathe. My chest rose and fell, covered in a thin layer of sweat that caused my skin to glisten. His tongue darted out along my neck, tasting it.

The shudder of ecstasy that rolled through me was divine. The whimper that escaped my throat was my demand for more. More of it. More of *him*. I no longer cared who or what he was. I simply *wanted*.

"You are *mine*," Korr'ok growled as I floated in front of him, naked and dripping.

"Yes," I agreed, delirious with desire. "*I am yours.*"

Fresh energy surged through him and into me. My body arched backward at the immensity of the pleasure suddenly inflicted on it. I was about to head over the edge of the biggest orgasm of my life, from the splash of water from a tap to barreling right over the lip of Niagara Falls. A cavern of blackness yawned wide, ready to accept me, knowing my mind couldn't handle what my body was trying to experience.

Korr'ok lifted his right hand and placed the red emblem on my chest, between my tiny, exposed breasts.

My eyes went wide, my body locking rigid

as I screamed in utter agony, the pain flaying me alive as it quite literally *rolled* out from the marking in a visible wave of red energy. I couldn't move, trapped in muscle spasms, as I tore my vocal cords to pieces screaming so loud and harshly.

Cold sweat puckered my skin as all warmth fled from me, taking with it the very precipice of bliss that I had been about to experience and turning it into the darkest, most forbidding nightmare.

"Make it stop," I heard someone gasp, the voice too torn to shreds for me to recognize it as my own. *"Please."*

"You are mine," Korr'ok intoned.

I started shaking involuntarily. My body couldn't handle the extremes he was putting it through. It was shutting down. My vision was fading around the edges, turning black. At least it wasn't red.

"Please."

Korr'ok stared implacably, unfazed by my suffering. "Say it."

"I already did," I moaned, the heat slowly frying my brain. Hadn't it just been cold? What was going on?

"Say it!" he bellowed, a hint of urgency underlying his tone.

Was he scared? I didn't know. All I knew was

that I had to make it stop. All of it. I needed it over. I had to say the words. Whatever it took to end the pain wracking my body, destroying me, fiber by fiber.

"I …"

The world spun. I had to get it out.

"Am …"

Korr'ok's eyes burned brighter than ever before in anticipation.

"*Yours!*"

CHAPTER SEVENTEEN

Mila

The next thing I remembered, I was waking up on a cloud of comfort, the likes of which I could not recall ever experiencing.

It was *too* comfortable. Too nice.

I'd never had anything nice, had never been able or allowed to. Therefore, whatever it was, it had to be *wrong*.

Without being truly aware of my surroundings, I scrambled away from the sensation—

And promptly fell out of a bed onto the hard wooden floor, the thin area rug not absorbing any of the impact.

Pain jarred up my elbow into my jaw, where my teeth slammed together so hard that it was a miracle I didn't chip them. Running my tongue over them just to be sure, I finally opened my eyes to take in my surroundings.

The source of my comfort, and then pain, turned out to be a gargantuan four-poster bed towering. I climbed to my feet, the top of the mattress nearly at my stomach.

How the hell is anyone supposed to climb in and out of this thing with ease? It's clearly not built for normal ... people.

Slow-returning brain functionality finally caught up with me, making the answer clear. That, however, brought with it a host of other questions.

I spent another moment admiring the bed, carved as it was from an onyx wood that had to be close to the color of Korr'ok's skin.

Had I really been sleeping in his bed? I forced down a shiver. There was no point in being afraid or disgusted. Whatever had happened—I did not let myself dwell on the courtroom just yet—had happened. It was over and done with.

A wave of nausea and exhaustion flooded me. The room wobbled, my legs warning me they were about to give out. I reached for the edge of the bed, flopping onto it as everything crashed around me.

My world was over. Done. Everything I thought I knew, thought I understood, was basically a lie. No, not a lie. None of it was *wrong*. It was simply … incomplete. There was so much more to it than I'd known.

And somehow, I'd ended up on the shitty side of it all. Again. It took my remaining strength, but I managed to pull myself onto the insanely huge bed before the last of my strength gave way.

I closed my eyes, simply too tired to continue.

When I opened them again, light was streaming through a window to my left. Had it done that before? I couldn't remember. Tiredly, I pulled myself up until my head rested on a pillow.

Exhaustion won yet again, and I passed out.

I must have awoken at one point before my next fit of awareness because I was back at the end of the bed when I woke.

Staring down at me was a pair of red eyes.

"Hey!" I yelped, scurrying backward. "What are you doing in here?"

Korr'ok tilted his head sideways but made no move to come closer, standing at the foot of the bed, wearing a simple black t-shirt and black slacks. "This is my bedroom," he rumbled as if that explained everything, his chest rising and falling in a slow rhythm, pulling the shirt tight across his pecs with every breath.

Not that I noticed. I definitely didn't stare.

"Do you not understand the concept of

privacy?" I fired back.

"You're in my house. You're in my bed. You're in *my* charge, tiny witch. You do not get privacy."

"I'm not a witch," I said, sinking into the comforters, suddenly wondering how I was wearing the giant nightgown. It was black, of course. Did the man own *any* color?

He's not a man.

"You used magic unlawfully and without training. That is called a witch," he informed me.

Shaking my head, I buried my face in my hands, taking deep breaths, trying to stay calm, all the while freaking out inside about the comfort of the stupid bed. Because of all that had happened, all the world-shattering changes, *that* should be the most uncomfortable experience for me.

"You look about ready to cry," Korr'ok observed. "Are you still unwell? In pain after the bonding?"

Bonding?

"No, I'm fine," I said. "Tears of happiness, probably."

The horned giant frowned, midnight skin wrinkling over his thick brow. "You are happy to be here?"

"Absolutely not!" I yelped. "No way, it's not that at all."

He waited patiently until I sighed.

"Do you realize that this is the most I've slept in a bed in years? I basically won the lottery by using that stupid book," I muttered, shaking my head at the hilarity of it all. I sobered quickly. "I just wish the people were okay."

Korr'ok sounded quizzical.

I looked up at the sound. "You know, Victor, the baker, and the mean girls who bullied me. I hope they survived it, at least."

"What are you talking about?" Korr'ok asked, suddenly next to me, leaning over the bed to look down at me, urgency etching lines into his face. "How do you not know if they're alive? You were there, Mila, were you not? Casting magic?"

I stared at him. "You mean you don't know? You people put me under arrest, and you don't even know what happened? I was stripped naked in front of the entire courtroom, Korr'ok!"

A giant hand covered my mouth, pinning me to the bed with such monstrous ease that I squeaked into his palm. The sudden demonstration of his strength was ... scary. My heart was thumping in my neck, my chest rising and falling with short, swift breaths out of my nose. Korr'ok leaned closer, filling my nose with hints of campfire and chocolate. It tickled my senses before settling somewhere deeper in me.

No. Not now. I fought down the desire to look up at him with eyes wide and pleading. I would *not* submit to him.

Korr'ok sniffed at the air but said nothing. Could he smell that I was turned on by the demonstration of his power? My cellmate had identified it easily enough.

"You must never refer to me by that name out loud," he growled in my ear instead. "You must address me as Lord Rokk. Do you understand?"

Reluctantly, I nodded, eager to get his hand off my mouth. I grabbed at it, pulling it away. I almost pushed it elsewhere. Lower. Where the heat between my legs craved for it.

"Why does it matter what I call you?" I asked.

"Later," *Lord Rokk* grunted. "First, you must tell me what happened. What did you do to those people?"

"Nothing," I said, thinking back to that night reluctantly. "I didn't do anything. It was ... a thing. I spoke from the book. Words I didn't even know. How did I do that?"

"It doesn't matter," he grunted, eyes flicking away for a moment. Did he even believe what he was saying? "Tell me more about what you did?"

"The ball of red," I said. "It was ... alive? It spoke."

"What did it say?" Korr'ok demanded hurriedly.

I closed my eyes, calling up the words. "First, it told me that I 'asked for this.' That I wanted it. Then it told me, '*You wanted this. You dreamed of it. Now you get it. Amateur. When I am done, I will come for you. Then I will be free!'"*

The tremble that hit my spine as I remembered the words was too hard for me to hide. Korr'ok saw and laid a hand on my shoulder.

"There's more, isn't there?" he asked in a calm, soothing voice.

My head jerked up to stare into his face. Never before had he spoken to me like that. With compassion. Truthfully, I didn't know it existed within him. Narrowing my eyes, I looked deep into those red orbs that were so unique to him.

Just how much more *was* there to Korr'ok/Lord Rokk? What had I yet to discover? And what more was he still hiding?

"I saw a face," I whispered. "In the power. I don't know who it was. But now I can't forget it."

Korr'ok nodded. He didn't question it, didn't call me crazy. He just accepted what I had to say, and that was that. Nobody had believed in me like that before. Nobody had *trusted* me like that.

"Get dressed," he said, pointing to a set of clothes sitting on a chair in the corner. "Quickly. We must go."

"What? Where are we going now?" I asked, not moving.

Korr'ok stared down at me from where he stood, with his face scrunched up like he couldn't believe I was dumb enough to ask. "Where do you think? We have to stop what you have unleashed. Before it kills you. We're going back to Earth."

CHAPTER EIGHTEEN

Mila

I looked over my shoulder as we ascended the ramp, the cliffs waiting for us, ominous in their darkness. Behind me, The Place Behind, or The Crack, as I'd started to think of it, bustled with life. It was weird to think that, despite the horrors I'd seen, life went on in the town like it did so many on Earth.

The Black Tower was a foreboding centerpiece to the town, its giant walls extending high above the buildings around it, but most seemed to ignore it. Even as we'd walked away from it, few paid us much attention. Those who knew "Lord Rokk" would show deference to him as his stature demanded, but most went about their days without a care.

More than once, I'd seen children—none

of them human, but children nonetheless—running in packs, laughing and giggling as kids were wont to do. It was a snippet of life I didn't expect to see.

"Am I free now?" I asked, conspicuously aware of the lack of restraints or bull-faced minotaurs. It was just the two of us on the climb.

Korr'ok—I would call him Lord Rokk around others, as he wished, but that was a fake persona, I knew that much—blew air from his nose as he glanced down at me.

"You are my responsibility now," he said. "I am to see to your punishment. Letting you simply 'go' would be a huge failure on my part. And I do not fail."

"Are you sure you're not my punishment?" I muttered. "Putting up with you certainly falls under the 'cruel and unusual' statute."

"Has it all been that bad?" Korr'ok muttered under his breath.

My head snapped up just in time to see his lips curl in a knowing grin. I stumbled as a wave of heat rolled through my body at that evil, taunting smile, moving out from the middle until all my lips burned. One with the memory of his kiss and what his mouth had felt like, the other with a nearly unceasing need to feel it for the first time.

He snatched my wrist, stopping me from

flailing further, although the press of his fingers on my flesh sent goosebumps along my arm and spine.

"Come," he commanded, gesturing with his head to indicate the hole in the cliffs ahead while somehow managing to make the word sound *far* more loaded. As if I could do that with a simple word from him. Nobody was that good.

I gathered my balance, tried to do the same with my composure, and stumped up the slope, leaving stupid-sexy-Korr'ok behind. Why did he have to be so alluring, despite his clearly inhuman origins? I mean, I'd seen black people before, but they had human skin that was simply black. Korr'ok's skin was almost a shiny metal. But it was warm. And soft.

I tried not to think about that. Instead, I shifted gears, forcing my sex-addled brain to think about escaping his clutches rather than jumping into them with no clothes. We were going back to Earth. To my home. It would be my chance to lose him. To find a way to leave that scary world far, far behind.

"How does anyone not notice?" I asked as Korr'ok waved away the false rock deep within the cliffs, returning us to the caverns behind the Falls, the sound of a tour guide speaking to his group reaching our ears. "Won't they notice us suddenly step out of nowhere?"

"No. Humans are, in general, oblivious. Their

minds will seek the easiest and simplest explanation for a situation. They will just assume they must have missed us before, that we were there all along."

"Yeah, that might work for me," I said, glancing back at him. "But what about your hor …"

The Korr'ok who stood behind me was not the one I was used to dealing with. While still quite tall, he'd shrunk to a much more reasonable stature that was only perhaps a few inches over six feet instead of closer to seven. Much *more* remarkable, however, was the fact that his horns were gone. Not covered but *gone*.

"Well, isn't *that* convenient," I said, reaching up to wave my hand through the space over his head, only to feel empty air. They were gone-gone, not just invisible. "I guess that could make this a bit easier. But your eyes … okay, fine, showoff."

His eyes had still been glowing red, but they rapidly cooled to a dark brown, concealing all trace of his inhuman heritage. Even his skin took on a more natural texture to it.

We joined the tour group at the back. A few people glanced at us as if surprised, but as Korr'ok had predicted, they quickly dismissed us, focusing instead on the tour guide.

"Does the sun ever set back there?" I asked under my breath once we emerged from the tourist center to see that the sun was low on the horizon.

"No. It is fixed. Come, we must hurry. Too much time has already passed," he said cryptically, refusing to elaborate when I pressed him.

I did as ordered, trying to shove aside the continued gnawing at my insides. The fact that Korr'ok was keeping me in the dark did not sit well. Had I done something even worse? Would I be sent back to jail when they discovered what had actually happened that night? I didn't know, and it ate at me.

The Green Line bus approached, and Korr'ok indicated we should get on it. It would take us up along the edge of the river, past the Clifton Hill tourist area, and toward the downtown, where I had made my home for the last decade or so.

Back to where the nightmare had begun.

As we climbed on, the bus driver nodded at Korr'ok, who tilted his head in response.

"What was that all about?" I asked, flicking my eyes back toward the front of the bus as we found a place to stand, all the seats already occupied.

"Tinsley is a fire elemental disguised as a human," he replied from the corner of his mouth. "He has been on Earth for a long time. He enjoys watching humans. They constantly change, from second to second, and that pleases his inner self. He finds it relaxing."

"Oh." I frowned. "Are there many like that?"

Korr'ok nodded slowly. "Yes. Niagara Falls is a locus point for the … for my world," he said, choosing his words wisely given the nearby people. "The biggest in the northern half of this continent. Not as large as New Orleans, for example, but bigger than any of the other northern hubs, mainly because of The Place Behind. You will find that there are many here who are … aware."

I sat back, wondering who else I'd interacted with over the years that might not have been human. There were so many weirdos. *Some* of them had to be that way because they were magical and not moronic … right?

The bus jerked into motion, every second drawing us closer to the bakery and what we would find there. Several days had passed, and I didn't know what to expect. Had Lily survived? Was she still there?

More people got on with each stop as we approached Clifton Hill. Tourist mecca. I licked my lips, a plan suddenly forming.

When the automated voice announced our stop, what seemed like *everyone* started heading toward the exit. It was simple. I let go of the pole and let myself be swept away before Korr'ok could react.

Once I was free, I ducked around people, moving swiftly through the crowd. If I could make it to the hill, I would be able to lose him in the crowd easily. It was my home. I knew every nook, every cranny, every place to dart around a corner and be out of sight.

No more prison. No more punishment. Nothing. I was—

I hissed as my breastbone suddenly grew warm. That couldn't be a good sign. I hurried up the hill, but each step grew harder than the last. I glanced back, but without his red eyes or horns, Korr'ok was much harder to spot in the growing gloom of the post-sunset hour. I didn't immediately see him, but that didn't mean much.

The heat intensified, stiffening the muscles in my body as I went. Eventually, I was forced to move off the sidewalk for fear that I wouldn't be able to take another step and I might be knocked down. So, I stood in the shadow of the wax museum, struggling against the heat shutting my body down.

What the fuck is going on? Why can't I move?

"What did I tell you?" Korr'ok whispered in my ear, the hot wash of his breath trickling down my neck.

I wanted to jump or shiver at his sudden closeness, but I could do nothing. I stared straight ahead, fully aware of his body behind me and his control over mine, but I was helpless against it.

"You said the words," he reminded me, the bass of his voice felt deep in my chest. "Did you forget already, tiny witch? You. Are. Mine."

Now a shiver ran down my spine. Because he let it.

"Perhaps I should give you a demonstration," he said. "Of just how strong my control is. Of what I can do if you force my hand. Should I do that?"

I tried to shake my head, to tell him no, that I wouldn't do it again, that I would be good, just please, don't hurt me. But the fire in my chest burned brighter, holding me rigid.

"Mila," Korr'ok growled in my ear, leaning over my left shoulder, not *quite* touching me.

I braced myself for whatever pain he inflicted upon my poor ...

"*Come* for me," he whispered.

And I did. Without warning, a blinding wave of ecstasy ripped from between my legs. It was so strong that I actually managed the barest hint of a whimper as air exploded from my nose. My eyes rolled back into my head as Korr'ok egged me on with an approving rumble.

My mind was pummeled by the intensity of the unexpected climax, my chest the only thing rising and falling as my lungs worked furiously, them and my brain taking the brunt of the physical impact of his command. Korr'ok stood behind me the entire time, never showing his face, never letting me see him. I heard his voice, felt his breath, and stood in his shadow.

People walked by, a few staring at me. I was on display and yet fully clothed.

"Blink twice if you promise to be good from now on," he said once my breathing returned to normal. "If you don't, I'll be forced to show you just how obedient you'll be to me."

Control of my body returned the instant I finished blinking. Spinning, I glared at him, disguising my arousal with anger. I shouldn't have been turned on by that. I should have been running. Yet, if he had *that* much control over me, he could have done worse. Much worse. I had been ready for pain. Not pleasure.

It was confusing. One moment I thought he was growing kinder toward me. The next ...

"Let's go," he said, and I followed, trying to sort out my brain and his actions.

We reached the bakery without further incident. I noticed the sheet was still covering my little alcove in the brick out back. Nobody had removed that. The door to the bakery, however, was unlocked and hanging open.

No police tape. No signs of life. No nothing.

Something was very wrong.

CHAPTER NINETEEN

Mila

"Why does everything look so ... normal?" I whispered.

It should have been night. That was a better time for skulking and talking so low. With the sun just now dropping below the horizon, I felt a little silly in my half-crouch, talking as quietly as possible.

"I'm not sure," Korr'ok said, sounding equally distrustful.

"He was burned alive in the oven. That should have been a crime scene. Yes, it's been several days, but I mean, it doesn't look like *anyone* was here. Look, my, uh, whatever, is still in one piece. Nobody has touched it."

I pointed at the sheet covering the entrance

to my little abode. Korr'ok moved to it, pulling the sheet aside to look within. His shoulder twitched, but he made no remark as he ran his hand through the air. I caught a hint of what might have been red light from the underside of his palm, but it was gone so quickly I couldn't be sure.

Had I seen that correctly? My eyes dropped to my palms, where in that very spot a few nights earlier, I'd held red magic in my palms. Did that mean Korr'ok used the same magic? What wasn't he telling me?

The tightness of his face when he pulled his head back told me he didn't like what he'd found.

"What? What is it?" I hissed.

"Inside," he growled, distinctly unhappy. His hand snatched my wrist, pulling me along in his wake.

"I hope Lily survived," I murmured to the empty bakery as we pushed through the open back door. "She was nice to me."

My nose wrinkled as I took my first breath of the air inside. "That's strong."

Korr'ok just grunted. Apparently, the scent of harsh cleaning chemicals didn't bother him. At least it was faded enough not to make me cough or my eyes water. I could only imagine what it must've been like at first.

"Could the police have come and gone? Crime

scene released back to Lily, maybe?" I asked. There were other scents in the air, though they were mostly overwhelmed by the cleaner. The bakery had clearly been in use. Ingredients were on the prep tables. A rack held some buns, and a quick glance showed they lacked mold. I touched one with a finger. It wasn't warm, but it was still quite fresh.

"Someone has been in here," Korr'ok growled. "Recently. Using this."

I glanced at the oven against the back wall. The one where Victor had been turned into a hot-cross bun. Nervously, I reached for the handle, unsure of what I would find. But when I pulled it open, it was empty. The stench of abrasive chemicals was stronger, however, proof that someone had cleaned up the evidence.

"Something is very wrong here," I reiterated. Nobody would reuse an oven with a body burned in it. That had to be illegal. So, why had it been cleaned, and why was it still here?

Looking inside, I couldn't spot any fresh residue. At least it didn't look like Lily or whoever had been cooking in it, but still …

The outside light was fading as the sun dropped lower, forcing us to rely on the dimmer interior lighting. Only the overheads were on, providing just enough to walk by, while the prep table lights were off. I went to turn them on, but Korr'ok grabbed my hand, stopping me.

"We should go," he said instead. "Now."

"What? Why?"

"Because I said so," he barked, and my chest grew warm at his command.

"Oookay," I said. "Temperamental, controlling, doesn't like to be questioned. Probably can't take constructive criticism, either. Perfect, perfect. I do love me a good toxic man."

Korr'ok stiffened. I thought he would lash out at me, but then he seemed to release. "Do you ever shut up?" he growled.

"I was taught not to speak with a full mouth," I said. "You could feed me. That might work."

His eyes blazed red for a moment from beneath his human disguise. "I don't need food to fill your mouth, tiny witch."

All the air was dragged from my lungs at his comment, leaving me frozen, unable to come up with a witty reply. Nor could I stop my brain from conjuring up various images of the outline of his cock under his pants or the bulge he'd sported in the courtroom.

I gave thanks for the darkness, knowing it would hide the absolute furnace that was my cheeks, a dead giveaway that I was thinking about his statement with more eagerness than disgust.

I should be disgusted, though. I don't want to suck on some monster cock. Ew.

"We're leaving," he repeated.

He gestured at the door the same moment it opened, and Lily walked through, stopping dead at the sight of us.

"You!" she hissed in abrupt recognition of me, her eyes widening until I could see the whites.

"Lily!" I gasped. "You're alive, thank goodness!"

I took a step toward her in relief, which just caused her to backpedal out of the doorway in terror.

Before she could turn to run, Korr'ok was there, moving like a blur until he snatched Lily's wrist and dragged her inside, pulling the door closed behind him and blocking the exit.

"Lily," I said, running up to her.

She backed away fearfully until her shoulders pressed against Korr'ok. That reminded her of his presence, causing her to pull away, forming a triangle between us. I skidded to a halt, not sure why she was so terrified of me—okay, maybe she had a reason to be. After all, the last time she'd seen me, I was wielding some sort of demonic light.

"I'm not here to hurt you," I said, holding up my hands placatingly. "But, Lily, what's going on here? What happened to your father's body? Why doesn't it look like the police have been here?"

Trembling in fear, Lily tried to pull away again,

but Korr'ok held her firm.

"I didn't call them," she squeaked, seeming to realize she was trapped. "I … couldn't afford to be shut down. We need the money. *I* need the money, I guess. We would have gone under if we closed down for them to investigate."

She sounded ashamed.

"What did you do with the body?" I pushed.

"Nothing!" she said. "It disappeared."

"What?" Korr'ok barked.

"I swear!" she said, struggling against his grip again, trying to shy away from both of us. "That thing you sent, it came back. I think it took my father's body. I don't know."

Korr'ok grunted. "It's going to come back tonight, then, too."

"How do you know that?" I asked, glancing at the smallish windows set high up into the wall. It was nearly dark out.

"Because I do," Korr'ok replied.

"What do we do, then?"

"*We* leave," he said, releasing Lily, who immediately scurried away, putting some tables between us.

"What about her?" I asked, pointing at the terrified young baker. "You want to just leave her?"

"There's nothing we can do about her," he said.

"If it chooses to go after her, it will. But it wants you. So, we're leaving."

"You can't be serious!"

"Deadly," he said, lifting a hand until my breastbone burned. "Let's go."

I fought against the mark, but slowly, one foot after the other, I started toward the exit. I looked behind me.

Lily watched us go, fear slowly replacing the look of helplessness as she realized Korr'ok was truly leaving her to her fate.

That bastard.

CHAPTER TWENTY

Korr'ok

I tried to contain myself, not letting my fear spill over.

"Are you scared of it?"

My snarl echoed off the brickwork of the nearby buildings.

"Absolutely not," I said with a laugh. "I have no reason to be scared of Irrtok."

Mila's arm muscles stiffened under my grip, revealing my first mistake as her shock momentarily loosened my control over her. Not that I enjoyed compelling her to behave.

Back on the hill surrounded by tourists, making her experience such sexual highs in public aroused me, turned me on. That was a fun game, and I would welcome a second round. The next time, I wouldn't give it to her so quickly. I would make it linger, use my voice to control her body and make her live in sexual agony for as long as I could before finally providing the release she would have sought.

But what I was doing? Forcing her to follow me, simply move along behind me? I did not enjoy that. There was no fun to it. It was ... boring.

"You know its name."

I refused to look back at her, to see the accusation on her face. But I had no choice. She stopped fighting my mental orders and surged forward until she could get in front of me and turn around, still walking backward.

"You fucking *know* what that thing is, *Korr'ok*, and you didn't tell me?"

Lunging forward, I grabbed her by the jaw, holding her still until our faces were inches apart. "What did I tell you about calling me by that name?" I growled threateningly.

"Then stop keeping secrets from me," she hissed defiantly, not backing down despite the pressure I exerted on her. "You're not going to hurt me anyway, not seriously, so you can stop with the tough guy act. We both know you'd rather fuck me than fight me."

Where was her backbone coming from? Was she speaking like that out of fear? Or was I seeing a new side to her, a more defiant, feistier side? Perhaps that was the *real* Mila? That wouldn't be so bad ...

"You know it. And you're scared of it," she said, deducing the incorrect answer from my pause. "Fuck. That means we're truly screwed, aren't we?"

"I am not scared of it," I said, glad to tell that little white lie. I didn't enjoy lying to Mila, which was a confusing sensation I didn't want to deal with now as we were in the middle of a situation.

"Are you sure?" she questioned, narrowing her eyes.

I let go of her jaw. "I'm positive. It's you, tiny witch, who should be scared of it. Now that you're back in the mortal realm, and as the one who holds sway over him, Irrtok will be looking for you. I have nothing to fear, but you ..."

"Then why did you want to leave?" she said sharply.

"To protect you!" I snapped.

"Liar," she said with far too much calm.

I hated when she read me so easily. Not that I was about to tell her the truth, that I recognized Irrtok indeed, that he matched the magic I'd easily recognized on the book. I didn't want her to know that he was a Fae. The truth was, I had nothing to fear from Irrtok if it came to a fight. He might easily overpower Mila, but me? I scoffed. I was one of the Sidhe.

Unfortunately, I didn't know Irrtok by reputation alone. That was why I didn't want to be around when he showed up. I knew him because he was fr—

A piercing shriek from inside the bakery assaulted my ears. Mila's head snapped around, holding a hand against her parted lips.

"Time to go," I said. "Time to return to The Place Behind."

I took one step forward before Mila moved to block my path, crossing her arms. "No."

"What?"

"We are not about to let her just *die* in there," she snarled as another scream came. "Especially if I am the one who caused it. So, you, Mr. Big-Bad-Whateveryouare, are going to march in there, and you are going to *kick its ass*."

"No," I said, shaking my head. "I am not."

I lifted my hand and gestured. Mila hissed in pain as the mark I'd made on her chest burned, compelling her to move aside and walk next to me.

"Why are you doing this?" she moaned through the pain, still trying to fight it. Didn't she know it was pointless?

"I'm saving your life, that's why," I said. "You should be more grateful."

The screams intensified. Metal crashed against

metal.

"Please," Mila begged. "Help her. Go stop it. I'd literally get on my knees and beg if I could move. Please, for once, do something *good*."

I laughed. "I'm not good, Mila. Haven't you learned that by now?"

"*Please*," she whispered pitifully. "I'll do anything. Whatever it takes. *Anything*."

The connotations of that offer were clear as day. I paused, considering it.

"Anything?" I replied.

Mila looked down, her tongue running over her lips. There was a long pause, but in the end, she nodded, her shoulders slumping slightly. "Yes," she said hoarsely. "Anything you want. I'll do it. I'll be a good girl. I promise. Please. Just *save her*."

She looked up at me, eyes wide and pleading. My cock burned, straining toward her. What was it about her that drove me so insane with lust? One moment she was weak and frail, and the next, she was strong and determined, willing to call me a liar to my face. *Nobody* did that and lived. Yet I hadn't punished her for it. She was infuriating!

"What are you talking about?" I snarled, disguising my anger at myself as anger at her by pretending to be oblivious.

Mila frowned. "I thought you wanted to ... you

know. Take advantage of me."

"Never," I growled.

I wanted to fuck her. Very, very badly. Throw her to the ground and mount her, claim her here where anyone could watch and see that she belonged to *me*. That I owned her body and soul, and nobody else could have her. The urge to do just that was nearly overwhelming, to the point that I started leaning toward Mila, my biceps twitching, eager to grip her with their strength.

But what I did *not* want to do was take advantage of her. I wanted her to come willingly. To want me to take her. Simply granting me access to her body was not enough. I already had that, if I so desired, I simply had to think it. I wanted more. I wanted her *mind*, too.

"What do you want, then?" she asked.

"A date," I said, likely surprising us both as the word came out.

Mila blinked. "That's … it?"

Another shriek.

I grimaced. If I went back in there and fought Irrtok, it would mean revealing things I didn't want to be revealed. So many years of work would be unraveled.

All for one woman? There was no way it could be worth it.

"Two dates," I said firmly. "Real dates. You have to try to have fun."

Mila nodded emphatically, her eyes bright and happy. "Okay. Two dates. I can do that. Now, go *save her*. Before it's too late!"

"You promise you'll act like they're real?"

"I promise!" she shouted. "Now, go, please."

I dashed for the building after memorizing the half-smile that had snuck across her face as she answered my final question.

CHAPTER TWENTY-ONE

Korr'ok

I burst through the door and skidded to a halt.

"Hello, Irrtok," I said as the red-glowing entity turned toward me, revealing itself to be a human body inhabited by the Fae.

There was a long moment as it stared at me. "Well, well, well. Now, isn't *this* unexpected," it chuckled.

I glanced at Lily, who was wielding a rolling pin along with several vicious-looking cuts, though they didn't look fatal. "Your father's body, I take it?" I asked, gesturing at the droopy-skinned human that had attacked her.

"Yes," she squeaked.

"Go outside," I ordered. "Mila will help you while I deal with this intruder."

"*Intruder?*" Irrtok hissed. "I did not ask to be here, to be bound to this body. Someone *forced* me."

"That's what you get for being a weak sack of shit." I grinned broadly while taunting him.

"It's been a long time, son of Char'ok. Much has changed since last you walked the halls of House Duloke," the Fae said with wicked laughter.

"Well, one thing I know *hasn't* changed," I hissed, wondering what he'd meant by that, "is my ability to kick your ass."

The saggy, drooping skin of the human body housing Irrtok shriveled and burned, flecks of ash floating away on a nonexistent breeze, revealing the incorporeal being behind it all.

Irrtok was as real as I, but his *true* body was back in Faerie, held against his will until he was released. Here, called as he was by magic, he was little more than an outline of his true shape.

But he felt pain, nonetheless. I flicked a hand forward, a red dart flying through the air. It split in half, then half again, and then again until dozens and hundreds of glittering shards of red magic were zeroing in on Irrtok.

He grunted and blasted many aside, avoiding others, which slammed into the stainless-steel oven behind him, turning the smooth face into a cheese grater. One took him in the side, but I knew it had been little more than a glancing blow. The fight was nowhere near over yet.

As he fell, Irrtok pushed off the table, sending the heavy baking surface skittering across the tiled floor. I had expected him to use magic, so the use of a physical object caught me by surprise. The table hit me squarely, driving the air from my lungs and throwing me backward. I landed against the cinderblock wall, my impact shaking loose all manner of dust and debris.

"Have you been hiding all this time on Earth?" Irrtok cackled, rolling to his feet and throwing magic at me.

I sucked in my stomach and slipped underneath the table, sending a pair of glowing discs Irrtok's way, no more than an inch off the ground. I then sent a foot-long spike of it on a different trajectory.

Irrtok leaped over my attacks, leaving him essentially immobile in the air. My third strike slammed into his shoulder, pinning him momentarily to the oven before it shattered into pieces, dropping him to one knee.

The Fae fell with a grunt, leaving wisps of red magic behind, indicating I had scored a solid hit. Not enough to send him back to Faerie, unfortunately, but it tilted the balance toward me.

"Damn you," Irrtok hissed.

As I said, he still felt the pain.

He grabbed a small rolling cart from where he was crouched and whipped it at me. I caught it mid-air, easily crumpling the metal into something unrecognizable before dropping it.

"You'll have to do better than that," I said, tossing my head back and laughing. "You haven't learned a thing."

"Oh, but I have," he said, lunging forward just as I snapped out a long cord of red energy, narrowly missing him with the magic whip.

He rolled between two ovens, momentarily leaving my sight. I heard something crackling, like thick paper being balled up. A moment later, a huge sack came hurtling over the top of the oven in a very high arc, right toward me.

"How is that supposed to hurt me?" I laughed, stepping aside and letting it hit the floor.

"It wasn't," Irrtok replied as the bag of flour exploded, white dust filling the air around me. I coughed, closing my eyes while my lashes grew heavy with the dust.

Irrtok slammed into me from the side with a blow worthy of a linebacker. I grunted as something gave way in my ribcage. Pain exploded up my other side as we hit the floor, my head slamming off the thick tile as it shattered under the impact. Blood dripped down my temple.

A blade of steel sliced over my stomach as

Irrtok rolled free, drawing yet more blood. He jumped to his feet, holding the kitchen knife low to the side, while droplets slowly fell from it, immediately absorbed by the mass of flour he stood upon.

"See. I've learned," Irrtok hissed.

"Or you got lucky," I said, slowly climbing to my feet, planting them both on the tiled floor outside the flour bomb's sphere of influence.

"You must be aware of your surroundings," Irrtok chanted, quoting someone like it made him all the wiser.

"Exactly," I hissed and flicked a ball of incandescent red fire at the flour while dropping a globe around it and Irrtok.

The summoned entity had a moment to realize his mistake before the flour pile exploded, filling the globe with fire and scouring everything into fine dust. I staggered, needing one hand to hold me up against the wall, the effort of keeping the globe in place requiring quite a large amount of magic. I hadn't cast anything that strong in a long time.

I could have just let it go and shielded myself, but that would have destroyed Lily's bakery, which would have hurt my chances of winning Mila's approval. Which I apparently gave a damn about.

"Damn all of this," I snarled to the empty

space, wishing it didn't have to go that way, that I could have remained hidden.

Now, though ... now it was only a matter of time. I just had to hope that the prize was worth the price.

I pushed open the door and went to Mila, still not entirely sure what the hell I was doing. But I was starting to figure out *why*.

CHAPTER TWENTY-TWO

Mila

We had our first date after returning to The Crack. I wasn't a fan of the name, but it was certainly a lot shorter than the formal name, and if humans were prone to anything, it was shortening things to speak less.

After leaving the bakery and ensuring Lily was all right, I allowed Korr'ok to bring us back. It felt wrong to just *leave* Lily like that, but she'd insisted she was okay and needed to get back to work. Korr'ok hadn't cared, she wasn't his problem anymore, but I couldn't help but wonder how she was handling everything so well.

I would have lost my shit and been in the middle of a mental breakdown. Not Lily. She was tougher than she looked. I just hoped she was processing things properly and not repressing until she exploded.

"Is the food okay?" Korr'ok asked, looking as if he were ready to summon the server to berate them if I said it wasn't.

"No, no, it's fine," I said, shaking my head to clear my lingering thoughts.

I had promised Korr'ok two dates where I would have fun, which meant giving him my full attention. Not *that* kind of attention. If he thought I would do that, well, he'd missed that opportunity when I offered it to save Lily. Instead, he'd wanted dates. So, he was getting dates. Just dates.

Not that he needs an opportunity, I thought, reminding myself of the orgasm he'd ordered me to have in public. My cheeks burned anew at the humiliation—and perhaps something akin to arousal came with it. It *was* kind of hot. If I ignored the mile-high red flags.

"Is there something else the matter?" he asked, leaning over the table until he was just outside of my bubble of personal space.

"I'm just distracted," I admitted, looking up at him.

The red glowing eyes were back, returning the instant we stepped into the passage behind the falls. So were the horns, his thick hair parted in rivers of black strands around them, the locks floating down the back of his head and behind his shoulders, stirring in the unceasing breeze passing over us.

Skin creased in his cheeks as he smiled, a gentle look that would have seemed wildly out of place to me a few days ago. The more I got to know Korr'ok, however, the more I picked up on nuances most were oblivious to. He might be a monster, but it was quickly becoming clear he wasn't *just* a monster.

"By what?" he asked, watching me with studied intent.

My chest rose and fell. Only a slight stiffness in the area reminded me of the mark I carried. His mark.

"Everything," I admitted with a sigh so heavy it bordered on dramatic. "I'm not sure I'll ever get used to dining next to a pair of werewolves or that there's a centaur birthday party going on outside. Including tiny children centaurs. The elves have an entire 'quarter' to themselves in the city. Dwarf bars exist. I'm *too tall* to be allowed in. I'm tiny. It's just a lot to get used to, Rokk."

I wrinkled my lip in disdain at having to use his fake name.

"You will adjust," he said with a conviction I didn't possess. "You are strong, tiny witch. Stronger than many and in ways that most humans will never possess. This will pass as you get used to the true world around you."

"Maybe," I said, noncommittal. "Maybe. But I just don't know anything about it."

"What would you like to know?" he asked, spreading his hands, inviting me to ask questions.

"Who are you?" I asked with a shrug. "Shoot, *what* are you?"

He pursed his lips, considering the question. It seemed like he wasn't going to answer.

"I am one of the Fae," he said, startling me with honesty. "Which I have mentioned. Fae are … Fae. You have heard the term 'fairy,' I'm sure. It is derived from us. Faerie is my home. Well, it is where I come from. Where my people live."

There was a slight undertone to that last sentence.

"Your people?"

Korr'ok grimaced as he nodded. "Your people come from Earth. Your people live there. I come from Faerie. My people live there."

That didn't sound right. But it also didn't have the vibe of a lie either. I wasn't sure *what* it was.

"Why do you live there, then?"

He smiled, his eyes empty. "Opportunity. Freedom."

Whether he meant it or not, some of his façade slipped just then, and my heart stilled at the intense depths of pain that peeked through the opening. Korr'ok was hurting and hurting badly.

It was something he had buried deep within him that he didn't want anyone to see.

But I'd glimpsed it.

"Have you been back?" I asked, eager to peer deeper, to learn more about the mysterious Faeman who controlled my body and my mind more and more. He certainly dominated my thoughts. And I wasn't just having dreams about being on top of him, grinding my hips—

"No," he said with a sternness that jerked me back to reality. "I have not. Nor will I. It is where I am from. But my home is here. The Place Behind."

"How long have you been here?"

"Long enough," he said, chuckling.

I didn't get the joke.

"Are you ready for dessert?"

The question preempted further interrogation, making it obvious he was shutting down that particular avenue of conversation. Not for good, though. I wasn't about to let that all slide. Something had happened to him, had hurt him in the past to drive him away, and I was determined to find out what.

"I could be convinced," I said, pushing my dinner plate away from me, careful to keep my napkin under my plate so it didn't blow away as the breeze picked up, pulling at his hair and mine.

We were sitting on a balcony high on the side of the Black Tower. *Very* high. The people moving around the busy town below were like ants, each a tiny speck that could be crushed with a finger. It was quite the sight, doubly so because there was no railing whatsoever, just a single layer of stone perhaps a foot high.

Korr'ok summoned our server. Apparently, dessert was platter-style, with little bits of everything. That sounded perfect. We ordered three. One for me, two for him. Fae apparently needed quite a lot of calories. Or calories mattered not at all to him. I wasn't sure.

"Can I ask you something?"

"You just did."

I rolled my eyes at the juvenile response as Korr'ok bobbed with silent laughter, his eyes twinkling with crimson light.

"Why me?" I asked. "Why a date? You aren't telling me everything. I know that."

He licked his lips, considering the question. "Truthfully, I have asked myself that same question ever since making the deal. I just ... it was what I wanted. You intrigue me, Mila. Most humans are beyond my notice. Yet I have a hard time taking my attention away from you."

"Ah, so this is an episode of *People Watching*?" I asked, suddenly feeling like I was under a microscope, my every action judged.

"What? No," he said, shaking his head. "But I don't understand you. There's something different. I can't place it."

"Great, now I'm a weirdo."

"Aren't we all?" he pointed out. "In our own way."

I looked at his abnormally dark skin, horns, and of course, his eyes. "You might have a point there," I admitted.

"Things have been ... weird between us in a way I don't understand," he said. "When I kissed you that first time, it was so different compared to anything before. I don't know how to explain it."

I thought back to the kiss. "You mean that time you took advantage of the fact that I was backed into a cell the size of this table and couldn't escape your clumsy attempts to plant your lips on mine? Is that the 'kiss' you're referring to?"

Korr'ok grinned. "You know damned well it is. You can snark at me all you want, tiny witch, but I remember how your body reacted. That was not clumsy at all."

I shrugged, trying to control myself. "If you say so. To me, I say it could have been better."

"You want better?"

"Did my leg 'pop'?" I challenged. "No. So, of

course, I want better."

"Leg pop? You want me to hurt your leg?" he seemed confused.

"No. Not that. I mean like this," I said, standing up and turning so he could see as I lifted my right leg. "When a girl's leg does this, it means the kiss is *good*."

Korr'ok looked me up and down, eyeing the blood-red dress he'd found for me. Then he stood.

"I guess I'll have to try again," he rumbled.

"That's not what I—"

My next words were stolen as he lifted me into the air, holding me over the edge of the balcony with both hands firmly around the small of my back. I gasped with fear as air rushed up, pulling at the hem of my dress, showing far too much leg to be considered classy.

"Put me down," I said.

"Not until your leg pops," he grinned, leaning just a bit more forward.

"K—Rokk!" I hissed. "Put me down. Now."

"Kiss me first," he growled.

"If I do that, will you put me down?"

"Maybe," he said before torching my lips with his.

Almost—but not quite—against my will, my head tilted back to make it easier, both my hands looping around his neck, fingers threading through his thick hair as my body responded to his kiss, despite the fear pounding in my chest.

And damn it, my leg popped!

A smile creased my lips as we parted for air, then found one another's mouths again. I was making out with a monster. And I enjoyed it!

I enjoyed it. I enjoyed being with a monster.

Just what did that say about me?

"Put me down, please," I said, suddenly feeling cold on the inside, unwanted memories boiling up out of nowhere. "Now."

"Mila?" he asked, concerned, though he returned me to my feet anyway.

"I need to go. Take me home. Now."

Korr'ok started to protest, then thought better of it.

"Very well," he said coldly, leading the way from the restaurant without another word.

I followed in his wake, lost in my thoughts.

Am I a monster, too?

INTERLUDE

Irrt'ok

The air grew thick and red, coiling in upon itself as light flickered off the thick stone walls of the dark room, the rock damp from the moisture so far underground. The boiling red maelstrom of cloud grew denser, generating more light with each tightening of the swirl.

There was a tearing sound, and then reality split open as something came tumbling through to land on the floor in a heap. The gash in the air closed while the red smoke curled down, binding itself to both wrists of the body lying on the damp floor, gasping for air.

"Damn him," Irrt'ok hissed, shaking his head, feeling the sting of the bonds, realizing what it meant.

Korr'ok couldn't kill him. Not in the mortal realm.

"Ten fucking years stuck here," Irrt'ok

growled, getting to his feet. "Great. Just great."

"I take it your return wasn't as enjoyable as your unexpected trip?" a figure asked, detaching itself from the shadows in one corner.

"No, my liege," Irrt'ok ground out unhappily, dropping to one knee. "They seldom are when the journey is made against your own desire."

"So, you let yourself get killed," the figure chuckled, shaking its head and heading for the door. "Come."

Irrt'ok rose, falling in step behind the figure, who towered above him, a pair of horns jutting from under his hair, the tips filed to a razor point. The click of shoes on stone sounded with each step his liege took.

"Who summoned you?"

"A nobody," Irrt'ok said, expressing his surprise. "I've never seen her before. I did, however, recognize the touch of her magic."

"Yet she managed to trap you?"

"No," Irrt'ok growled. "Someone bound the spell to summon me to a book. She simply read it."

"And you let such a nobody banish you back here for a decade? Come now, Irrt'ok, I thought better of you than that."

"I'm glad to hear that, my liege," Irrt'ok said, dipping his head toward the ruler of House Duloke, the strongest faction in Faerie. "Because it wasn't her."

The click of footsteps on stone stopped. "Then, who? Surely not some mortal."

Irrt'ok's face spread wide into a smile. "Oh, no mortal at all."

The leader of House Duloke turned, noting the smug smile on his subject's face. "You seem inordinately proud of yourself. I hope, for your sake, the answer is worth making me ask."

The minor Fae's smile faded immediately. "My apologies, my liege. But yes, I think you will find it quite worthwhile. You see, the one who defeated me was none other than your brother."

Red light lit the corridor as a pair of scarlet eyes burned bright. "Really? My brothers are dead, Irrt'ok. I watched them die myself. You know that. You were there. Are you saying one of them lived?"

"Rill'ok and Priv'ok, yes," Irrt'ok replied, the smile returning. "But no. I was referring to *Korr'ok*."

Silence ruled as moments turned to seconds. Then, a millimeter at a time, the smile on Irrt'ok's master's face grew wider.

"Come, Irrt'ok, there is apparently much to discuss," said Kraw'ok, the leader of House Duloke. "Much to discuss indeed."

CHAPTER TWENTY-THREE

Mila

I stared through the ceiling, seeing visions I had long repressed or forgotten about. The guest room was quiet, and Korr'ok had left me alone since we returned. Perhaps he was pissed at the sudden ending to the date, or maybe he realized I wasn't in a good state. Either way, he'd given me space and time, both of which I desperately needed.

Am I a monster?

The question circled ceaselessly through my brain, coming and going with an ebb and flow like the tides. Sometimes, I thought hard, without an answer, and other times, I was so lost in myself that I barely considered it.

But it was a valid question to ask. I had killed Victor. I was responsible for his death. Maybe I hadn't known what I was doing, but then again, maybe I had. When I reached for the book, I felt the malice contained within. On one level or another, I had to have known that by opening it, nothing *good* would come. Which meant I had embraced the evil. I had become the monster.

And that wasn't even considering what may or may not have happened to Sarabeth and the others. Were they even alive? I didn't know. There could be more blood on my hand.

"My fault," I whispered to the empty room. "I have to accept it. There's no changing what's been done. Only the future."

Could I change who I was becoming? Or had my fate been sealed, dooming me to end up like my parents? Monsters in their own way.

I shuddered as, all of a sudden, I was back in the kitchen of the house I'd grown up in. A two-story affair located on a quiet cul-de-sac. No picket fence, but ivy had grown up some of the brick walls. There were two clean, new cars in the driveway, and we took two vacations a year.

Everyone thought it was idyllic.

"A fucking C? You got a C? All that money we paid for a fucking tutor, and this is the best you could do, you stupid shit? How are you going to get into medical school with a C? You need to do better!"

I shrank away from the memory as the wooden spoon turned my backside red, bruising it so bad it hurt to sit for a week.

That was first grade. First fucking grade.

The next year had been no better. A spoon for a low grade. A belt for specks of dust I had missed while cleaning the entire house.

"You don't pay any rent. We don't have any freeloaders in this house. You have to learn your place. Now get to work! The real world won't just let you live for free. It's time you figured that out."

That was my father. He'd alternated between telling me that I was gone the moment I turned eighteen, that I was so stupid I would end up on the streets selling my body for crack, and that I needed to shape up if I wanted to get into Columbia or any of the other "good" schools.

One time I'd asked him which one he wanted. He beat me, breaking a rib, for my "insolence," as he put it.

I ran away after that and ended up in Mrs. Johnson's "Home for Hurting Youth" at the tender age of ten. Even thinking the name brought a snort. Why had nobody ever thought to look into the irony of the name? You didn't go there for help. You went there to *get* hurt.

If I'd thought my father considered me a freeloader, Mrs. Johnson was on another level. Then, of course, there were the other kids, who took their cues from Mrs. Johnson. They'd learned that violence against the weak was the way to go.

By fifteen, I had fulfilled my father's prophecy. Living on the street, trading whatever I had, sometimes my body, for money or food to survive. Nobody liked to think about that aspect of society. It made their skin crawl.

Well, fuck them. I had lived it. They could go back to their precious ivory towers and pretend like it didn't exist. Like the world was somehow better than that. I knew it wasn't, and I had the mental scars to prove it.

I would have the physical ones, too, except my body healed everything in time. There were men who would pay extra knowing you could take it, that the evidence of their darkest desires would never be permanent.

A tear rolled down my cheek, sadness for the girl in the past. She, at least, had been free.

The laugh that exploded from my lungs caught me completely by surprise, forcing me to swiftly smother the sound, even as my body shook. It doubled, then doubled some more until I was heaving, barely able to breathe. Tears streamed down my face.

Perhaps cackling was the better term for what I was doing in near silence. But it didn't matter.

The irony of it all was lost on me somehow. I was "free" living on the streets, perhaps. But my "punishment" at Korr'ok's hands was anything but that. I was living a life of absolute luxury compared to before. The bed under me was softer than anything I had slept on in years. I had a real pillow. Meals whenever I wanted.

And I was getting ready to abandon it all.

Outside, the sounds of Korr'ok moving had ceased well over an hour ago after he'd retired to his room, announcing he was heading to bed. The last time I had left my room, ostensibly to "get a snack," the light had been off under his door, and no noises could be heard from within.

It was time.

Pushing aside my melancholic thoughts of past and present, I slid from the bed as softly as I could and padded to the door, doing my best not to make a sound. Thankfully, the smooth stone floors of the Black Tower were *excellent* for not conducting sound. It was the only thing that gave me a chance.

The door was unlocked. It took me nearly five minutes of painstakingly slow movements to open it without so much as a squeak. Every fiber in my body screamed at me to open it and run as fast as I could, but I knew that wouldn't be the way to do it. I had to move cautiously, carefully. Once I was out of his earshot, I had to move like I belonged.

Like I wasn't terrified that my head would be ripped off if Korr'ok caught up with me. That would be the hard part, but I had to try. I couldn't stay there forever. I just couldn't.

After another five minutes of armpit-drenching patience to close the door, I was off, making my way toward the stairs that would lead me out. Out of the oppressive building, out of that wild place, and out from under the thumb of the hottest man I'd ever met.

Once free, I would find a way to remove his hold over me. Someone had to be able to detect whatever he'd put in my chest and remove it. Or maybe I would just hop on a bus and move away forever. It wasn't like I had anything tying me down. Niagara Falls was home, but if it was home or prison, well, that choice was clear.

The never-setting sun caused me to squint as I exited the tower on the ground floor, my quads aching from the descent down the many stairs. Ignoring it, I headed for the gates. And freedom.

Breathe, Mila. Just breathe. You can do this. You're allowed to be here. In fact, you belong *here. Look at everyone else coming and going. You're just another one of them. Don't look at the guards for permission. Just walk past, blank-eyed stare. Your mind is elsewhere because this is a regular occurrence for you.*

The minotaurs let me pass without so much as a huff or grunt. I fought back a shiver. I wasn't done yet. Not by a long shot. I had to get up the ramp and into the caverns behind the Falls.

"Easy does it," I murmured, shoulders rising

and falling as I took a deep breath, taking a roundabout way to the edge of the city.

I wasn't running. Wasn't escaping. I was simply making the journey to the other side, that was all. That was what I needed everyone around me to believe.

At the bottom of the ramp, a trio of human-looking beings gathered and started up. I hurried, catching up just enough to walk behind them, hoping I wouldn't stick out. I was wearing the same clothes I'd worn to the bakery. Pants. Shirt. Low-cut boots. Nothing that called attention.

As we hiked, the back of my neck burned. The urge to turn around grew stronger. I wanted to know if I was free. If I'd made it.

"Don't do it," I hissed under my breath.

"What did you say?"

"Nothing," I replied, giving my head a quick shake.

Other than a raised eyebrow, there was no response. We ascended the ramp and, one by one, slipped into the crack that would take us out of there. Finally, it was my turn, and I walked forward, head held high.

I'd made it. We exited into the caverns and went our separate ways without a word. I hiked for the exit, eager to put as much distance between myself and my hometown as I could.

I'd always wanted to visit Vancouver. Perhaps it was time I went cross-country. Mind made up, determined to start fresh, I put a smile on my face and picked up my pace. I was finally free.

Up ahead, the rock wall began to glow, reflecting light from around the corner.

A purple light.

CHAPTER TWENTY-FOUR

Mila

"Shit, shit, shit," I cursed, turning and hurrying in the other direction.

I knew what that light portended and what would come charging out from it. My shoes slapped hard against the rocky ground, but all that mattered at the moment was speed. I had to gain ground on the stupid Gray Knights before they got organized and came after me.

"Come on," I hissed, looking at my hands, trying to summon the fire from within, the energy that might help me somehow escape from their clutches.

The roar of the falls grew louder as, instead of heading for the elevator that would take me *up*, I went deeper into the tunnel, toward the platforms that emerged alongside the towering funnel of water. The walls were white and painted there, the floor slicker than before from mist that worked its way into the corridors.

Behind me, the minotaurs were deploying, not worried about being found down there at that time of day. How they had found *me* so quickly was a different question, one I would ask later after I had escaped their clutches.

"Halt!" a voice barked from somewhere behind me.

Did they ever expect people who were running away to listen? It made no sense to me. I just put my head down and ran faster. There was only one hope of escape now. One way out.

My clothing did a poor job repelling the water, the fabric sticking to my skin as it was quickly drenched by the unceasing torrent pouring over the edge high above me. Up ahead, the tunnel abruptly ended. A gate rose halfway up the wall, blocking the way, with four or six feet of floor on the far side before it suddenly dropped away.

"This is stupid, Mila," I hissed, pulling myself over the barricade as fast as I could, careful to monitor my footing. "Really, really stupid."

Footsteps could be heard over the tremendous crashing roar of the water as it raced by, not five feet from me. I was truly *behind* the Falls, about a third of the way up from the base. I wasn't on a platform farther down where I could safely climb over the side and run.

It was a true waterfall.

"Come *on*," I hissed, pushing at the spot in my mind where I'd felt the magic or whatever it was on previous occasions. "Please."

"That's far enough," a commanding voice ordered as a minotaur strode out of the mists.

I backed away until my foot slipped on the very edge of the lip, halting my progress. The minotaur smiled. He must have thought I was trapped, not understanding just how badly I wanted to be free again.

"I'm not going back," I stated. "I won't."

"You can't escape us," he said.

I pushed harder at my mind, anger at my situation building. I did not want to feel helpless. I wanted to feel strong. To be respected. Not laughed at. The heat of my fury stirred, the fires of anger stirring in my belly. I stoked it more. Adding my hatred of the injustices cast upon me, of person after person deciding how my life would be run. For once, just once in my life, *I* wanted to be in control of my destiny.

Again, I nudged my mind, ordering it to respond.

A soft red glow bounced off the whitewashed walls of the tunnel. The minotaur's eyes grew wide. He didn't retreat, but he did drop his fingers to a thick-shafted mace strapped to his side, gripping the wooden haft firmly.

"Back off," I growled, pulling harder at the little spark I could feel in my brain, teasing more of it free and into my hands. "Now."

"No."

I cursed. I could make my hands glow, but I didn't actually know how to *use* the power any more than that. Fighting wasn't an option. It couldn't be, not with the other Gray Knights filling the hallway behind their leader. I was outmatched.

"Damn it," I moaned.

Protect me, I ordered the power, imagining it like a cocoon around me. Shielding me. Keeping me alive.

Light swirled brighter as the balls grew bigger in my hands.

With a snarl, the minotaur ripped the gate free from its hinges and came at me.

"Sayonara, cow-face," I spat and flung myself back off the platform.

Water rushing downward at an incredible rate slapped at me, spinning me around wildly as I screamed and curled into a ball, knowing it wouldn't be long before—

I hit the surface like a cannonball, air driven from my lungs on impact, while the force of millions of gallons of water falling from above pushed me deep under the water, keeping me away from any easy source of oxygen.

The turbulent waters tossed me around like a blender while my lungs screamed for air. I wanted to uncurl and stroke for the surface, but that was a surefire way to die. There was too much water coming down too hard.

I balled up tighter, willing myself to survive, fighting hard to keep calm and slow my heartbeat to let my precious oxygen last just a little bit longer. It was my only hope.

My chest was ready to explode, and my body was shutting down when, at last, I finally bobbed to the surface. The thunderous roar of the falls was behind me, only a light mist drenching the air.

I gasped, fresh panic taking over for a moment as I paddled awkwardly to stay afloat. After all, I had never learned how to swim.

My four-limbed pawing at the water seemed to work, however, because I didn't sink. The river swept me away, and I didn't fight it. I tried to steer myself slowly toward shore, but by the time I found footing steady enough to stop myself, I was half a mile downstream.

Of course, I knew the Gray Knights wouldn't give up. Their portals would let them close the gap quicker than I liked. Which meant, as exhausted as I was, I had to continue.

That was when the reality of it hit me. I *could* carry on. The red glow had long since vanished from my hands. But I was *alive*, and not only that, but I was also essentially unharmed. Soaked to the bone in frigid water and likely at risk for hypothermia if I didn't keep moving, but no broken bones, nothing.

"It worked," I whispered, smiling to myself. "Holy shit, it worked!"

I would have to practice and practice frequently, but if I could do that? I could do anything! Maybe I could use this newfound power to lift myself out of poverty. Live a life the way *I wanted*.

Sorry, Korr'ok. But living in your shadow, under the constant threat of you taking control of my body, is not a healthy relationship. I didn't choose any of that.

My shoes soggy and squishing with every step, I moved off, heading downriver. The slope grew less steep the farther I went. It would be faster to stay in the river, but up ahead was the first of a series of rapids, and I was smart enough to know better than to pit my meager swimming skills against the Whirlpool Rapids.

So, instead, I clambered over rocks, moving as fast as I could. With any luck, the Gray Knights would assume I was dead and not give pursuit.

A portal opened to my left without warning, the purple glow diffusing swiftly so that those farther away would be hard-pressed to spot it.

"That *would* be my luck," I hissed, heading

toward the river as Gray Knights poured out.

We weren't even that far from where they'd captured me the first time. It was like a repeat all over again. There had to be some meaning behind that, didn't there?

"That's far enough," the same minotaur growled as they fanned out, weapons at the ready. "Come peacefully, or we'll have to use force."

Tired and aching, despite the protection of my magic, I set my jaw and feet. "No," I said calmly, reaching deep inside me to that wellspring of magic I was learning to touch.

It took less effort that time. My hands glowed red at my side.

"Very well," the leader growled, gesturing with his head.

Two of his men came at me in a rush, on opposite sides of the line. With a shout, I thrust both hands up and *pushed* at the magic in my palms.

Balls of red light shot out. One flew straight and true, slamming into the shin of the beast on my right. He yelped and went down in a tumble. The other twisted at the waist, taking the impact in his arm, and continued coming.

"Oh, crap."

I summoned more magic but was forced to dive out of the way, narrowly missing the swing of his weapon, a simple staff of wood. It was a good four inches in diameter, though, making it more than "good enough" to drop me if it connected.

With another yell, I pointed both hands at him as he wound up to attack again and let fly with everything.

A wave of nausea and exhaustion ripped through me, but I watched with great satisfaction as both balls hit the minotaur in the chest, tossing him back into the river, where he disappeared below the surface.

My legs wavered, making it hard to evade the third and fourth Gray Knights, who came in with the leader on their heels. I dropped low, dodging their strikes, but one of them lashed out with a boot that caught me in the knee, spinning me around and dropping me on my back.

"Ahh!" I cried, crossing my arms over my face as the leader tried smashing my face with the butt of his weapon.

A crimson shield burst into being in front of my arms, stopping his attack. The minotaur grunted and tried again but was denied.

"Fuck you," I spat. "You'll never have me."

The bull-headed beast snorted, then kicked me in the head with a boot. Stars danced across my vision as I rolled away, my ears ringing from the blow.

On he came. I tried to focus, to call up a shield to stop him, but my brain wasn't working right, wasn't responding how I wanted it to.

"You're mine now," he snarled, hauling back and slamming his fist into my nose, breaking it.

As I tried to respond, he drove a punch deep into my stomach, causing me to convulse upward. "No more jokes."

I clawed at his eyes, but he batted my hands aside, slapping some sort of restraint around my wrists, pinning them together.

"I'm going to enjoy this," he growled as the Knight I'd dumped in the river clumped his way free of the soggy bank, fury evident in his gaze.

A fresh punch further broke my nose. I cried out, curling into a ball, ready for the next one to land.

There was a burst of light, which I initially attributed to another blow to my head. But no agony followed it. Instead, a wave of cold settled over me as the minotaurs shouted.

Thwack. I grimaced at the sound of flesh on flesh, then retched as something very large *snapped*. The scream was cut off abruptly, followed by a deep snarl that ran through the very rocks on which I lay.

"She. Is. *Mine*," Korr'ok snarled again, radiating a fury I'd never seen in him before.

"She's a fugitive who broke the confines

of her punishment," the lead minotaur said, not backing down. "A punishment *you* were supposed to be overseeing, Lord Rokk."

"Are you challenging me, Divecto?" Korr'ok asked in cold tones.

"No," Divecto replied, though it was clear much was implied by the exchange.

"I thought not," came the angry reply. "I will bring her back. You have my word."

A long silence followed before Divecto eventually grunted an understanding. Purple light came and then went, leaving me alone with Korr'ok.

"Get up," he ordered without coming to see me.

My chest burned immediately, forcing me to comply. I stood, staring sullenly at the ground as blood dripped from my nose.

"Enough of that." Korr'ok snapped his fingers at me, and my nose exploded in blinding pain, enough to force me to cry out.

Once it faded, however, so did the pain and swelling that was pushing my eyes closed.

"How?" I gasped, lifting my bound wrists so that I could tentatively touch the healed area.

"That's not important," Korr'ok growled, marching over to me until he was so close his size was almost oppressive. "What is important is that we go back. Peacefully."

"I won't go back," I said quietly.

"You can, and you will. Then you will accept whatever punishment is meted out for breaking the rules. I cannot protect you from that."

I frowned. That wasn't all … "There's something you aren't telling me, isn't there?"

Korr'ok sighed. "By breaking the rules, you have shown my claim on you to be … incomplete. Others will come now and challenge me."

"Challenge you?" I asked, my stomach tightening with nerves. "For what?"

Twin eyes burned scarlet in the dark, making me their sole focus. "You."

CHAPTER TWENTY-FIVE

Mila

I pushed open the door to Korr'ok's quarters but stopped short of disappearing into my room. Was it my room? Or a glorified prison cell?

Does it matter?

"I don't understand," I said, spinning on him and crossing my arms.

Korr'ok just looked at me, waiting with that annoying stillness that belied a patience level I could only ever dream of. Why couldn't he show a *tiny* bit of interest in what I was about to say? Grrr ... men!

"You said I would be punished," I told him. "When you stopped the Gray Knights. You said I would have to take whatever punishment the Court gave me. I was expecting solitary or lashing, hell, maybe a public execution. But all they gave me was ... more house arrest and supervision under you? That puts my entire 'punishment' back into your hands."

"Yes, it does," Korr'ok rumbled, my chest glowing faintly with the outline of the magic he'd branded me with. I flinched at its heat. "So be good."

"No promises," I said, trying to ignore it. "But you made it out like I would receive more. Much more. But I didn't. Why not?"

Korr'ok looked away. "Because I gave Dannorax something he wanted more than to punish you."

"You did? What did you give him?"

"My spot on the Jury," Korr'ok replied evenly, his face turning to stone, preventing me from determining just how he felt about it.

"What? He wanted that?"

For a moment, the glow of his eyes dimmed ever so slightly. "Yes. For some time now."

"Why?"

"Because I am the only one who could conceivably challenge him for the spot as Judge," Korr'ok explained. "Dannorax knows who I am. Well, perhaps not *precisely* who I am, but what I am. He knows he would be unwise to challenge me. The outcome would not be a guaranteed win for him. Or me."

"He fears you?"

Korr'ok snorted. "Dannorax is a *dragon*, Mila. He fears few things. Even most *gods* would do well to avoid him. But he does respect my capabilities in battle. As I do him. The Place Behind is his domain and has been for a long, long time. Ever since he and—"

My eyebrows went up. "Ever since he and …?"

"No," Korr'ok said firmly with a shake of his head, changing the subject back. "The point is, he's happy to have me gone, even if I had no intentions of ever trying to take his spot."

"I still don't get it," I said. "Why do it, then? Why give that up?"

"For you," he said with heavy gravity, the words slamming into my chest like a cannonball, shaking my legs. "You are mine, Mila. Not his, not any of theirs, but *mine*."

The last word was like a bullet, cracking the sound barrier as it filled the air around us. Korr'ok's eyes burned with an intense scarlet flame that I'd never seen before, turning the space around us into a thick soup of heat. My lips parted slightly, my lungs working harder to breathe.

Nobody had ever tried to claim me before. Certainly not that way, not so passionately. How did one respond to that? How would *I* respond?

"O-oh," I managed to stammer, eyes still locked with his.

Quick, think of something else to say. It doesn't have to be an address to world leaders. Just say something!

"Th-thank you," I said a little more evenly that time, trying to ignore the fire spreading down the back of my neck. "I appreciate you doing that for me."

We were standing several feet apart in the middle of the common room, but the stillness of everything made it seem like he was right there. In front of me, mere inches away, like when he came to my solitary cell. Just me and my monster.

Only there was nothing to stop him. Or me.

A fresh wave of prickling spikes of anticipation rolled through me, settling swiftly between my legs. Was it really going to happen? Hours ago, I was ready to leave him, to run away and never look back.

Now, after knowing he'd given up something important for me, I was changing my mind?

Or was my mind never really made up to begin with? Was it Korr'ok I was running from or this entire place? Do I really know? And now he's leaving it voluntarily. For me. Because of me. Which is it? Does it matter?

"Mila," Korr'ok rumbled, his words carrying across the gulf between us like the early warnings of a spring storm.

"Yes?" I whispered, not trusting myself to speak properly.

"There is something we must address." He came closer.

"Okay," I squeaked, trying to stay still so I didn't tremble, his broad, powerful chest inches from me as I looked up into a face I had once thought scary.

Now I just saw him. The eyes could be unnerving still at times, but in them, I no longer saw a spooky monster out of my nightmare. I simply saw him. The, well, maybe not *man*, but he was definitely man-*ly*. Very manly.

"After this, if you try to escape from me again," Korr'ok said, one hand caressing my jaw, forcing my head to tilt farther back, "bad things will happen. I will not have the power to stop them. Not without violence, and I cannot risk that at this time. Not what it would take to bring them all down to save you."

"What are you saying?" I asked, breathing out slowly through pursed lips, trying to ignore the billowing heat infusing my entire body from his simple touch.

"That I need to know if I can trust you," he said.

"To do what?" I breathed.

"To stay with me. To not run away." The tip of his index finger hooked under my jaw, sending a tremor through my body that saw me swaying slightly closer to him. "Can you promise me that?"

"I ... I'll try," I replied, unsure why I couldn't lie to him.

I didn't want to leave Korr'ok. At least, not yet, but I loathed being anybody's prisoner. Even his. If he asked me without that clause, I wasn't so sure what my answer would be. The thought of being tied up and at Korr'ok's mercy was ... well, confusing didn't even *begin* to cover it.

"You'll have to do better than that," he growled, arms flexing as he laid his hands on my shoulders, fingers draping down onto my upper back.

He was so *big*. I was so little.

A shiver ran down my spine.

Shit. Did he notice? What does he think? Is he assuming it meant I'm afraid of him? But I am. Sort of. But, like, I don't think he would hurt me. Not ... not like that. He's given up so much to keep me safe.

Why? Why would he do that? Does he expect me to repay him by hopping into bed with him? No, that doesn't seem like his way. If he wanted me, he would just come for me. I have serious doubts about whether or not I would even try to stop him. Do I want him to stop? What if his hands slid down my shoulder? Across my breasts? What would that be like?

My inner monologue was brought to a screeching halt as he cupped my chin.

"I need you to promise that you won't run away from me," he said softly. "You don't have to promise anything else. Just that you'll stay."

"For how long?" I said with a whimper as he leaned toward me, his face right *there*, so close to mine.

The glow of his eyes had softened to a dim illumination. There were levels to him, I was discovering. Levels I would never have suspected upon first sight.

"Until—"

He whipped around at the sound of wood breaking, keeping me firmly behind him with one arm. The soft, gentle giant was gone in a heartbeat, replaced by a towering monster whose growl made the very air quiver in fear as he placed himself between me and whatever was coming through the door.

CHAPTER TWENTY-SIX

Korr'ok

It came sooner than I'd expected. I had hoped for several hours of reprieve, but it seemed that I wouldn't be granted even that much. Word would have spread that I was no longer on the Jury, which meant my claim on the woman was now considered 'open to the highest bidder.'

A.k.a. 'the one who could take her from me.'

Unmated human females were rare and highly desirable in The Place Behind, and I had harbored no doubts I would have to defend my claim to her.

That didn't bother me. The trick would be doing so and *not* giving away the true strength within me. There were few I wouldn't want to face in battle, and fewer still who fell into that category and would try to come for Mila. It didn't matter, though. I would win.

As I had told her, she was *mine*. More and more, I was no longer viewing it that way out of duty or a desire to figure out just who she was or why her magic was so tantalizingly familiar, like a word on the tip of my tongue. No, I saw her as mine because I *wanted* her to be mine.

The door shattered, revealing the first challenger to come for her, his eyes alight with golden hunger.

They could come for her, but they would never get her. She might be scared of me, but I would show her that she had no reason to fear. Not anymore.

And that started by protecting her.

With a mighty roar, I charged Gunnar, the living embodiment of a bloodthirsty Viking. The giant bear of a man, nearly as tall as I, was perhaps larger, given his muscles were swathed in a layer of fat, all of which were covered by animal skins draped over his body.

The demi-god swung a short-handled axe at me, matching my bellow with his own. I slapped the flat of the blade away and ducked inside his reach, lowering my shoulder and delivering it into his midsection.

Priority number one: get him away from Mila.

We crashed through the door, destroying it beyond repair, and Gunnar's back slammed into the stone wall of the hallway, whipsawing his head back against the rock. It rebounded with a sickening thud, but the pain and splitting of skin only further enraged the Viking warrior.

That was the problem with those types. They were battle-crazed, and pain wouldn't stop them or even slow them down. I was fairly certain Gunnar didn't even *feel* pain.

"Your claim is weak," he spat, shoving me away with a mighty bounce of his chest, creating a gap. "I will take the woman and show her what a true man is like. She will lay before me and experience proper treatment."

A red hue descended over my vision at the thought of Mila lying beneath Gunnar, exposed, vulnerable, being taken against her will.

His axe sliced in, but I again batted it aside, growling thunderously as I charged at him with abandon.

But Gunnar wasn't as dumb as he acted. The taunt had been testing my defenses, and it had worked, finding a weak spot. Enraged, I had charged in blind to his other hand, which whipped around, bringing a stout but sturdy war hammer into play by connecting the flat side with my skull.

The lights went out briefly as more stars than I could count blinded me, sending me to my knees, where a beefy kick to the midsection tossed me down the hall. I rolled, hair whipping around, until I came to a halt, staring at the ceiling.

"You have grown weak, *Korr'ok*."

My blood stilled as he used my true name.

"Yes, that's right. I know who you are," Gunnar drawled. "Third son. Outcast. *Failure*."

I snorted, getting to my feet and setting my shoulders as Gunnar clomped down the hallway toward me. Everything seemed to slow, turning his approach from a balanced warlike stance to a clumsy, plodding trot. Behind him, Mila's head appeared in the hallway, concern dotting her features as her jaw tightened in dismay. She must have seen the blood dripping from my temple where Gunnar's hammer had opened a gouge.

"You think, by divulging that information, you have an advantage," I said, the hallway taking on a red hue, but that time for an entirely different reason. "That you somehow one-upped me. But you're wrong, Gunnar. So very, *very* wrong."

"And how is that?" the Viking demi-god chortled, whirling his axe around casually. "I am going to kick your Faerie ass and take the woman, and everyone will know about it. You're screwed."

"No," I said, inhaling and then exhaling. "You're wrong."

"I am?" he said with a mighty snort that

befitted his stature. "How?"

"Because now I am *free*."

Red lightning cracked from my hand, shooting out and catching Gunnar in his prodigious gut. The impact tossed the Viking down the hallway, leaving fur and skin behind him in a streak, even as he cradled the blackened and charred skin from where my blow had impacted. Mila ducked out of the way as he flailed past.

I snarled and stomped past him, pausing in front of my door.

"I'll be right with you," I said, leaning in and kissing her. Hard.

She inhaled sharply, body stiff, before melting into me, her hands coming to grab my jaw—and pulling away, slick with blood.

"Sorry," I said, meeting her eyes.

"It's fine. Go kick his ass," she said, swallowing nervously, suddenly unsure of what she had just done.

I nodded once sharply, and turned away. There would be time to unpack her look. Later. First, I had to finish dealing with Gunnar.

"Ha. Ha, ha, ha!" the brute chuckled, getting to his feet with surprising agility. "Not bad, Korr'ok. Not bad at all, for a washed-up *has-been*. He said you might do something like that, though."

Alarm bells started ringing in my head.

"So, he prepared me for that eventuality."

Gunnar set himself, both weapons in front of him. *"Glavardo!"*

I blinked as he uttered the single word, a Fae word of power. Red light burst from both weapons as lines appeared on them, sharp and straight like they were trying to contain the magic but slowly shattering into a million pieces.

Someone had gifted him with a very powerful enchantment on his weapons. I hadn't expected that at all. Nor did I have time to study its implications.

Gunnar came on in a rush, the air screaming as the axe blade split it apart, leaving a long gouge down my chest. I backpedaled as fast as I could, unprepared for the speed of his strikes. The hammer caught me in the shoulder, and magic exploded from the contact, sending me down the hallway like a ping-pong ball. The Viking tossed back his head and howled with laughter and battle fury all rolled into one.

When he came at me again, all thought had left his eyes, leaving him with just a crazed desire to kill.

I guess someone should have told him about the side effects of Faerie magic when used like that. He'd become the tool of whoever gave him the power. A tool meant to be discarded after use.

Unfortunately, his use was apparently to kill me, and he was coming annoyingly close to it. I had hoped to spare his life and simply beat him, but it was increasingly apparent that such an outcome was no longer feasible.

"*Enough*," I barked, throwing magic at Gunnar.

The axe sliced through the magic while the hammer connected with my jaw. I left the ground, my horns smashing up into the rock, momentarily pinning me there.

Gunnar used that moment to bring the axe back across my midsection in the reverse swing, cutting deep through my black skin and spilling my blood. I roared in agony as the touch of his metal burned deep.

He punched me in the face with the top of his hammer, and the impact snapped one of my horns off, spinning me around, spraying blood everywhere as I catapulted away and hit the ground.

"This was fun," Gunnar taunted as he approached, his weapons dripping my blood. "We should do it again sometime."

"I think I'm going to be busy that day," I grunted as he hoisted me up by my other horn, with his axe hanging at his side and the other hand gripping the hammer.

"Okay, then I'll just kill you today," he spat, tossing me against the wall and swinging his hammer so fast it connected before I'd even fallen.

My leg shattered under the impact of

the enchanted weapon. A weapon enchanted *perfectly* to hurt me. By someone who had intimate knowledge of me and who I was. Someone who could provide such magic. But who?

"I expected a better fight from you," Gunnar barked. "You're even weaker than he said you would be."

My eyes narrowed. That confirmed someone had *actively* sent Gunnar to kill me. But there was no animosity between the demi-god and me. Not as recently as several days ago, the last time I'd seen him in Court. What had happened to make him like this? What changed?

Gunnar raised his hammer and brought it down—

And I intercepted it with a blade of glowing red magic that extended from my right forearm. Gunnar's eyes went wide.

"You were used, Gunnar," I whispered. "Used and lied to. And for that, I am sorry."

The blade from my other forearm punched up through his stomach and out the other side, blood sizzling into vapor from the heat of the magical weapon. I tossed the badly wounded Viking aside and got to my feet. Foot, really, since the other leg was useless. I balanced heavily on my left leg, shunting the pain aside, ignoring it for the moment even as it hammered against my brain.

I thrust a hand at him, and red magic flowed from the weapons and into me.

"See, that's the thing about using tailor-made magical weapons," I said. "They work great when you have the element of surprise. But they're easily countered after that. That magic is my magic. It's part of me. And it *responds* to me."

Gunnar smiled, which was very unsettling. "But did I fail?" he grunted.

"Yes," I said. "And you gave away the fact that someone is looking for me and wants me dead. You were a bad move on their part. You should have said no."

And then I took his head from his body, leaving a score in the stone under his neck from the sweeping strike of my blade.

Gunnar's eyes blinked, the golden light fading.

"You don't say no to *him*," he cackled amid a stream of blood.

He smiled at me as he died, all the light fading from his eyes.

I frowned, trying to puzzle out that last cryptic comment. Who had forced Gunnar into confronting me? And, more importantly, *why did they want me dead?*

CHAPTER TWENTY-SEVEN

Mila

As soon as the brilliant red blades of death disappeared, I ran up to Korr'ok, mentally pushing down the wave of revulsion at the headless body. I'd seen corpses before, not including Victor, but that was by far the most gruesome death scene I'd witnessed.

"Are you okay?" I exclaimed, stunned he was somehow still standing.

When he turned to look at me, I gasped at the state of his face. Gashes streamed thick onyx blood down his face, and a weird viscous red ooze leaked from the shattered horn. His left shoulder hung limply, and the way his right leg hung from his body did not look right at all.

"What can I do?"

Korr'ok grunted and flicked his right hand at

the body. Flame far too red to be natural erupted from the body and blood stains, quickly eating away at the corpse.

"My room," he said through teeth clenched in pain. "There is a wardrobe. Open it. Remove the center drawer and bring it to me. The contents are not important. Just the drawer."

I rushed down the hall and threw open the door to his room. On the left stood his wardrobe. When I pulled open the doors, I was greeted with a row of black and gray shirts hanging from a rack. Below that were three drawers with ornate gold knobs.

Snatching the center one, I yanked it open and off its rails, dumping the watches and other myriad jewelry to the floor as I dashed back up the hall, holding the deceptively heavy wooden drawer.

"Here! I have it!" I cried, skidding to a stop, noting that the floor was conspicuously absent of any of the attacker's remains.

Korr'ok reached out and casually tore it apart with one hand, tossing aside everything but the base. That he gripped in one hand and swung against the wall. The wood shattered, revealing a second layer. From it fell a medallion that glittered softly with dark scarlet tones.

Grabbing it mid-air, Korr'ok inhaled deeply. Magic flowed from the medallion and into his hand, tracing its way up his arm like spider veins before disappearing under the seam of his shirt. They reappeared up his neck, across his face, and down his other arm. I could see it spreading across his entire body through the exposed skin.

The medallion continued to glow as time went on, ten seconds, then thirty. A full minute passed before Korr'ok slumped over, the magic seemingly drained. He pocketed the item, then motioned for me to move aside.

Awkwardly, leaning heavily on the wall, he stumped his way to his quarters without help. Not that there was much I could do. He was too big for me to be of much assistance, leaving me hanging around like a gnat, hovering and annoying but unable to actually *do* anything.

It was not a pleasant feeling.

"Can I get you something?" I asked once he fell into his bed, staining the covers with his blood. "Water? Food?"

"Water would be nice," he said, eyes drooping low.

"Are you going to make it?" I asked nervously.

If he died …

"Yes. Just … need to recover first." He coughed, which didn't do much to convince me of his words.

My gaze lingered for a few moments as he settled deeper into the bed, then I hurried to bring him a glass of water. He accepted it and drained it in two gulps. I brought two glasses the next time. His lips quirked upon noticing, a look that left my skin tingling despite his beaten and bruised face.

I wasn't about to forget how he'd paused mid-fight to kiss me. My body had boiled itself alive in those few heartbeats. Only the sudden strength of Gunnar had brought me back to reality. If the fight had been over then, and Korr'ok had come to me, eyes ablaze, muscles stretched and taut, his body next to mine ... I wasn't sure what would have happened.

"Will your horn grow back?" I asked. "It looks pretty nasty."

"Yes. Not the first time one of those things has been removed from my skull. Not a pleasant experience, though."

"Right. Well, that's good. You look better with two."

He eyed me. "You like them? They don't scare you? Humans are always so afraid of them. They see me as the devil."

"So did I at first," I admitted shyly. "But you know what they say about not judging a book by its cover and all. Besides, I'm not exactly normal myself now, am I?"

I lifted a hand, managing to summon forth a bit of my magic. It sparked and swirled around my hand, a dancing line of red that I still had no idea how to control.

"There is something different about you," he said, reaching up with his good hand, an answering line of magic darting through his much larger fingers. "I just don't know what that is yet. You're unlike any human I've met."

"Thanks ... I think?"

He smiled, and I suddenly wanted to open a window to let some cooler air in. How could he be lying there, covered in blood with a horrifically broken leg, busted shoulder, and massive gouge in his stomach, and *still* fill me with butterflies with just a smile?

Because he doesn't smile like that at anyone else. Just you. With everyone else, he's the mighty Lord Rokk. Fierce warrior. Even fiercer than a grumpy old man who hates today's kids. But with you ...

I swallowed that thought. There were things I wasn't ready to think about or admit to myself, and that was one of them. Not yet. Maybe not ever. I didn't know.

"What was that thing with the medallion?" I asked, feeling bold.

"Energy reserves," he said.

There was more to it than that. I considered pushing, trying to get him to just tell me more, but I didn't. Perhaps I should have.

"Why didn't they do anything to heal you, then?"

"I am healing," he said. "It's just not instantaneous. Nobody can do that. Not from weapons that have been imbued with magic designed specifically to harm you."

"I see. Who would do that?"

The softness left his face, replaced by the hardened features of the person everyone around me feared.

"I don't know," he growled, shaking his head and then wincing as he remembered how hurt it was. "But I intend to find out."

I leaned forward, brushing away some of his hair that had gotten caught in the blood on his face. My fingers dragged across his skin, and Korr'ok inhaled sharply, looking up at me.

There was surprise on his face. Not from my actions, no. From my touch? Did he feel the same way I did when he touched me?

I caressed his cheek without thinking, more focused on testing the theory than anything else, including the consequences of my actions.

Korr'ok's body went still. "What are you doing?" he asked cautiously.

"Learning," I whispered, placing my hand on his chest just above the biggest cut, feeling the beat of his heart through my palm on his bare skin.

It was so strong. And fast. Was he nervous, or was it still adrenaline from the fight? I knew that was why my heart was still racing. Being so close to danger and seeing someone else get hurt while defending you was a rush. It just hadn't calmed down yet.

"What is it you're learning?" he asked, laying a hand on mine but not removing it.

"I ... I'm not sure," I stammered, my voice betraying me.

"Try," he urged.

I licked my lips, the little movement drawing a lingering gaze that had all *manner* of connotations that I wasn't sure I was ready for.

Are you not ready for it? Or are you scared you'll like it?

"I'm learning you aren't the scary monster I assumed," I said, forcing the words out.

"No, that's not it," he said. "I *am* a monster, Mila, and you would do well not to forget it."

I smiled tightly. He was right. "Fine. You're not *just* the scary monster I assumed when I first saw you. You're more as well. I thought you mindless, full of rage. But you're smart. There's a person in there under the anger and, well, cruelty, I guess. And that person isn't always an asshole."

"Then I'm not trying hard enough," he rumbled, one side of his face twitching.

"You don't *have* to try around me," I said. "*That's* what you need to be learning."

"I don't want you to forget and assume I'm safe

and cuddly," he said, baring his teeth.

"I won't forget that, trust me. But you can let me see the rest of you, too."

Then I leaned down, and for the first time, *I kissed him*.

CHAPTER TWENTY-EIGHT

Mila

I wasn't prepared for the reaction from the rest of my body as our lips touched. Before I knew it, I was all but rubbing up against him, desperate to feel more of his touch. His mouth was scorching hot, forcing my head back as he parted my lips with his tongue. I might have initiated it, but within seconds, he took control of it. Of me.

For a moment, I hesitated, wondering if that change was natural or if he was using the brand within my chest. Determined to differentiate the two, I pulled back, searching his eyes for any sign that he was frustrated with me for disobeying.

"Is something wrong?" he asked. "Did I hurt you?"

I shook my head, wordlessly reaching for the back of his head to pull him down to me again.

My fingers brushed one of the cuts, however, drawing a wince.

"I'm sorry," I said, gingerly withdrawing my hand. "I just …"

Korr'ok's chest rumbled with thunder, a laugh not given full form. "It's fine. Perhaps we just put this on hold. I should shower to get clean. By then, the worst of it will be healed. That way, you won't get covered in more blood."

"More …?" I looked down at myself. In the heat of the kiss, I hadn't realized I'd pressed so hard against him, staining my clothes with blood. "Damn."

"We'll get you some more," he said, bracing one hand on the wall and limping toward the broken remains that were once his door.

I followed with my hands out, ready to do whatever I could to help if he faltered. *I'd probably just cushion his fall, wouldn't I?* There didn't seem to be much point. If Korr'ok started going down, I wouldn't stop him. He was too big.

Thankfully, we got back to the room without issue. The cuts on his body were already healing, having stopped bleeding during the short journey back. They were still ugly and swollen, especially the huge one across his chest, but he seemed about right in saying that by the time he got out of the shower, he'd be in better shape.

I let him go into the bathroom, waiting

outside with crossed arms, unsure of what to do next. Just standing around waiting for him to finish seemed awkward. Yet what more was there to do?

A grunt from the other side of the door drew my attention. Soft cursing followed.

"Are you okay?" I asked, worried he'd hurt himself.

"I'm fine," he assured me. "Just struggling to get these things off. They're all torn up. My arms don't want to bend that way."

"Oh. Here, I can help with that," I said, pushing open the door, figuring I could help pull his shirt over his head.

"Wait—" Korr'ok started to say, but I'd already pushed my way in.

Only to find his shirt already gone and Korr'ok's pants halfway down his legs, exposing his thick cock.

"Oh, my," I said in a rush of breath, my eyes locked between his legs, almost forced there by the downward V-shape of his lowest abs that pointed toward his impressive dick.

Korr'ok watched me. I could feel his eyes roaming over my body. Probably wondering what I looked like without clothes on. Did he want to see? Would he like it? I didn't have the tits, ass, or hips most girls had. I'd often thought of myself as a rectangle. All corners and edges.

Nothing soft and womanly about me.

"Stop that," he growled, reading my mind.

Strong fingers cupped my chin, gently prying it upward against my will, forcing me to lock gazes with him. I did, and my body came alive as I saw the fires burning deep in those ethereal orbs. I wasn't sure when I'd learned how to read them, but there was no mistaking what I saw.

"I don't know what negative thought you're having," he told me. "But I can assure you, it isn't warranted."

"Okay," I whispered, not sure I believed him.

"*Believe it*," he growled powerfully enough to make my heart skip a beat and my mouth go dry.

I tried to gather my thoughts, which was particularly difficult when the tip of his cock brushed against my stomach, announcing his arousal.

Korr'ok shifted, and something tore. Fearful that he'd ripped open a cut, I looked down past his thick shaft, only to see that he'd used his massive strength to tear apart his pants. Leaving him entirely naked and mostly covered in dried blood.

"Um," I squeaked.

"Come with me," he ordered, backing toward the giant glass shower.

I just nodded, doing as ordered as he turned the shower on and drenched us in water that was somehow instantly warm. Blood sluiced from his body while the liquid plastered my clothing to my body.

"That can't be comfortable," Korr'ok said, lifting my shirt over my head without waiting for an answer.

It was a struggle that involved some shaking, a little hopping, and more laughs than the mood had initially called for, but eventually, we were both naked, my clothes in a pile in the corner, and smiles on our faces.

"Well, now," he said with a shake of his head. "I think that may have used up enough time to let me heal well enough."

"Well enough for what?" I asked cautiously.

"To do *this*," he growled, grabbing my waist and lifting me from the floor, pressing my back to the tiled wall.

"Oh," I whispered, gently wrapping my legs around his waist to ensure I didn't hurt him. "I like that."

"Good," he said in a rumble that vibrated through my body. Then he covered my mouth with his, stealing all the oxygen from my lungs with the heat of his kiss.

It wasn't just the intensity of the moment either. He was genuinely *hot*. As if his body temperature ticked up the more turned on he became. Was that even possible? I didn't know, nor did I have the brain power to think about it because he was pushing me farther up the wall so that his mouth could explore my body.

I all but melted as his mouth covered one of my nipples, teasing it with his tongue, rolling over it in soft, warm circles that sent their sensitivity skyrocketing.

"Oh, fuck," I moaned, grabbing onto his horns without thinking.

Korr'ok's throat erupted with a growl that sent my palms flat against the wall.

"No," he said. "Put your hands back. That was good."

"Like this?" I whispered tentatively, wrapping my hands around his horns again, noting that the one that had been broken off was already mostly regrown. He wasn't kidding about healing fast.

"Yes," he rumbled. "Just like that."

He knelt without warning, still easily holding me up, but now he had the height to put his face between my knees without sending my head crashing through the roof. I was thankful for that.

Then his tongue hit my clit.

"Oh my *god*."

My sexual experiences growing up had not been anything pleasant. Most had been desperate trades for food or shelter during the winter, selling myself for a place to sleep. Nothing I was proud of or wanted to relive.

Korr'ok was the first man to touch my body who cared about *my* pleasure. A fact I was made blissfully aware of several minutes later when I had the first real orgasm of my life given to me by someone else.

I cried out, holding tight to his horns, using them to push my dripping cunt hard against his tongue while my hips shook. Hands gripped my waist, squeezing tight to remind me who controlled me.

And I came harder than ever before. Every muscle tightened, and I writhed in his grip as ecstasy rolled out from between my legs like a shockwave, ripping through my body, turning every nerve end into a fiery ball of bliss that then reported back to my brain. My nerve centers went into lockdown, and I shut down, unable to control myself or do anything more than ride it out, holding onto Korr'ok's horns as his tongue stroked my clit masterfully over and over again.

"Holy fuck," I moaned as the climax faded, leaving me limp in Korr'ok's arms. "I ... *wow*."

He laid me on the tiled floor, shielding me from the shower spray with his giant body. That brought a smile to my face. Although he called himself a monster, in moments like that, I knew it wasn't totally true.

"I'm glad you enjoyed that," he said, pushing

his way between my legs, though they spread willingly enough.

"That's putting it mildly," I joked as he lined himself up with my opening, gripping his shaft with one hand, running the tip over my pussy lips, coating it in the wetness that dripped freely there.

I'd thought I was ready, but when he guided the tip into me, I moaned at its unexpected tight feeling. He was big. I was small, and it had been a long, *long* time.

Korr'ok grunted. "I'll go slow," he promised, moving to cover my body completely with his, resting on his forearms, giant biceps next to my head.

He did just as promised, taking his time entering me. At some point, I wanted more, and my fingers dug into his chest as I struggled to stretch to fit him. Eventually, it became a challenge. I'd come this far. He had so much buried inside me. I *had* to have it all. Every inch of him.

"*More*," I growled at him several times, wrapping my legs around his waist, pulling him down into me, capturing his thick shaft, and conquering it inch by inch.

He might claim that I was his, but I intended to make him *mine*.

And I did. Eventually, he could thrust no more,

his hips pressing hard against mine. We rested like that for a bit, rocking against one another while my body adjusted.

But eventually, I wanted more. He read my mind and, without a word, began to thrust into me. I held onto his neck, my body on fire, his cock sliding in and out with smooth motions that made my limbs tremble.

"Do it," he ordered in my ear. "Don't hold back. Let yourself go, Mila. You're *mine* now."

Something about how he said it flipped a switch in my brain, and I lost control, screaming out wordlessly as my cunt clamped down over his shaft repeatedly. The action drew grunts from him, and I saw his face strain. His cock swelled, driving my orgasm to another gear, but he didn't explode.

He did, however, thrust harder. And harder. The shower continued to run. Korr'ok's groans grew louder. My fingers dug into his back.

When the end came, I had a moment to gasp as he erupted inside me, warmth spilling from my insides as he never stopped thrusting. My own body was triggered by his climax, and we stared into one another's eyes as we came and came hard.

Soon, he sagged over me, both of us breathing hard, unable to form words. The shower sprayed everywhere, but neither of us cared.

"Wow," I managed to utter finally, my body beaten and pleasured in the best ways.

Korr'ok grunted and slowly withdrew, leaving me feeling empty, like I was missing something.

Just physically, I told myself before I could overanalyze the sensation.

We got up, finished showering, and dried off before flopping down on his bed. I ached slightly between my legs, and his cum slowly leaked from me, a sensation I'd never experienced before. It brought a smile to my face instead of a cringe.

It was a pleasant reminder of the intense moment we'd shared.

Perhaps, I wondered idly, now would be a good time to try to get him to share something else.

"So," I said, rolling onto my side and draping a leg over him. "I think, maybe, after all that, you can tell me why you go by a name that isn't yours? What are you hiding?"

Korr'ok looked at me sharply enough to slide a sliver of fear into my stomach. Had I pushed too far?

CHAPTER TWENTY-NINE

Korr'ok

"That's what you want to talk about right now?"

Mila's eyebrows lifted as she gazed at our naked bodies, entwined with one another, her pale human skin against my midnight monster flesh, the sheets a tangled mess.

It was quite the tale of opposites, but the feel of her against me was unlike anything I could describe. I didn't want it to end, especially because of how she might react after learning the truth.

The fact that I was even considering telling her everything didn't register at that moment. I hadn't told a soul who I was in a long, *long* time. But if she asked, I knew I'd tell her.

"Given what you just did to me," she said wryly, "I think maybe it's allowed."

I casually ran a hand along my regrown horn. "If I recall correctly, things were done to me as well …"

The warmth of her touch was still a present memory in my mind. Never had any of my bed partners been brave enough to hold them while they rode me. I had felt like little more than a play toy for her while she did it. And I'd enjoyed it.

"Maybe," she said with a wave, her cheeks turning rosy, "but you know what I meant."

"Perhaps," I agreed with a sigh. "Tell me, what do you know of Faerie?"

"That it's a place. You're from there. That's about it, really," she said thoughtfully. "Are you in trouble with someone there? Is that why you ran away?"

I snorted. "Despite whatever ridiculousness Gunnar might have spouted, I didn't *run* away. Certainly not from someone. I left of my own accord. I didn't tell anyone I was leaving or where I was going, so perhaps my leave could be construed as having run away, but I left to pursue a life I wanted. Not the one assigned to me."

"You didn't have free will there? Were you a prisoner?"

"In a way," I said with a small shrug, not

wanting to disturb her body. "Faerie is ruled over by the Sidhe. The strongest and oldest of the Fae creatures. The Sidhe are organized into houses. Ten Great Houses and numerous affiliated minor houses. Each Great House rules a section of Fae."

"And you're a Sidhe," she surmised.

"Yes," I said, a strange weightlessness coming over me as I told someone the truth. No more hiding behind lies for the first time in forever. "I am of House Duloke."

"Is that where the second half of your name comes from?" she asked, noting the similar ending to both words.

I nodded. "Precisely. I was born the third son of four to Char'ok, head of House Duloke."

"You had three brothers?" she exclaimed with a shudder. "That sounds chaotic enough in a human household. But when you're all, well … like you, that just sounds like a disaster waiting to happen."

I didn't bother holding back a chuckle. "I'm sure there were times when I was a child that were, shall we say, *trying* for our keepers, but when you're born to the head of the ruling House of Faerie, you learn at a young age how to behave."

"If Duloke is the ruling house, and you were the son of one of its leaders, wouldn't that have made you a sort of bigwig? An important person?"

"Not particularly. My eldest brother, Rill'ok, was set to succeed my father. Priv'ok was the second son and head of the armies. Third son and fourth son? Unnecessary. A girl would have been better. Then my father could have married her to another Great House to forge bonds. But I didn't want to be a part of that life. Politics? No, thank you. So, I left to make my own way. I changed my name and never revealed my heritage. I ended up here, in The Place Behind, and that's that."

Mila's blue eyes were focused and thoughtful, slightly narrowed as she considered all I'd told her.

"What about your other brother? What did he end up doing?" she asked.

"Kraw'ok?" I shrugged. "No idea. He was still young and unfocused when I left. He was coddled by my mother a little too much. I doubt he made much of himself. Too weak."

"I see." Thankfully, she didn't push the subject.

I grunted and shrugged. "And now you know."

"What have you been doing in the meantime?" she asked. "How did you end up involved with the Twisted Court?"

"It's fun," I said with another, stronger shrug. I'd noticed the way the first one caused her breasts to jiggle. Which was even more pleasant to the eye.

"Stop that," she said with a giggle, pulling the sheet up.

"Never," I growled, tearing the sheet away from her entirely, leaving her body exposed to my greedy gaze.

She pouted but made no effort to reclaim her cover. "Now you have to tell me about what you do. Do you really enjoy seeing people tortured and hurt?"

"They deserve it," I growled.

"Did I deserve it?" she fired back.

"You broke the law," I pointed out. "And I left my spot on the Jury for you. This is different."

"And how many other women have gone before the court to be claimed by someone else and had worse done to them?"

"I am who I am, Mila," I told her coldly. "I am a Fae. It is in my blood to see the scales balanced. Things must be made even. Sometimes those who break the rules must be punished. Like the man I brought here. He was beating his wife and raping his daughter. Should I have just left him be?"

"Well, maybe not," she said. "But that's what prison is for …"

"Prison is for those who can be redeemed. Minor crimes. The man was doing despicable things to a *child*. Call me any name you want, think me however evil. I do not care. She was a child. She had nobody to help her. So, I helped her."

"You help in the worst sort of ways," she said, shaking her head. "How am I supposed to accept this?"

"Just accept it," I said with a shrug. "It's who I am, Mila. Take it or leave it."

It was a little brusque, and I hoped she would stay, but I wouldn't change. Not when it came to punishing men like Abhed.

She mulled that over. "Is being on the Jury all you've done?"

"No," I said. "I have a job. And before you ask, I kill people."

"But not children," she said, pulling away from me slightly.

"No gods, no innocents, no children," I repeated my mantra.

"So, what, you only kill bad guys?" she scoffed.

"There are very few people in my world who can so easily be classified as good or bad," I explained. "Much of that is determined by your point of view. After all, you got at least one person killed, if not others. Does that make you evil? Are you bad?"

She looked troubled.

"There are many shades of gray," I told her, softening my tone. "I evaluate each case and make my decision. I will not pretend to be a 'good' person. Nor am I despicably evil like Abhed or others like him, whom I view as the lowest of the low. I just don't hide behind a fake front."

There was a prolonged silence as Mila digested my words. I let her work through it, my grip around her waist comfortable, not preventative. If she wanted to get up and move away, I would let her.

But she didn't.

"You're an interesting person, Korr'ok of House Duloke," she said at last. "I'm not entirely sure what to make of you. Some things you say appeal to me. But then you turn around and support that ass of a dragon, Dannorax."

I gave her a tight smile.

"Why is he so uptight and mean anyway?" she asked.

"I'm not sure," I told her. "Nor would it be my place to tell his story. There is a reason, I'm sure, but he chooses not to share it. And as to why I support him, well, he's been put in charge of this sector of the world, and that's the way it goes."

"You seem unwilling to defy him, which seems unlike you."

That time, I laughed. "As I said before, he's a *dragon*, Mila. Challenging him would not be a smart career move for either of us."

"Even for one like you? A Sidhe?"

"Even for one like me," I confirmed.

"So, you couldn't beat him?"

"You don't win a fight between us," I said. "You just don't lose it. Such a battle would be a pyrrhic victory at best, if not a total loss, with both of us dying."

"I see."

She didn't sound disappointed or surprised. Prying for more information, perhaps, to learn the extent of my strength? I wasn't sure, but I wouldn't put it past her. Mila was smart. For someone who'd grown up on the streets, it was slightly unexpected. Perhaps that was me judging a book by its cover. I wasn't sure, but I was quickly coming to realize I shouldn't underestimate her.

"Are you satisfied now? Have your answers?" I teased, running a finger down her shoulder, watching her skin pucker and tighten from my touch.

"Almost," she said, not stopping me. "What happens next?"

"What do you mean?" I asked, my finger pausing just shy of her clavicle, deciding whether to dip lower or continue back up her neck.

"To me. I'm your prisoner, aren't I?"

I looked her body up and down, blood filling my cock once more as it lusted after her. "I think it's probably safe to say you're becoming a bit more than that, don't you?"

She grinned, noticing my visceral reaction. "So, I'm free to go, then?"

I laughed. "Only if you want to challenge Dannorax and have him reverse his ruling."

"Well, isn't *that* a convenient way for you to keep me around," she drawled.

"Yes. How fortunate for me," I said.

She giggled.

"Now, if you would be so kind," I implored, pushing her down onto her back, spreading her legs with a knee, kissing my way down her body, over her breasts, the pink nipples hardening on their own as I watched. "I have to finish something before we take care of business."

"Oh," she cried softly as my tongue found its mark. "This isn't business?"

"This is most definitely *pleasure*," I growled around her mound.

"Okay," she hissed, gripping the covers. "But what's next?"

"Finding out who sent Gunnar after me," I said, sliding a finger into her damp hole, eliciting a louder moan. "Now shut up and focus on me."

CHAPTER THIRTY

Mila

When Korr'ok told me we'd be looking for information about who had sent Gunnar, visions of seedy men in dimly lit taverns and secret back-alley meetings filled my mind. Where information would be bartered, threats offered, and danger abounded.

None of that came to be. Instead, after our personal, ahem, *business* was concluded to the mutual satisfaction (several times over) of both parties, we'd showered, dressed, stopped for food, and then gone to the library of all places.

"I'm confused," I stated, looking around at the various creatures with their noses or other appendages stuffed between the pages of books, magazines, and other forms of physical media. "How will a library give us the information we need?"

"It's not," he admitted. "But before I go poking around, asking questions about House Duloke, I need to get caught up on current events. Hence, the library."

"*Current* events?" I repeated. "But a library isn't really that current. Unless ... Korr'ok, *how long have you been gone?*"

"Almost two centuries," he said offhandedly as if it were nothing. A footnote.

"Oh."

"Yes, now come on, everything to do with Fae is on the fourth floor."

"Right." I trailed along in a daze. Korr'ok had made it sound like he'd left only a couple of years ago. Maybe ten at the most. But if the ratio of time at home from time gone held up ... "Uh, how old are you?"

"I don't know," he said. "Two hundred or so Earth years? Something like that. Fae don't really keep track. Not precisely, at least."

"*Two hundred ...*" I gaped at him.

"Get used to it," he said with a grin. "My father is *much* older."

"Okay." I felt a little lightheaded as my brain tried to process just how much Korr'ok must have seen in his life. Two hundred years! Insane.

I trailed after him, not really paying attention, as we went up to the library's fourth floor.

While he perused books, updating himself on his House, I stared out the window at the Black Tower several blocks away, its shadow an oppressive covering of the buildings to my left, a sullen reminder of the lord who dwelled within.

At some point, Korr'ok came to me, frustrated. "There's nothing here. No changes."

"Then we have to look for newer news, don't we?"

He nodded. "Yes. I have some contacts within the city. Let's go."

I grinned. Now we were talking. Shady secrets, hidden hideouts, that was the fun kind of stuff! Not well-lit libraries with perfectly labeled and organized books.

"Why are you grinning?" he asked.

"'Cause we're going skulking!" I exclaimed. "I've always wanted to do that. Do we go sit at a bar and wait for someone to approach us? Or are you going to go in and use your rep to get an audience and then kick the ass of someone who doesn't want to help?"

"What? Where did you get all those ideas?" he asked.

"Uh. Books? I read a lot from the library. There isn't much else to do when growing up on the streets," I said awkwardly.

"Right. Well, we're not going to do any of that. We're going to go to one of my contacts who does a lot of business in Faerie. Then I'm going to ask him what he's heard. He works in the marketplace. It's going to be boring."

"I guess that makes sense," I said, sad we wouldn't get to sneak around.

Korr'ok just shook his head and led me from the library. The trip was brief, only several blocks. The closer we got, the thicker the push of people around us. Ahead, I could hear the sound of vendors hawking their wares, people chatting excitedly, buyers haggling with sellers, and the cries of *"Make way!"* from those who thought they were better.

I thought I was prepared, but then we turned the corner into the open-air marketplace in a giant square. I'd clearly had no real idea what I was getting into. Scents hit me in the face like a mallet—freshly cooked food mixing with savory spices, burning wood and incense, but also sulfur and less pleasant aromas.

"Busy place," I remarked as we plunged into the sea of people without hesitation.

Korr'ok took my hand to ensure we wouldn't be separated, but even there, people moved aside for 'Lord Rokk' as best they could. We made swift time to the other side of the square, where the stalls were larger, the people finer dressed, and the oppressive throngs of bodies more spread out.

We approached a short tripodal being with

two big eyes on the side of his head and a pair of antennae sticking up. His skin was brown like mud with a slightly moist sheen to it. There was no hair anywhere on his body. He was standing in the middle of a tent, surrounded by tables laden with articles of clothing piled high in a multitude of bright and fun colors.

"Arresh," Korr'ok greeted, crossing his wrists in front of him and bowing his head.

"Lord Rokk!" Arresh exclaimed, bowing from the waist and going a near ninety-degree bend. "It is good to see you. Come to buy the pretty lady something nice?"

I started to speak, but Korr'ok gripped my hand tighter in a warning.

"Yes. Do you have anything new?"

"Hmmm," the merchant said, looking me up and down. "A robe, perhaps. She would look good in blue, no?"

"Red," Korr'ok said immediately.

Arresh shot a look at the Fae but simply shrugged and nodded. "Yes, red is also an excellent color. Perhaps something like this would suit the lady's tastes?" He clomped over to a table and pulled up a beautiful scarlet robe with thick cuffs and collar and gold embroidery over the seams.

It was absolutely not my taste—how it could be, I'd never owned a robe before! —but when

I ran my fingers over the material, I was immediately won over. The softness was *to die for*. I almost started purring just feeling it, and when the odd merchant draped it over me, I practically melted.

"I think we'll take it," Korr'ok said with a smile.

"Very good, very good," Arresh said, clasping his hands together. "Anything else I can help you with?"

"Information," Korr'ok said, keeping his voice low so it didn't carry, though with the din around us, I wasn't sure he had anything to fear.

"Of course. What do you seek?"

"News, mostly. Have there been any changes in Faerie lately? Things not making the public rounds just yet?"

Arresh frowned. "You have not heard?"

"I rarely care to stay abreast of the news. You know this. What is it?"

Arresh grinned. "House Duloke, the greatest of the Houses, is purportedly under new management."

"Purportedly?"

"They have not confirmed anything, but rumors are circulating that there was a coup of some sort. The father and several brothers were taken out."

I stifled a gasp. Korr'ok's family was dead?

"But nobody is talking about this?" Korr'ok demanded.

"Not publicly, not yet."

"Why not?" he mused, his hand gripping mine tightly.

I squeezed back, making sure he knew I was there. That I would support him. I couldn't begin to imagine what was going through his mind. How was he staying so composed?

"Again, I do not have firm information, Lord Rokk," Arresh said, spreading his hands out, palms upward. "But the rumor is about 'consolidation.' Perhaps they fear a challenger?"

I couldn't have been the only one who detected an undercurrent to Arresh's words.

"A challenger? To whom? Who is ruling the House now?" Korr'ok did his best to sound confused.

I wondered if Arresh was buying it.

"Word on the street is that it was the youngest brother who orchestrated it all," Arresh said, smiling broadly. "Maybe he's afraid he didn't get the rest of the family? Perhaps the rumors are wrong, and someone survived?"

"Perhaps," Korr'ok said, sounding thoughtful. "Thank you for the information."

"You are welcome. Please, what else can I, humble merchant, tell you about the state of Faerie?"

"Nothing," Korr'ok said. "We're done here."

"There must be more I can do to provide service to one such as you, Lord Rokk," Arresh supplicated.

I stared at the merchant. There was something —

"He's stalling," I said, just as Korr'ok jerked his head around.

"Get down!" he shouted, throwing me to the floor as something sailed past our heads.

A second later, Arresh's stall exploded.

CHAPTER THIRTY-ONE

Korr'ok

The explosion threw us sideways, through the side of a canvas tent. I bounced once before catching myself in a crouch and sliding sideways across the sandy ground, my feet and fists leaving trails behind me.

"Mila!" I barked, looking around wildly for her as chaos reigned outside the tent following the explosion.

Another cylinder came sailing in through an opening, trailing red smoke. I snarled, gathered it in one hand, and spun, hurling it back the way it had come in a single smooth motion.

The canister exploded, the shockwave rippling against the canvas sidewalls of the huge, mostly empty tent I'd landed in.

"Mila!" I shouted, scouring the tent as I moved

toward the entrance. Only a handful of tables had been set up so far, though many more were stacked flat behind the upright ones. Beside them were crumpled boxes stacked higher than my head, full of garments and reams of material.

As I passed the boxes, they moved. I froze, red blades shooting up from both forearms as I prepared to defend myself.

"Show yourself!" I barked.

A groan filtered out from deep within the stacks of boxes.

"Mila?" I asked, blades disappearing as I tossed boxes aside to reveal her battered form.

"What the hell happened?" she asked, getting to her feet. The boxes might have actually softened the blow of the explosion.

"Magic grenades," I grunted, pulling her close and drawing strength from the feel of her body pressed next to mine. All that time, I'd thought that it was her strange magic that intrigued me, pulled to me, but maybe I was wrong. Maybe it was *her* ...

"From whom?"

There was motion at the doors of the tent.

"I'm not sure," I growled, "but I think we're about to find out."

Four hulking figures in all black entered the room. Thick-shouldered and broad-chested, with skin the color of a midnight sun, identifying them was easy.

"Sidhe assassins," I spat.

"Huh?" Mila mumbled.

"Faeries. Deadly ones. Stay behind me."

Without a word, the four foes spread out in a shallow arc, keeping us pinned against the boxes. I grunted. Taking on four assassins was a tall order. I could do it. But could I do it *and* keep Mila safe? Having to devote some of my attention to her would make things difficult.

I gathered my power as they attacked, moving in silent unison. Magic unfurled from between my gathered hands like a mushroom cloud, moving sideways toward the assassins. The red wave caught two of them unprepared, tossing them back across the tent.

Immediately, I spun to my right, blades sliding up from my wrists. I blocked one attack down low with my left hand, then sliced hard with my right above, but the attacker was already moving out of range. My spin took me the rest of the way around, with the remaining attacker stabbing high with two metal daggers that dripped with what I assumed was poison.

My blades were completely out of position to stop the attack. *If* I had continued turning like normal to plant both feet. Instead, however, I had shifted my weight as I turned, leaving my left foot planted hard. My right came up and connected solidly enough between his legs that Mila cringed audibly behind me.

However, the assassin was skilled, and he rolled back, away from my killing blow. By then, the first attacker had recovered and lunged in. He wielded a long blade with a slight curve at the top, a style I wasn't familiar with.

"Who sent you?" I snarled, moving to keep Mila directly behind me. The assassin pinned me down, reducing my mobility and creating clear avenues of attack, giving me a higher chance to predict what they would do.

Trade-offs, all around.

The leading assassin pulled his lips back in a smile but, as was traditional with their sect, said nothing. They wouldn't give up anything.

Fortunately for them, I didn't *need* them to be particularly vocal to give away their allegiance. There was another way. A simpler way.

Just as silently as they came at me, I went on the attack, magic striking against Faerie steel, driving them back, keeping them separated as the other two recovered from my initial magical attack and rejoined the fight.

I drove down low on one, then with a gesture, flung sand in his eye. A wall of red darts half a foot long came at me, but I turned them aside with a gust of wind, forcing two attackers to dart from the path or be impaled. The entire tent glowed red, the color of most magic in the world, a deadly hue.

The first to fall was the attacker on my far right. He came in hard on the heels of a failed attack from one of his fellows, trying to drive me back toward the boxes. I tossed a magic ball to my left, aimed at the middle of the three remaining assassins. It went off, a mostly harmless explosion designed to force them back.

The shockwave caught my attacker in the back. He stumbled forward, right onto my blades, which drove through his chest, only my forearms stopping his forward progress.

He looked at me without care, then died. His body disintegrated around my blades as thousands of tiny red marbles cascaded to the ground before swiftly dissipating into matching smoke.

"I should have known," I spat, glaring at the three remaining Sidhe. "House Duloke sent you."

"How do you know that?" Mila asked from behind me in the lull that followed the death.

"Red is the color of House Duloke. When a Fae dies outside of Faerie, they don't really die. They're simply banished from any other plane for ten years. Only within our realm can they truly die."

"And when one of you dies, you die like that?" she asked.

"Yes."

The other three came on. I drove two of them back with swift cuts of my blade, forcing them to dance backward or be opened from waist to shoulder. I spun, stabbing a blade at the third. He caught it between his two daggers, the tip a solid six inches from his face. He winked at me as if to say, *You're too short.*

I grinned, and the blade lengthened another two feet in the blink of an eye, piercing through his winking eye and out the back of his head. Marbles fell to the sandy floor before fading in a swirl of red smoke, just like the first.

Before I could recover, the other two were on me in a flash. By clearing out others, I'd given them more room to work, and those two moved like they had trained for it. They drove me back until Mila was climbing onto the boxes to give me room.

Angry at the sudden change in fortune, I pushed outward with a wave of magic that I hardened. No explosion, no tricks. Just a solid wall that I poured copious amounts of energy into.

Sidhe steel stabbed deep into the wall on my right. I brought both blades down hard on the sword with the hooked end, snapping it free at the hilt. The wall came down, and I slammed my head into the assassin's brow, shattering his nose as he staggered back.

The other Fae had tried to sneak past, heading for Mila. I leaped at him, landing on his back, my blades fading as we rolled to the ground. I took several hard blows, and he ended up knocking me free with an elbow directly to the temple, which stunned me for a moment.

I expected him to get up and go for Mila to finish her off.

Instead, he drew a poisoned blade and stabbed it at my throat. The move caught me by surprise, forcing me to dodge to the side, wasting precious seconds before I could explode upward, driving through his defenses to use my superior strength. My arm snaked around his neck, and with a snarl, I crushed his windpipe and kept squeezing.

A few seconds later, the body collapsed as he was banished back to Faerie.

I got to my feet, ready to end it—

Just as the last assassin hurled the stump of his blade at Mila.

She tried to duck out of the way. Instead of taking her in the chest, it sank deep into her side. With a cry, she slumped to the ground.

Magic shot out from my hand, scarlet tendrils wrapping around his torso. I yanked him toward me and, without preamble, drove my blade up through his chin until it protruded from the top of his head.

"Mila!" I bellowed as the body fell apart. My feet crunched red marbles as I raced to her side, cradling her in my lap, looking horrifically at the wound in her side.

Her eyes were glazed with shock, the pain from the wound likely overwhelming her.

"Hi," she whispered. "Your arms are big."

"Hey, it's going to be okay," I whispered as blood soaked her clothing, pouring out from around the blade.

"Liar," she said, staring up at me, the blue so bright and prominent. "You would be healing me if you could."

"It doesn't work like that," I said. "You'll have to use your magic. I don't have that kind of power. A broken nose I can heal with your own strength. But this ... drawing the strength to heal this will kill you."

"Teach me?" she asked weakly, concentration lines creasing her face.

Her right hand started to glow. Even mortally wounded, with a sword more than halfway through her body, she could still call forth some magic. It was impressive. I'd never met a human with a strength like hers. She was unique.

"I'm sorry I wasn't fast enough," I whispered, stroking her face as the magic faded.

As she faded.

"It's okay," she whispered. "I should have

ducked."

"Mila."

She smiled. "Yes?"

"I …" my throat closed up.

"I know," she whispered, the light fading from her eyes.

"Mila!" I bellowed, my thighs sticky with her blood. "Mila, come back!"

She went still, and my blood froze as the first inkling of pain latched its fiery tendrils deep into every part of my body. Most pain I could fight my way through. But this hurt, this *loss* would consume me. I needed her back. I needed her body to be full of life, of zest, and the feistiness I associated with her.

Mila. Please. I need you.

But it did nothing. She was still, cooling rapidly.

Then her body collapsed into thousands of tiny *blue* marbles that fell through my fingers and evaporated into smoke.

Blue smoke.

CHAPTER THIRTY-TWO

Korr'ok

I stared at my empty hands, frozen with shock, unable to process what I was seeing.

Outside the tent, the bedlam was slowly dying as the square emptied after the explosions. That wasn't my concern. My focus was on my hands. Hands that a moment earlier had held Mila's dying body. She'd felt so frail and weak instead of just tiny.

For a moment, she'd felt like I *expected* a human to feel. Something I was totally oblivious to *not* feeling in her before. She'd been my tiny witch, but I'd used that as an apt label rather than an insult.

Perhaps more apt than I'd expected.

"A Fae death?" I whispered, my fingers closing

and opening again, as if her body would still be there, just invisible. "Impossible."

It should have been. There was no way she could have slipped past me like that. All the times we'd touched. We'd fucked, I'd been deep inside her, listening to her moans as I filled her tiny body and stretched it full, and yet I'd never noticed she was *Fae?*

"Not possible," I restated to nobody, getting to my feet, lost in the puzzle that was the woman.

My pain was fading swiftly, only to be replaced by confusion. Mila, it turned out, was not dead. Not quite. I hadn't lost her.

But did I ever have her? She hid this truth from me the entire time, somehow. Lied to me about who she was and what she was doing. All of that was fake. She was fake.

And so was what I'd felt between us.

My heart was already hardening as the realizations started to add up. She was a decoy. Designed to get me out into the open. Nothing more. I'd revealed myself to her in a moment of weakness, and now, the entire life I'd built for myself was unraveling.

All because of *her*.

All because she'd lied to me.

"You're a fool," I hissed, looking around the tent for answers to questions I hadn't yet fully formed.

Aside from one.

Who was Mila, really? And why was she working with Kraw'ok, my brother? She wasn't even of House Duloke! The blue marbles and smoke gave her away as House Mirgave. The biggest rival of Duloke for the rule of all of Faerie. She wasn't an ally. She was an enemy.

None of it made any sense!

She'd tricked me that entire time. But how? Who could have tipped the Houses off to my true nature?

There was only one answer to that. One being who knew who I was, who could have given me up.

I stormed out of the tent, a ball of red fury that scattered people from my path. Those who were too slow were simply bowled over. In my rage, I didn't even notice. Too intent was I on my target.

I'd long avoided giving any reason to challenge him. There had been no need, for we had been in accord. Something, however, had changed that. Had driven him to oust me from The Place Behind. Why he had chosen to do it that way instead of simply asking me to leave, I didn't know.

But I was about to find out.

The door to his private chambers flew open with a heavy blow of my foot, and I walked out onto the platform that looked down over the lush garden with its river and hot stone, heated by reflected sunlight down through the Black Tower. As I expected, I found Dannorax lounging comfortably in the heat.

His head came up at the unexpected intrusion, flames gathering in the back of his mouth, signified by a rushing *whoosh* of air toward the dragon.

I had my magic up and hardened, ready to deflect the flame at one of his prized giant flowers.

"Rokk, what is the meaning of this?" the dragon burbled angrily, the words distorted by the fireball he was prepared to unleash.

"I should ask you the same!" I shouted angrily, drawing in more magic and preparing a strike of my own.

The dragon tilted his head slightly but did not back down. "Explain."

"You did this," I snarled. "You exposed me, told them where to find me. Why? I demand an explanation of this injustice!"

The dragon drew himself up to full height at my challenge. The air trembled, but I flung aside the oppressive nature of fear that poured from the dragon, a natural intimidation tool designed to weaken all those who faced him. The wave hit my magic and shattered into a thousand tiny pieces. I snorted in disdain. He knew better than to try that shit with me.

"You forget your place, Rokk," the dragon rumbled ominously, smoke drifting from one nostril. "This is *my* court. You will show respect and not slander when speaking to me!"

"Respect is a two-way street between us," I hissed. "When you betrayed me to the Houses, you lost that respect."

The dragon's yellow eyes opened wide in surprise, the pupils narrowing to slits. "Betray you to the Houses? I did no such thing."

I hesitated, unprepared for such denial. The facts all pointed to someone exposing me. How else would Mila know where to come looking?

"Bring forth your evidence," Dannorax said. "I have great respect for you, Lord Rokk. I choose to believe you would not make such an accusation idly."

It was the first time he'd used my title in conjunction with my fake name. A name he continued to use, even though there was no longer a need. Perhaps he was telling the truth?

I told him of the attack in the marketplace. Of Mila's true nature.

"Your logic is sound," Dannorax rumbled, sounding thoughtful. "I see how you came to believe I was behind the deception. However, I was not."

Dannorax was a crusty old dragon with a cruel

streak wider than his wingspan. But he wasn't a liar.

I glanced behind me at the broken door. "You have my apologies, then, for how I burst into your quarters."

The dragon, perhaps to avoid further confrontation, something neither of us truly desired, waved it away with a flip of one giant wing.

"Rest assured, Lord Rokk, that if I *had* known the truth of her nature, I would not have punished her as a human but as a Fae. And you know such a penalty is death. Do you dare say I wouldn't have done so?"

He was challenging me to say he wouldn't have followed the law. If I did, I'd be saying he wasn't fit to be the Judge of the Court. And such a challenge would result in a battle.

I gritted my teeth. I was still furious about being duped by Mila, but it seemed the conspiracy ran in another line. One I had yet to uncover. But it didn't involve Dannorax.

"No," I told him. "I will not say such a thing."

"Good." The dragon curled back onto his heated rock.

"She fooled us all," I rumbled. "Does that not concern you?"

"Me?" Dannorax replied, closing one eye, the other still fixed on me. "Why should it concern me? She is *your* charge, Lord Rokk. What are you going to do now?"

I eyed the dragon. "I'm not sure yet. However, I will find out who the betrayer is and bring justice to them."

"That is your own endeavor. I shouldn't have to remind you that you took responsibility for her. Therefore, you must go get her."

I sputtered. That was not something I'd intended to do.

"You branded her," Dannorax said in hard tones. "You took personal responsibility for her, something you *requested* from me. Anything she does is on *you*, and I *will* hold you to that under the law."

Biting down on my temper, I took several deep breaths. It wasn't Dannorax I was mad at. He was right. Mila was my responsibility. She had to be captured and brought back to the Court to be tried properly.

As a Fae.

One way or another, I would have to deal with her. Which meant I had to get her.

I sighed.

That meant returning to Faerie.

To home.

CHAPTER THIRTY-THREE

Mila

I blinked awake.

That was the first surprise. I was alive. Somehow. Hadn't I died? It was all a bit blurry, but I could recall the pain in my side—

"The sword!" I yelped and looked down at my side.

My unblemished side. There was a giant hole in my shirt where the blade had pierced it, but my side was pale and unharmed. No sign whatsoever of the gaping wound that should have been there, filled only by the steel of the sword that had plunged into me.

But it was gone. That was surprise number two.

In the distance, a haunting cry filtered

through the air. It was cut short as the unmistakable piercing screech of a predator silenced it. I shivered, sitting up and looking around.

The first clue that I wasn't in The Place Behind anymore was the sky. It was a dim purplish hue. There was no sun, just a violet hue filtering through the numerous clouds.

I could hear the sounds of water burbling nearby, a river or stream of sorts. The noise was partially blocked by the trees, however, making it tough to discern from where it was coming. The trees were a sickly orange color, with leaves of red and brown that grew in hexagonal shapes.

The entire place gave me shivers. Unfortunately, I'd woken up in a clearing in the middle of an entire forest of the things, which meant, regardless of where I went, I would have to go through them.

Shapes moved in their shadows, high up among branches, and more than once, I picked out eyes that gleamed in the dull light. Watching me. Perhaps waiting for me to enter their clutches.

"Where *am* I?" I whispered. The ground under my feet was soft and almost spongy, a far cry from the hard sand and rock of The Place Behind. I wasn't there, but I also wasn't on Earth, that much I was sure of.

"Think, Mila, *think*," I urged myself, trying to

come up with a plan.

Another shrieking cry of a hunter sent shivers down my spine. It sounded close and rather large. I didn't want to get caught out there in the open by whatever beast belonged to that cry, that much I knew.

I snatched a rock from the ground, holding it tight, my only line of defense against anything that might try to—

A blur of light zipped out of the forest and past me, blowing my hair out behind me as it went.

"What the—?" I yelped, spinning to follow it as the ball of light stopped and buzzed past my face again.

"Stop it!" I snarled, trying to strike it with my rock.

I might as well have been trying to stop spilled milk with a colander. It was pointless. The thing dodged all my attacks with contemptuous ease.

"Hey, what's the matter with you?" it squeaked as I spat at it. "That's fucking nasty!"

My eyes bulged right out of my head. "You talk?"

The blur of light slowed just long enough for me to realize it was a person. A very tiny person, no more than six inches tall. He wore a loincloth and not much else. His thick black hair was pulled up in a messy topknot, revealing extremely smooth facial features and a sharp nose. Both ears ended in pointy tips instead of rounded curves.

Sprouting from his back were four tiny wings, beating so fast I could barely see them.

"What are you staring at, bigfoot?" he piped, hovering in front of my face. "You got something to say, you overblown sack of water?"

I couldn't help it. I laughed.

The little guy darted in and socked me right on the bridge of my nose, toppling me back onto my ass in a rush of pain that had me blinking back tears.

"That's right, ya crybaby. Don't fuck with me, got it? I'll mess you up."

I arched an eyebrow. "Will you now?"

The little thing came at me again in a rush —and I exhaled the breath I had been holding, sending him tumbling backward.

"Peace," I said softly. "I don't want to fight you."

"Of course not," he said in what was most definitely a snarl, not what I would call a cheep. Not to his face, at least, unless he continued to talk shit to me. "You know I'd fuck you up, you crusty hag."

"Hag?" I scoffed. "Now that's a little too far, don't you think? I'm only twenty-two."

The things eyes narrowed. "Twenty-two *what*? Decades? Centuries?"

"Years."

It laughed. "Yeah, right. Don't lie to me, lady. I can see the wrinkles on your face from here. You're ancient."

"Now that's just rude … whoever you are."

"You can call me Touk!" he said proudly, beating his chest with one tiny hand.

"Okay, Touk. Can I ask you something? Where am I?"

The little creature darted closer, peering at my eyes. "Gee, I must have hit you real hard. Which isn't surprising. I'm strong. But you must be dumb, too. That would explain it. You were already dumb, and I knocked you hard enough to make you even dumber."

"That could well be," I muttered, fighting back a smile. "But it doesn't answer the question. Where am I?"

"The Forest of Desolation!" Touk shouted, doing a spin.

"Oh." That told me precisely nothing. "And the Forest of Desolation is … where?"

"Wow, you really are stupid, aren't you?"

I stared, trying hard not to hit the little flying man. It wasn't easy. "Pretend I'm extra stupid, Touk. Where is the forest? What is this place as a whole?"

"The forest is right there!" he said excitedly, pointing. "And right there! It's all around us!"

"Right. And outside the forest? What's there?"

"In what direction?" Touk said with a sigh, crossing his arms with a sigh.

"Touk. Pretend I know absolutely nothing."

"That's easy enough," he said.

I took a deep breath, steadying my growing temper.

"What *realm* am I in, Touk? Since I take it I'm not on Earth or The Place Behind anymore?"

Touk stared. "Are you lost?"

"Very, very lost," I said. "I was somewhere else, and then … then I got stabbed. Then I woke up here."

"How stupid does a Faerie have to be to get lost in Faerie?" Touk asked, shaking his head. "You're hopeless, crone. Age taking your memory already?"

"What do you mean?" I asked.

"If you died and woke up here, that means you're a Faerie," Touk said in a boring monotone. "A Faerie who wakes up in Faerie but doesn't know they're in Faerie? Stupid, stupid, stupid."

I stared at him. "But I'm not a Faerie."

"If you die and wake up in Faerie, you're one of the Fae," he repeated, growing bored, looking around.

"And what about you?"

"I'm a sprite!"

"Of course," I said. "And you, Touk, are you King of the Sprites?"

"What? No way! That guy is so old. He's practically ancient, like you!"

I rubbed my temples to try to dispel the oncoming headache. "God, I wish Korr'ok was here."

In a flash, Touk was next to my face, placing his tiny hands on my mouth. "Shhhhh!" he hissed, looking around wildly.

I casually reached up and pinched his waist, pulling him away. "What are you doing?"

"You can't say their names around here!" he said. "It's forbidden by the Dark Lady."

"*What* is forbidden?"

"Saying the names of House Duloke," the sprite said, then clapped his hands over his mouth. "You bitch, look what you made me say!"

"And why can't we say that, Touk?"

"Because you're on House Mirgave lands," the tiny man said, putting his hands on his hips. "They're archrivals to Du … to that other place! They hate one another. The Dark Lady of Mirgave has banned all mention of them. How can you be one of them and not know this? Were you dropped on your head as a baby? Can you even remember that long ago?"

"I've lived my entire life on Earth, Touk," I told him. "As a human."

"Well, you aren't," he said matter-of-factly. "Do you remember your Fae parents?"

"No. I was raised by humans."

'Raised' being a generous term, but I wasn't about to try to explain *that* to the childlike sprite.

"Ew, that sounds terrible. Why?"

"I ... don't know," I said. "That's why I wish Korr ... why I wish *he* were here. I need to find him."

The sprite stared at me as if I'd announced I wanted to throw myself into a meat grinder. "*Why?*" he gasped.

"Because I know him? He could help me explain this."

"Or he could *kill* you," Touk pointed out. "Which is what the Dark Lady or her agents will do if you mention his name again. Try, for once in your ancient life, not to be stupid like that, okay?"

"Why is this such a big deal?"

"Because you woke up here after you died," Touk said. "That means you're a Mirgave. You belong to their House. You're a part of them and must obey the Dark Lady. Boy, you really are no better than a child."

Part of the Mirgave? At war with Duloke? That made no sense. I *couldn't* be part Fae. Could I? Who were my parents then? They hadn't been Fae ... had they? It was confusing. Why would they have hated me so much if that were the case?

"Touk, I can't stay here," I said. "I have to get out of here. Will you help me?"

"You want my help?"

"You're Touk! Greatest of the sprites. Who else would an idiot like me turn to when they needed help?"

Touk tapped tiny fingers against his tiny chin while glowing with praise. "Good point. Well, if you want to die, that's your choice. Come on, this way, dumb-dumb. Hurry before the soldiers get here."

"Soldiers?"

"Yes. The Dark Lady will have sensed your arrival and want to know more about how someone so stupid and old got here. Come, we must go!"

And off he went in a ball of light. I stumbled after him, still trying to puzzle things out. Maybe I *was* dumb as Touk had said because, to me, none of it made any sense.

Yet.

CHAPTER THIRTY-FOUR

Mila

I ran through the meadow, the grass growing longer and redder the closer we got to the forest's edge.

"Are you sure it's safe to go in there?" I asked Touk nervously as the piercing cry of the unseen predator echoed again. Closer that time.

The ball of light came to a stop. "Would you rather sit around here and wait for the Dark Lady's soldiers? They're not exactly known for being polite to dumb-dumbs. Especially ones who are friends with stupid Dulokes like you are. It's your choice, though."

"Fine," I grimaced, clenching my jaw and pushing forward.

I'd already died once. What was a second time?

Eyes gleamed in the dark of the forest, the pupils reflecting the barest hints of light that reached that deep under the canopy. Odd-colored leaves crunched like wafers under my feet, far thicker than anything I'd ever seen on Earth. Creatures scrambled out from under the piles, but I didn't stop to look.

Other, larger things lurked in the dark at the edges of my vision. I could sense them, but any time I turned my head to try to focus, they disappeared, so I stopped trying. Either Touk would lead me to safety, or I would die. Given my complete ignorance of where I was, I had no real option *but* to trust the little guy.

"Come on, faster!" Touk said. "Use your old legs for once in your fucking life, will you?"

"You're very rude," I huffed. "Has anyone told you that?"

Touk burned brighter. "Really? You mean that?"

"No," I said, not sure why that was considered a compliment.

"Oh. Fuck you." And he took off faster, my tiny legs churning to try to at least keep him in sight.

I scrambled over a rock covered in baby blue lichen, hunks of it coming off and sticking to my fingers. I peeled it off, retching at the mass of suckers on the underside of the moss, grasping and moving, trying to find a grip.

"God, this place is made of nightmares," I moaned, seeing Touk's light in the distance and giving chase once more.

The nightmare fuel burned brighter when I heard the first shouts from far behind.

"Come *on*," Touk urged, suddenly right next to me, his light dimmed, making it easier to see his features. "The Dark Lady's soldiers are coming. If you're going to escape, you have to reach the border to the Duloke lands before they get you!"

"How far are we?" I gasped, my side aching. For a Faerie, I didn't seem to have any of the strength or speed that Korr'ok did.

Talk about unfair.

"Far. We must run. Stop being such a fucking wuss and run. I'm not even going fast. They're going to catch you. Probably take your stupid head and leave your old body behind. That's what they do to intruders."

"Great," I muttered, but I took off.

Not that I was sure why. The voices of the soldiers were growing closer faster than I could move. They would catch me in no time.

As if to make sure my internal prophecy came true, the ground started to slope upward. I tried, but my legs just weren't up to the task. My quads were already burning and trying to run up a slope just made it worse.

"I can't," I gasped to Touk. "I can't."

The sprite hovered nearby. "You old people never work out. You should run more often."

"No kidding." I kept moving, but it was slow now.

The flicker of warning in my periphery was all I got before a soldier in royal blue armor appeared out of the darkness, whirling a rope around his head.

Without thinking, I reached into myself, grasping for that place in my brain that came alive when I used magic.

Now. Please.

My hands glowed red, and with a very feminine grunt, I reached out for the oncoming soldier. Instead of trying to push him back, however, I grabbed hold of him with my magic and pulled as hard as I could.

With a yelp of surprise, the Fae hurtled past me before bouncing off a tree trunk and spinning away into the darkness.

I didn't bother to see if he stayed down. I was already running.

"Wow, that was awesome!" Touk cried, zipping around my head repeatedly. "Do it again!"

"To whom?" I asked as we ran on.

"Them?" he suggested, flying while facing backward and pointing past my head.

I glanced over my shoulder to see a squad of blue-armored soldiers closing in on me fast.

"Fuck," I moaned, stumbling to a halt as they surrounded me, weapons drawn, all the pointy edges aimed my way.

Spreading my hands wide, I once again reached out for that place in my mind, trying to draw more energy from it. Anything that would buy me time. As before, the power came slowly until my hands glowed.

And then it was ripped from me.

I stared at my empty palms as sinister laughter drifted out from the forest.

"So clumsy and slow," the male voice taunted, coming from several directions, giving me no opportunity to locate it.

The soldiers chuckled. They were all bulky-looking Fae, like smaller versions of Korr'ok.

"Who are you?" the voice asked with wicked curiosity.

"I could say the same for you. Show yourself!"

A figure detached itself from the darkness and moved in a blur until it was right in front of me, forcing me to lean far backward. "Is that what you truly want?" he asked, the face narrower and more aquiline than the broader, flat faces of the soldiers.

Nobility, perhaps, given the way his long hair was styled, something he could do without a helmet.

"Yes, I thought not," he spat, stepping back

behind the circle of soldiers and walking in a slow path around me. "The lady will have many questions for you, yes, many indeed. An unknown intruder? Unaligned, but with Mirgave blood? *Most* interesting."

I tried to pretend like I knew what all that meant. I had a vague idea, given what I'd learned, but the *how* of it still made no sense. I wasn't a Fae.

"Nothing to say for yourself?" the leader asked.

I gave him a cold look, going for the only option available to me. "Not to a lowly servant like you. Take me to the Dark Lady."

"A bold move," the Fae chuckled. "Considering that you're most likely a Duloke spy, this close to the border and trying to reach it. And once the Lady has extracted all the information from you that she needs, I will take *great* pleasure in executing another traitor like you."

He smiled broadly as I paled. "Come! Let us go. The Dark Lady awaits."

So much for my plan.

CHAPTER THIRTY-FIVE

Mila

With the helmetless Fae in the lead, I was marched through a portal and into the halls of House Mirgave.

I was led through a stone hallway with high ceilings and thick arches that spanned the corridor every so often. Huge painted tapestries several dozen feet tall hung from the wall to my right, painted in brilliant, vibrant colors. Each one depicted a different Fae. Past rulers of the House, perhaps. I wasn't sure. On my right, matching-sized stained-glass panes let in the purple light from outside.

The flickering of torch fire cast shadows crazily, turning the blue-carpeted floor into some sort of nightmarish sea we crossed, the soldiers marching in perfect lockstep on either side of me. They weren't looking at me, but their weapons were drawn and ready.

If I moved, they would cut me down without hesitation.

There were little alcoves at the base of the arches, perfect for two or three people to sit and chat. We passed some people, courtiers, I figured, leeches who served no real purpose but to be seen. None of them said anything, though they all glanced at me, then leaned in to speak in hushed whispers after I'd passed.

"Charming place you've got here," I remarked.

One of the guards drove the butt of his sword into my side, bruising a rib. I hissed in pain but didn't falter. Now, I sensed, was not the time to show weakness. I had to be strong. Show the Fae that I belonged. That would be the only way I stayed alive.

We stopped at the end of the hallway in front of a pair of doors cast from dull bronze. The helmetless Fae turned, his eyes blazing with malevolent energy, turning a much darker shade of blue as they did.

"When we enter the Dark Lady's chambers, you will show respect. I would just as soon take your head from your body here and now, but she has insisted on bringing you before her. If you do not act as her station accords, I will show you the true meaning of pain. This, I swear."

"Anything else?" I asked, trying to appear bored.

He leaned closer and grinned. "I can smell your fear. You don't fool me, half-breed."

Then he straightened and pushed open the doors, leading me into a hall that was even grander than the one we'd just left.

Deep rich royal blue velvet carpeting ran down the center of the throne room, leading up the steps to a huge chair carved from some sort of black metal shot through with streaks of cobalt that glittered from the roaring fires that blazed merrily on either side of the seat.

But it wasn't that which caught the eye, nor the lofty arches that disappeared into darkness high above, where azure *things* darted in and out of view. Empty rows of pews carved from rich hardwoods did little to keep one's attention, nor did the multitude of art on the wall or various pedestals.

No, all focus was immediately drawn to the woman sitting on the throne. Draped in living shadow, all I could see—besides the slender shape of her definitely feminine body—were her eyes. They were twin ovals of perfect ultramarine, so vivid and piercing that all focus in the chamber was drawn to them.

Which was probably just how the Dark Lady wanted it.

Evil rolled off her in waves, practically filling the room with malevolence. An act, I wondered, or just her natural state? It was impossible to tell, but regardless, I knew her power wasn't something I wanted to trifle with. She would squash me flat with less than a thought.

"Bring her forth."

I shivered at the Dark Lady's voice. It was cool but hard. Like spring water frozen into diamonds, it reached out and captured me, urging me on with a life of its own. I tried to resist the pull of her magic, but I was a babe before a master, a match flickering before an out-of-control wildfire.

I stood no chance. The guards paused while their leader alone escorted me closer to the foot of the throne. It was only as we got close that I realized just how huge it was. The lady must have rivaled Korr'ok in height, and the throne was built to size. She towered over us, looking down from her position.

"Interesting," she said as I came to a stop. Her head tilted slightly to the side.

I bit back my natural reply of *If you think so*. What she thought was interesting, I didn't know.

"How did you come to be on my lands?" the Dark Lady asked.

I started to shrug, but a vitriolic look from the Fae captain stopped me. "I'm not sure," I admitted. "But according to him, I'm a Fae who was killed and thus banished back here."

"You aren't a Fae?"

Now I did shrug. "He's telling me otherwise, but I've lived my entire life among humans, *being* human. I find it hard to believe I'm some magical creature. How could I have been oblivious for so long?"

The figure shifted on the throne, shadows parting for just a moment, giving me a glimpse of the woman's face. Her beauty staggered me, nearly driving me to my knees as my brain tried to process and failed. She was perfection. Every inch of skin flawless, every curve perfect.

She was everything I, and every other woman, was not and would never be.

And I hated her for it.

"There are ways for such things to happen," the Dark Lady said, her perfectly plump limps curling upward into a wicked smile. "Especially for a half-breed."

I stiffened.

"Oh, yes," she replied. "That is what you are. I can smell your human heritage from here, a truly unpleasant odor. It betrays you, you know. I can all but taste your fear, your nervousness. It is rife in the air. You are no Fae, but nor are you truly human either."

"Then … who am I?" I asked nervously. "How

was I tricked into coming off as human?"

The Dark Lady lifted a hand, and a spark of blue leaped from her index finger and plunged into my stomach. I hissed at the pain, but it was gone just as quickly as it came, carrying a trace of me back to the Lady.

She examined the magic, moving her long, delicate-fingered hands in weird ways, seeing things only she could see.

"Well, well, well. Isn't *that* interesting," she murmured. "Mich'av, you were just full of secrets you didn't tell me. Coming back to cause me trouble one more time, are you?"

"I didn't mean to cause anyone trouble," I protested.

"Not you, half-breed," the Dark Lady said contemptuously. "Rather, your father."

I went still. "You knew my father? My real father?"

"Oh, yes," she said, the reply devolving into an angry hiss. "I did."

I frowned. "He's dead, then?"

"Oh, yes. Him and all his line." She tapped a chin with one long finger. "Well, *almost* his entire line. I had thought they were all gone, but now it seems he left one last surprise. You."

"I don't understand."

"He got you upon your mother, a human. As for your power, he must have bound that away from you. Tied it to something."

I stiffened. The book?

"Ah, so there *was* something, was there?" the Lady asked.

I didn't respond.

"You'll tell eventually," she said. "I must make sure there are no further surprises left by your father. He was an ambitious one. I'll give him that much. His plot to take the throne quite possibly would have succeeded ... if Aurr'av here hadn't secretly been working for me and turned him in."

The Fae who had brought me to the foot of the throne graced me with a broad grin.

"It took me quite some time to stop him and his loyalists," she mused while Aurr'av and I stared at each other, him with contempt, me with fury.

My attention was wrenched away, however, when the Dark Lady flicked a finger, and blue magic swirled up to take the shape of a face.

One I'd seen before.

Instantly, I was back in my hovel behind the bakery. Magic was swirling around, erupting out of the book as I read the words I didn't know from the page.

And for a brief moment, an image appeared in the red energy. Of a man with slanted eyes and pointed ears. He had black skin, darker than any human, just like Korr'ok, and his eyes glowed. In my vision, they had glowed red, but I realized now that it was just the magic. Because in the Lady's conjuring, his eyes were blue. Like hers.

Like mine.

"My father?" I whispered.

"Oh, yes. Your *traitor* of a father."

I swallowed a giant lump at the reminder that the Dark Lady had eliminated his entire line. Which seemed to be what she was leaning to with me. The last thing she needed was a reminder of my father's attempt at a coup.

Before she could pronounce my death, or any other sentence, the air in the room seemed to still slightly.

"My, oh, *my*," the Lady said, her voice distant but focused. "Now, isn't *this* a coincidence?"

She flung a hand outward, and between us rose the image of a figure standing on grassy plains at the edge of a line of trees.

He stood seven feet tall, with huge muscles and two horns that I knew all too well.

"I call upon Lallandri'av!" Korr'ok called in the vision. "Dark Lady of Mirgave. I am Korr'ok. Son of Char'ok of House Duloke. I seek an audience."

The Dark Lady's eyes focused through the vision on me. "First, a half-breed who shows up out of nowhere, and now, the long-lost son of my most hated rival is at my doorstep, asking for an audience. My, oh, my, Aurr'av, isn't *that* a coincidence."

The Fae captain inclined his head in agreement.

"What do you make of that, half-breed?" the Lady challenged.

"I don't know," I said, just a bit too quickly.

"Yes, I think you do," she replied, lifting a hand toward me.

Cobalt tendrils sped from her fingertips, wrapping around me like the tentacles of a kraken, lifting me in the air until I hovered in front of her.

The other hand came up, and a single line of blue magic pierced my breastbone. I screamed as the bond mark Korr'ok had implanted there glowed a bright red, revealing itself.

"Yes, I think you *do* know him," she cackled. "Aurr'av, gather an escort for our wayward foe. This shall be interesting."

The bond marker burned again, eliciting another ragged scream from my throat.

"Very interesting indeed," she said with a happy purr as she leaned forward, her eyes burning in their sockets.

CHAPTER THIRTY-SIX

Korr'ok

I'd never been to House Mirgave before, but it was about what I would expect. Ostentatious and over the top, with references to the glory won by the house. And it was blue. Blue everywhere.

We're not so different, are we? I thought, reminded all too clearly about how House Duloke was no different. *We just use red instead.*

With the two Houses on the brink of open warfare, I took a huge risk by appearing at the border. However, given my prolonged absence from Faerie and my younger brother's apparent coup, I banked on the Dark Lady's curiosity to work in my favor.

Killing me would further stabilize her archrival. Letting me live, on the other hand, would provide her with an opportunity to sow discord and perhaps even weaken the House if I chose to go after my brother.

Unfortunately for her, I had no intention whatsoever of doing anything of the sort. I despised Kraw'ok for what he'd done, but Duloke was not my home. Not anymore. I was there for Mila and nothing more.

"She awaits you inside," said Aurr'av, the Dark Lady's captain, who bowed respectfully as he pushed open one of the bronze doors, the huge metal panel swinging easily on perfectly balanced hinges.

I strode inside, bracing myself at the sight of Mila, held high in the air by the Dark Lady's magic.

"Korr'ok!" she shouted, turning mid-air to reveal the red glow of the brand I'd placed within her chest. The Dark Lady's magic was testing it, causing it to show itself.

That couldn't feel good. Mila had to be in a lot of pain.

"Enough!" I barked, surprising myself with the break in protocol. "Put her down."

"Who are you," the Dark Lady hissed, azure flames exploding from the fires to either side of her ominous throne. "to come into my hall, into *my* home, and make demands of *me*!"

I glared at her, knowing my eyes would be

blazing as bright a red as hers did with blue. My magic shunted aside hers as I marched down the blue carpet toward the two women, doing my best to ensure I didn't burn footprints behind me out of spite. It was tempting, however. The arrogance of the Fae had never sat well with me.

The Dark Lady was powerful beyond doubt, but I was the scion of an equally powerful family, and she would not intimidate me. My powers might not be *quite* equal to hers, but they were more than enough to ensure she didn't want to risk getting into a knockdown fight with me.

After all, if she *lost*, I would become ruler of House Mirgave. I was pretty certain the faction would implode at the idea of a Duloke being in charge. It was so tempting that I almost wanted to try to see it. Almost.

"You know who I am," I replied instead. "I am Korr'ok, eldest surviving son of Char'ok, and I am here to bargain. But only if you put her down."

I shouldn't have cared so much about Mila. She was a liar and no longer meant anything to me besides being my prisoner. Thus, her pain shouldn't have mattered. But it did. I was furious beyond measure at the sight of her trapped in the air, the Dark Lady's magic inflicting pain on her with every passing second.

"This one is the half-breed offspring of a traitor," the Dark Lady said, Mila not moving from where she hovered in the air to my right.

"Tell me why I shouldn't finish the job before she tries to do as her father did?"

Half breed? I tried to smother my surprise. That was new information.

"Because she is my charge," I said, pointing at her breastbone. "You can see the mark I have made. I have *claimed* her, Lallandri'av. If you kill her now, I will have to take issue with that."

The air hung heavy before us. It was exceedingly rare that a lord or lady of a Fae House was ever challenged. That was, essentially, what I'd just done. I didn't want to fight her. But if she killed Mila, then I would. Protocol demanded it.

"We seem to be at an impasse," the Dark Lady said. "I want her dead, to tie up loose ends. You want her alive for the same. How do you propose we deal with this?"

"A trade," I replied, holding up the sack I'd been holding. "Her, for this."

The Dark Lady stared curiously from beneath her shadows, keeping her face mostly veiled. I could have pierced the magical concealment if I chose, but I didn't, letting her have her fun.

"What do you have to trade for her life?" she asked.

"The book that her powers were harnessed to," I said. "That's how she passed into my territory without me realizing who she is."

"And that matters to me why?"

"Whoever bound her power to it also bound a Fae from House Duloke into it," I said. "A traitor, working within your own house. Sound familiar?"

"And how do you know I haven't already killed this traitor? It was likely her father."

I smiled tightly. "The magic has a woman's touch to it."

That got the attention of both of them. Based on Mila's story about where she'd gotten the book, I'd figured out that the woman running the bookstore must have been a Fae, someone aligned with House Duloke. Given that the Dark Lady was saying Mila's father was a traitor, that theory now stood on shaky ground. I didn't know what her father had been planning, nor did I care. All that mattered was that there was still a chance the person who had bound Mila to the book was still alive.

The Dark Lady looked from me to Mila and back. "What is your angle here, son of Duloke?"

I shook my head sharply. "I do not associate with them. I left a long time ago. We stand apart."

She snorted. "One does not leave their line behind," she chuckled. "Things are changing in Duloke."

"If you mean to hint cryptically about my brother's coup, I assure you, I know, and I intend to do nothing about it. I am here for the woman and the woman only. Do we have a deal?"

Lallandri'av looked down at me thoughtfully. "You seek to appear aloof and uncaring, Korr'ok, son of Char'ok. But I sense great turmoil in you. You hide it well, but a woman's intuition is often stronger than any magic. You branded this woman, but you act as if she's your prisoner. You care not for her?"

"No," I said gruffly after taking a second to gather myself.

The grin was more felt than seen. I wasn't fooling her for a second. I was furious with Mila for lying, but I couldn't bring myself to hate her. Not yet. I had let myself grow too close to stay impartial.

A failure that I will not repeat.

"I shall think about your trade proposal," the Dark Lady said. "I shall respond within two days. Until then, Korr'ok, I extend to you the hospitality of my House. You may stay here, and I vow not to order any of my servants to kill you."

Of course, that wasn't the same as vowing they wouldn't try such a thing. She simply wouldn't tell them to. A slight but important difference. I would have to stay on guard.

"I will respect your timeline, Dark Lady," I rumbled. "However, I must insist on being able to talk in private with the prisoner in the meantime."

"Of course. Aurr'av will show you to a secure room."

Meaning a room the Lady could easily listen in. She was playing me, stalling for time with this "I need two days to think" bullshit. That much was obvious. What I needed to figure out was *why*? What was she waiting for?

I shoved that thought aside as Mila was lowered to the floor. I longed to catch her, to hold her tight, but I kept my distance, letting her gather herself without help. Without my touch. I had to be cool. Collected. Withdrawn.

Then I could ask her why she'd lied to me and find the answer to at least *one* of the questions on my growing list.

Her answer is bound to be interesting, if nothing else, I thought, looking out of the corner of my eyes at her, trying not to remember her lying under me, her body slowly writhing with pleasure, her moans tickling my ear as I filled her with my hard cock, taking her. Making her mine …

Conflicted, I followed Aurr'av out of the hall.

What would I do next?

CHAPTER THIRTY-SEVEN

Mila

The excitement I'd felt upon first seeing Korr'ok was rapidly fading as we were escorted down a small hallway and into a room. From the moment he'd shown up, he hadn't given me any familiar response.

He'd cut himself off from me. The final piece had been him telling the Dark Lady that he didn't care for me. That he was there because I was in his charge. I was a package for him to collect, nothing more.

Aurr'av closed the door behind us, locking it, ostensibly to give us privacy. Somehow, I doubted that.

"They're probably listening to us," I said, trying to break the ice.

"Probably," he said gruffly. "I would in their

place. Ensure we aren't planning any sort of escape or further trouble. Which is easy enough to do since we aren't."

"Korr'ok," I said, reaching out to touch him.

He pulled away, my hand falling through open space instead. That flinch hurt more than anything else he'd done so far.

"I don't understand," I whispered. "Why are you acting like this?"

I thought I would never see him again. Now I wondered which was worse—not seeing him or his flinch. His rejection wasn't easy to handle.

"You can stop with the bullshit, Mila," he growled, "and just tell me the truth."

"What are you talking about?" I hissed, hands on my hips, moving to stand right in front of him, glaring up at him. "You're the one acting all weird. Why are you pretending like you hate me?"

"Pretending?" he scoffed. "*Pretending*? How could I not hate you, Mila? Even now, you won't drop the act. Just rubbing it in further, are you? Enjoying the pain you caused, is that it?"

He snarled and spun away, stalking to the far side of the room, moving around the circular desk and its chairs before resting a forearm on the wall.

"What act?" I managed to splutter, astonished by the outburst. "*What are you talking about?*"

"You!" he bellowed, bouncing his fist off the wall, his voice pained. "I'm talking about *you*, Mila. You lied to me!"

I stared at him. "I did?"

The red in his eyes blazed further, his jaw muscles standing out in stark relief. "You're doing it even now! You hid yourself from me. On purpose. Lied to me about who you were. About what you were. This is all your fault. I'm not here to win you back. I'm here because I took responsibility for you, and I intend to see it through until your punishment is complete."

My jaw refused to work in the wake of his accusations. He had it all *wrong*. Everything was so twisted, and I just wanted to sort it out, but Korr'ok clearly had no interest in doing so. He just wanted to be mad.

"You don't understand," I whispered.

"Oh, I understand perfectly," he growled. "I know why you did it. I know why you tricked me. And it worked. So, there you go. I hope you're happy. Because once the Dark Lady releases you into my custody, you're going back to jail instead of staying with me. I'll take my brand back, and you can rot."

Blinking furiously, trying to keep my tears from falling, I shook my head at him. "You're wrong, Korr'ok," I said in a pained whisper. "I didn't lie to you."

He scoffed.

"I didn't. I told you everything. I showed you everything. I *gave* you everything I had," I said, reminding him of how I'd given my body to him in full trust. "I let you in, in ways I haven't let *anyone* in. Ever. Do you understand?"

Korr'ok shook his head. "I trusted you," he said as if he hadn't heard a word I said.

"And I trusted you!" I shouted back.

"You took advantage of that trust, and you hid from me."

"Men," I spat. "You're all the same, human or not. Stubborn, pigheaded, unable to realize the truth even when it slaps you in the goddamn face!"

Korr'ok snarled at me angrily.

"Yeah, go on, be all big and tough," I said, shaking my head. "'Cause that's been so much help so far. You idiot. I didn't know. Get that through your head. *I. Didn't. Know.* I thought I was *dying* in your arms in the marketplace. And you know what was the last thought going through my head? Do you want to know?"

He glared sullenly but didn't turn away.

"I thought that it sucked. Because after surviving a shit life for so long, I had *finally* found someone who seemed to actually care for me. Someone who didn't bully me or take advantage of me when they could easily have done so," I said, yanking my shirt down to reveal where he'd marked me.

Korr'ok's eyes fell on my skin, but he still said nothing. Which was fine by me. I had more to say.

"I was finally experiencing what most people take for granted. I thought, for a brief moment, that maybe I could be *happy* with you. What a fool I was. It was all just an act from you, wasn't it? That's how you're able to be such a dick now. I should have seen it. Should have realized you weren't real. You're just a monster, after all."

"You expect me to believe you've been oblivious your entire life that you weren't a Fae? That you weren't different?" he barked. "Even tying your power to the book doesn't make you completely human, Mila."

I hesitated.

There had been things that were odd. I healed faster than most. Not, like, immediately, but I'd always recovered quicker than the other kids who received beatings at Mrs. Johnson's foster home.

"Exactly," he said, shaking his head.

"That doesn't mean I knew what it meant or that I was actively trying to fool you," I said.

"So, it's all real, then? You really cared about me, and you weren't trying to expose me, to bring me out into the open?" he challenged.

"No!" I shouted. "No, I wasn't trying to do that at all. Yes, I care about you. Cared about you. I don't know."

"Prove it, then," he said suddenly.

"What?"

"Prove that you cared about me."

I frowned at him. "How do you expect me to do that?"

"I don't know," he replied. "But if you do, you'll find a way."

I licked my lips, thinking furiously. What could I do? Did he want me to tell him that I loved him?

Instantly, I knew that was what he wanted. He wanted me to say it, to make that irrevocable act, to take the next step in a relationship that neither of us had really been aware was developing until it was suddenly there before us.

I took a deep breath. Could I say that? Was I ready to?

I hesitated again, unsure of what to do. What if I told him, but I was wrong about myself? I didn't want to say it just to make him happy, to show him that I cared. But I also wanted him to know I wasn't making it up. That he'd wormed his way deeper into my heart than I'd ever had any intention of letting him.

That I cared deeply, I could say that, but it wouldn't be enough to sway him. I had strong feelings, yes. I just maybe didn't love him. Not yet.

I looked away, unable to say the three words he so badly wanted to hear.

"Exactly," he said sadly.

CHAPTER THIRTY-EIGHT

Korr'ok

The door opened before more could be said. Aurr'av strode into the room, uncaring of what may or may not have been going on.

"Come," he barked officiously. "The Dark Lady will see you again."

"Already?" I asked, narrowing my eyes suspiciously at the Mirgave captain. "That was fast."

The high-ranking Fae—as high as one could be without being one of the Sidhe—curled a lip at me in a sneer. "In House Mirgave, we respect our rulers." He snorted. "That means when given a command, I obey it. I don't have a temper tantrum and try to kill my House Leader."

The comment was clearly designed as a jab against me, but it slid off like water and oil.

While I didn't think my family deserved death, I was a Fae—and a Sidhe at that. Familial attachments held little sway with us. Therefore, Aurr'av's comment didn't hit the mark.

Perhaps, I wondered, *House Mirgave feels slightly differently about their blood? An interesting insight.*

Aurr'av, realizing he hadn't pierced my armor, gestured impatiently into the hallway. "Keep the Lady waiting at your peril," he growled. "Not mine. Let's go."

With a casual shrug, as if to say I really didn't give a shit about him—which I didn't—I moved past him, then waited for Mila to go through the door first. She looked up at me while moving past, eyes searching mine for something. When she didn't find it, she looked forward and set her shoulders.

She was strong. Stronger than I'd ever given her credit for.

Was that enough, though? I was confused. She continued to insist on ignorance, but clearly, she knew *something* about her was different. The fact that she'd been willing to admit to that much suggested she was telling the truth ...

Unless that's exactly why she revealed she suspected herself to be different somehow. So that her story becomes even more believable.

What I couldn't figure out was if she was

trying to maintain her cover, *why*? Why keep the lie going? I'd been forced into the open. I'd entered Faerie for the first time and proclaimed myself to the head of another Great House. Word would get around that I was still alive. My brother would probably come for me at some point, which was just another thing to be wary of. All the hard work I'd put into staying out of the way, hidden in The Place Behind, a wayward back-alley pocket dimension, was undone. Because of her.

If that wasn't her game, then what was?

A growl of frustration rumbled in my chest, prompting looks from both parties. I ignored them.

I wanted to hate Mila. To take her back to Dannorax, remove the bond mark, and put her into the hands of the Jury's justice. Rid myself of the entire thing, move on, and find a new place to go where I could just be myself without the worry of my past coming to find me.

Kraw'ok could have House Duloke, for all I cared. I just wanted peace.

Mila stepped slightly closer as Aurr'av moved past us to open the huge doors into the Dark Lady's throne room. As she did, a hint of her magic tickled my senses, driving itself deep into my brain.

Against my will, images of us were conjured forth, cascading through my mind like a slideshow on fast forward. Clenching my teeth, I tried to push the memories away while remaining calm. She wasn't mine anymore. I didn't want her. It had meant nothing!

My body didn't agree. As we reached the moment of our first kiss, Mila standing in the doorway of her solitary cell, my cock began to stir. An ache throbbed deep in my balls as I relived standing behind her in public, smelling her scent as she had an orgasm in front of all those people, unable to move.

Then we were together. Her body on top of mine, her hands wrapped around my horns, using them to guide her hips down and then as leverage to grind hard into me, capturing my cock deep inside her tiny body. I clamped down hard on a groan as I recalled the sensation of emptying my seed deep inside her.

Claiming her in an entirely new way.

I hunched over slightly, breathing hard, trying to contain myself and stop from reaching out and grabbing her and taking her lithe body right there, right then. I didn't care if anyone was watching. And neither would she when the heat came to her. My touch would be irresistible, and she would melt. Just the way I longed for.

Aurr'av threw open the door and announced us into the Dark Lady's presence. Still breathing deep through my nose, drawing curious stares from Mila, I entered the room.

The sight waiting before me turned my blood to ice, sucking the breath from my chest at the same time.

"Welcome!" the Dark Lady of Mirgave said, waving us both forward.

"Who is that?" Mila asked, her eyes darting from me to the figure standing at the base of the throne, fingers interlocked behind his back, waiting for us with a broad smile etched into his midnight skin.

Two horns, just like mine, poked up from his skull. Eyes the color of rubies glowed with pleasure as they landed on Mila, then me.

"That's my brother," I rumbled. "Kraw'ok. The new head of House Duloke and the one who killed my family to get where he is."

"Oh." Mila didn't sound nearly concerned enough. "Why do you think he's here?"

"I don't know. But whatever it is, it can't be good," I growled. "These two Houses are supposed to be at each other's throats, on the verge of war. Why would she admit him here unless it was for her benefit? And the same goes for Kraw'ok."

"How do you know it has to do with us?" she asked, a bit more nervous.

"Because of me," I said. "He knows I'm alive."

"I don't get it," she murmured as we walked down the azure carpet between aisles of empty pews. The entire room seemed ominous in its empty, cavernous state.

"Kraw'ok is the youngest of four brothers," I reminded her. "He killed the other two and my father to gain the throne as his by right."

The sudden sharp intake of breath showed Mila had clued in. "And with you showing yourself now, you have a better claim to the head of House Duloke."

"Exactly."

"So, he wants you dead."

"That is my assumption," I confirmed, my eyes locked with Kraw'ok's. "I want nothing to do with it, but he can't risk that. He needs me dead. Or at least, under his control somehow."

"How would he do that?" Mila asked nervously.

"Through you, of course," Kraw'ok gloated as we approached. "Hello, dear brother."

Mila's face paled as she began to understand the gravity of the situation.

"What do you want?" I growled.

The Dark Lady chose that moment to intervene, probably for the best. I wasn't sure I could have kept myself from attacking Kraw'ok. I didn't want the throne, but I still despised him.

Just not for the reason everyone assumed.

"Lord Kraw'ok has just arrived," the Dark Lady

said, taking control of the conversation, "and he has made a most excellent proposal for what to do."

"Has he now?" I asked dryly. "And what proposal is that?"

"Peace," the Dark Lady said. "His troops will withdraw from our borders. As will ours. A gesture of goodwill from both parties."

"How generous of him," I said, rolling my eyes. "And what did you have to do to get him to do that?"

"Why, nothing," the Dark Lady said. "Which is why it's so beneficial for me. I simply do *nothing* about either of you two, and I benefit. Isn't that remarkable?"

"So, you're going to let him take her then, is that it?"

"No, no," the Dark Lady said. "I'm not going to *let* him. I'm simply not going to stop him."

"That's the same thing," Mila said. "You're just letting him do whatever he wants. And you get nothing out of it."

The chamber went cold. Beside me, Aurr'av stiffened in alarm as the hair on the Dark Lady's head floated freely, the only thing moving at the moment.

"No, it is not," she said icily. "Context matters greatly. Kraw'ok is going to *take* you. I am not *giving* him to you. Once he has you, he will have what he needs to secure his borders, and the recent unpleasantness between our Houses will subside. Do I make myself clear?"

I covered Mila's mouth with a hand. She shot me an angry glare, but it subsided after I gave her a tiny shake of her head. Arguing Fae logic was useless and a waste of time. The deal had already been decided.

"As the offer is better on a large scale for my House, I must therefore decline yours, Korr'ok," she continued in a normal tone. "Thank you for your time. Aurr'av will show you to the border when you're ready. Please do not ever come back."

Kraw'ok just grinned over at me. "No hard feelings, *brother*. But she'll make a better concubine for me than she would ever do for you. Best you not make an issue of it. Otherwise, I might have to change my mind on how I treat her."

An image of Mila, pinned to a bed underneath Kraw'ok, came to rest in the front of my mind.

"Just like old times, isn't it?" he said under his breath, fingers closing over Mila's arms. "They always want me more."

I snapped.

CHAPTER THIRTY-NINE

Korr'ok

Kraw'ok had just enough time for his eyes to go wide before my uppercut took him in the chin, lifting him clear of his feet and throwing him back ten or more feet to land in a heap.

"*SHE IS MINE!*" I bellowed loudly enough that dust and bits of stone fell from the arched ceiling far, far above.

There was no magic. No weapons. Just raw brute strength. I landed on my younger brother like a wolverine, kicking, clawing, and driving home whatever attack I could. No skill or plan. I was enraged beyond all definitions, and it had turned me feral.

The initial attack had stunned him, but Kraw'ok was a Sidhe and no slouch. I took my fair share of blows until one of them finally dislodged me, sending me rolling off to the side, coughing as I struggled to breathe from the sharp elbow to the stomach.

In a flash, I was on my feet, just in time to greet Kraw'ok with a bear hug as he came at me. Holding tight, his feet off the floor, I roared in anger yet again. My arms squeezed, and one of his ribs gave way.

His head smashed into mine, causing me to stagger back as blood poured from my nose.

"MINE!" I shouted, lunging for him, ignoring the pain. "She is mine!"

We went down in a heap, the combat wholly uncivilized. I didn't care.

"Too bad you didn't fight like this the first time," Kraw'ok taunted as we grappled on the floor of the Mirgave throne room. "You might have stood a chance. Might not have lost."

I snorted, then spat blood. "You just don't get it, little brother. And you never will because nobody loves you. They just fear you, and for that, I pity you."

His knee came up and caught me in the groin. I rolled away with a loud groan of pain, narrowly missing Mila, who scampered out of the way.

I planted my fingers in the blue velvet carpet and used it as a foothold to spin myself wildly to the side. My foot lashed out, spilling my brother. Then I was on my feet and onto his back. Snaking my arm around his neck, I tried to squeeze, but he threw his head back fast enough to catch me in the jaw.

Momentarily stunned, I lost my grip, allowing him to escape. Kraw'ok got to his feet at the same time I did. Both of us stared at each other, eyes full of rage and hatred.

"You're as pathetic as the rest of them," he snarled.

I laughed. "Because everyone thinks you actually defeated father and our brothers in combat and not with a blade to the back when they couldn't defend themselves."

The flash of incensed scarlet in his eyes told me the barb had gone home.

"Coward," I added, shaking my head.

"You're going to end up like the rest of them," Kraw'ok said. "The throne is mine!"

"I've been gone for ages, you imbecile. What makes you think I *want* it? You're a sniveling coward, and someone will usurp you before long, too. But it won't be me. I quite literally want nothing to do with you."

"Then why are you back?" he barked, circling me while I matched him, step for step.

"For her!" I snarled, pointing at Mila. "And only for her."

"You care about the half-breed?" Kraw'ok chuckled. "You're more pathetic than I thought."

I couldn't help it. His comment got the better of me. I flung myself at him, and we went down again, each struggling for the upper hand, neither quite succeeding. Despite my comment about him stabbing our brothers in the back, it was clear he'd trained a lot while I was gone. Fighting had never been something he was particularly good at, but that had changed.

"She's going to make a fine trophy," he cackled as I struggled to move his arms to the side to deliver a blow to his smug face. "I'll treat her well. You know I will."

Red magic formed in my hand, and I slapped him across the face with it, tearing a gash from his temple to his chin.

"*Enough!*" a female voice barked over the din of combat and the blood roaring in my ears.

Kraw'ok bellowed in anger as feet clattered down the carpet from the door toward us. He renewed his attack, blood leaking down the side of his face. I smashed my forehead into his again and then again, drawing more blood.

"I'll make sure she knows the true touch of a man!" my brother coughed through blood just as hands grabbed my arms and hauled me free from him.

Furious beyond reasoning, magic exploded from my body, tossing the hands free as I lunged for Kraw'ok's throat.

There was a flash of blue, and the next thing I knew, I was sailing through the air uncontrollably, bouncing off the carpet and slamming my head into one of the bronze doors, leaving a tiny dent in the metal and a huge bruise on the side of my skull.

"I said *enough*," the Dark Lady of Mirgave hissed into the silence that followed.

My vision, as wonky as it was after the blow, was still able to spot her as she hovered in the air halfway down the steps of her throne, azure magic held ready in both hands, one pointed at each of us.

At her feet, standing by my brother, were a handful of her soldiers, including Aurr'av, who looked slightly disheveled.

I calmed instantly, realizing my error as it sank in whose hands had tried to grab me.

"You," the Dark Lady said, crooking a finger at me.

Slowly getting to my feet, I walked back down the aisle, staring straight ahead. I avoided looking at Kraw'ok, knowing his smug look would do nothing but ignite my rage again.

He'd won. His comments had provoked me past the point that was acceptable. Now I would pay the price.

"You have my apology for my actions, my lady," I said, bowing my head as I reached the group. "As well to you, Aurr'av."

The Mirgave captain glanced at his lady, who tilted her head slightly.

"No offense taken," the captain said gruffly, though the cobalt fire that burned in his eyes said otherwise. He stepped back and, along with the other foot soldiers, withdrew toward the door, leaving the four of us.

"You broke the rules of hospitality and used magic on my lands," the Dark Lady said.

"I am sorry for that," I said respectfully. "It won't happen again."

"Of course it won't. But the damage has been done." She turned to Kraw'ok. "Go now while my patience with you is still somewhat intact. Don't think I'm stupid. I know what you did. I'm tempted to deal with both of you, but protocol states you were the victim. Begone."

"Of course, Lady Mirgave," Kraw'ok said. Then he took Mila by the upper arm and dragged her down the aisle.

I watched her go, something dark and angry stirring in me. Something I knew I wouldn't be able to contain for much longer.

"I'll come for you," I mouthed at her before I could stop myself. *I swear it.*

Then they were gone.

CHAPTER FORTY

Korr'ok

The ominous silence lingered as the doors closed behind my brother and a woman who, at the worst time possible, I was coming to realize meant more to me than I'd ever suspected.

A woman who I would go through hell to be with again, as I had just vowed. It was a vow I would keep. A vow she was *worth*. I might have marked her as mine at the start of it all, but I wanted her to be mine now in so many other ways. Ways that would send me back to a place I'd vowed never to step foot in again.

House Duloke.

"You used your magic in my halls," the Dark Lady said, settling back onto her throne, the fires burning blue on either side of her, a surefire sign she was not impressed.

"I did, yes," I admitted. "I lost my temper and let it get the better of me. Not something of which I am overly proud of."

My blunt admittance and refusal to try to dodge her charge caught Lallandri'av by surprise. I could see it in how she stiffened and her jaw worked, though most of her was still hidden behind her magic.

"You're an intriguing one, Korr'ok," she mused. As she leaned forward, she exposed the perfect lines of her face and midnight skin, leading back to her wondrous mane of hair, the strands a voluminous deep blue that rippled and practically glowed of its own accord.

"Not really," I replied courteously. "I'm just not interested in politics."

"You are a Sidhe," she countered. "That comes with the territory."

"Life is a lot more fun when you don't play the game."

She laughed in a frosty tone that echoed off the walls. "Oh, really? And what do you call what you were doing in The Place Behind on Dannorax's court? You played your own game there. Punishing those you wanted. Including the half-breed."

My eyes narrowed. "How did you know about that?"

"Word travels fast." She refused to say more.

"Perhaps it was a game," I acceded. "But it was not politics like this. I despise it. Having to pretend to feel one way, to gain the loyalty of someone needed to betray a third party, all while gaining solely for yourself as best you can? Manipulative and entirely devoid of any sort of respect."

"You would be very good at it."

I shrugged, not caving.

"You attacked my men," she said. "On my land. They are considered an extension of my persona. Given your status within House Duloke—whether you like it or not—that could be seen as an act of war."

"So, go to war then," I said bluntly. "It doesn't benefit you in any way. Even with Kraw'ok in charge, you're still weaker, albeit only barely. You might be able to use your superior intellect and experience to outmaneuver him, but it would have to be by enough to win swiftly. Otherwise, they will grind you down."

The Dark Lady leaned back, crossing her legs with a flourish. "Your tactical analysis is impressive. Even for one gone so long."

"I like to stay informed," I replied.

"I could use one such as you."

I laughed. "Just kill me now. Your offer is generous," I added to assuage any insult, "of that there is no doubt. But I do not wish to live amid a den of vipers who would sooner see me dead than use my help. Thank you, but no."

"Then what shall I do with you? In the past, I have had others executed for such offenses."

Taking a deep breath, rolling my head from side to side, I locked gazes with her. "You could try that," I said, the barest hint of a challenge underscoring my words. "But you know as well as I do that there's no guarantee you would win."

The Dark Lady might have an edge in raw power, but she had sat on her throne for a long time. Her combat skills were not up to par. Not enough, I would wager, to offset the power differences between us.

"I must do something," she said. "I would appear weak if I let such a thing slip by."

"Of course. You *could* try to have me executed," I said slowly, a plan forming. "Or …"

"You have an alternative suggestion?"

"I might," I said. "Mila is a half-breed. Of your house."

"Yes," the Dark Lady said tightly. "Her appearance raises many questions. The potential that a traitor is still amid my ranks is … irritating."

"Then let me rid you of two problems," I suggested, not quite able to believe that I was thinking of going ahead with the plan.

Not because it wouldn't succeed. There was a high likelihood I could pull it off. That wasn't it, but rather what my pulling it off would mean.

For Mila *and* me.

"I'm listening," the Dark Lady said, leaning forward as her lips curled upward in a wicked smile.

And so, in slow terms at first, but with growing confidence, I set the future of Mila and myself into stone.

I just had to hope she was interested in the idea.

CHAPTER FORTY-ONE

Mila

One thing I had learned about the Great Houses of the Fae was that Duloke was supposed to be the strongest, "most grand" of them all. That was what I'd been told by several people. If that were the case, I had to wonder how.

"Talk about depressing," I muttered as we stepped through a portal into a dark-lit hallway, the walls and floor barely visible. Far in the distance, a single torch flickered pitifully, its light struggling to keep back the dark. The walls were dank, and I was sure if I reached out to run a finger along them, they would be covered in slime. "You live here?"

Kraw'ok sniffed haughtily. "*I* don't."

"Ah, we're in the dungeons then, are we? Dank,

dark, and depressing. Got it. Gonna throw me in a cell and forget about me until I'm nothing but bones?"

The head of House Duloke looked down at me. I shivered, trying to shove aside the eerie similarities between him and his brother. There was no mistaking them for anything but brothers. Korr'ok was taller, more muscular, and with less of a hatred-filled sneer permanently etched onto his face, but the jaw lines and strong, straight nose were clearly family traits.

"Do you ever stop running your mouth?"

"Not until it's fit," I snarked back under my breath.

"Huh?"

"Never mind. It'll go over your horns."

Kraw'ok tightened his grip on my arm, using it to shove me hard against the nasty walls. "You will learn to show some respect. I saved your life, *half-breed*."

"My life was fine before you got involved with it, traitor. Killer of your own blood."

The Fae snorted and started walking again, dragging me with him. "That means nothing in this world. Only humans cling to that silly delusion."

I recalled how Korr'ok had reacted upon hearing his family had been slaughtered. Fae might not care to the same extent humans did, but he had certainly experienced *some* emotion. Far more than Kraw'ok displayed, that was for sure.

Okay, so he's a psychopath. Sociopath. Whichever the insane emotionless one is.

I could never remember. Labels didn't matter, but it did mean I would be on a knife's edge the entire time I was imprisoned there. Hopefully, that wouldn't be long, but I couldn't bank on it. There were bound to be defenses that Korr'ok had to bull his way through before he got to me.

If he'd even meant it.

Things between us were … well, confusing was a generous way to put it. Our relationship, such as it was, had started on dubious terms, to say the least, when he'd basically branded me in front of his Jury peers against my will. Yet, despite those actions and his distinctly harsh outer persona, I'd be a liar if I said there wasn't something more.

A spark that had pushed us both past the usual boundaries of what such a relationship should entail. He hadn't punished me—not really—and I hadn't come to hate him. In fact, just the opposite. Reluctantly, he showed me the new world I was exposed to, teaching me about it bit by bit.

Ensuring I wouldn't break the law again. He was, in a way, protecting me.

It wasn't until I'd lain dying in his arms, however, that I'd broken through. Seen the real side of him. A side that he never showed anyone. After all, if they knew he had emotions, if he *cared*, then how would he be seen as a monster?

But his anguish had been real.

I sighed heavily, understanding why he'd acted so betrayed upon seeing me. To him, he'd lost me ... only to find out he hadn't really known me to begin with.

As it turns out, I never really knew myself, either. A half-breed Fae-human mix?

It explained a lot, and I was glad to be alive, but I feared that in doing so, I might have lost Korr'ok forever.

Please, give me a chance to show you that I wasn't faking any of it. Let me show you that I l—

"I bet you're wondering why I went to such lengths to steal you out from under Korr'ok, don't you?"

I was snapped out of my thoughts as we paused in front of a blank spot on the wall. The only sign it was different was it looked clean*er*. Definitely still not clean, just not slime covered.

"Not really," I sighed. "It's fairly obvious."

"Oh, is it?" he taunted. "Please, enlighten me."

"Leverage. You killed your family, ensuring you could sit on the throne without any challengers with a better claim to it. Korr'ok turns up alive, and since he's older, he has a better claim to it than you. He's also not a known traitor, so he probably could have a lot of support from the rest of the House. You take me, threaten to kill me if he tries anything. Leverage."

"That is certainly part of it," he agreed. "But there's more. You see, I do have support in the rest of the House. And I make sure to reward that support well."

"What does that have to do with me?"

Kraw'ok chuckled nastily and pressed on a stone in the wall, causing the entire section to slide away. Inside, a glowing red entity turned to face me, giving me a very familiar lopsided grin.

"Hello, *Mila*," Irrt'ok hissed, shooting toward me.

I stepped back, but Kraw'ok's bulk prevented me from going anywhere. Irrt'ok reached the edge of the room beyond the hidden door and abruptly halted.

"Irrt'ok is confined to these chambers," Kraw'ok explained. "Once he's better, however …"

I retched at the implication that I would be handed over to the disgusting Fae. The last time I had seen him, he'd been inhabiting Victor the baker's body, and I couldn't get that image from my head.

"Now that you know your ultimate fate," the

Dark Lord of Duloke rumbled, "come, let me show you the *other* reason."

He yanked me away hard enough to nearly dislocate my shoulder, pulling me up a set of stairs after him. I stumbled to try to keep up with his long legs but was pulled along forcefully.

"How far away is this 'real reason'?" I asked.

"She's not far."

That time I lost my footing out of surprise. "She?"

"Oh, yes, *she*," the head of House Duloke confirmed. "The *real* reason Korr'ok left so long ago."

I felt my stomach sink. "He said he left because he was bored and knew he'd never rule, so he wanted to go make a life for himself elsewhere."

"Is that so?" Kraw'ok laughed heartily. "I wonder how long it took for him to start telling himself that. Does he believe it now? Probably."

We exited the stairwell into a nicer but still dim section of the House. My eyes saw signs of scuffling. Broken pictures, marks on the wall, pieces of crumbled stone not cleaned up.

The evidence of Kraw'ok's coup was still fresh on the minds of anyone who walked the halls. A reminder, perhaps, of what lengths he would go to for power? I wouldn't put that past someone like him.

"And this is where you will stay," Kraw'ok

announced abruptly, pushing open one side of a set of standard double doors. "I can't stay, business to attend to, but I'm sure you two have *lots* to catch up on."

He shoved me through the door and then closed them behind me. The sound of a lock sliding shut followed.

"Great," I muttered, staring around the room. It, at least, was brightly lit. Chairs and a couch decorated the center of the room, with several small tables holding myriad objects pushed up against the walls.

There were three more doors, one on each wall. Torchlight glittered everywhere, giving the place a golden hue to it.

"Trust me," a soft, feminine voice said. "You want it this way. It's better than when he shows interest."

The shudder that accompanied the voice was palpable. Footsteps announced the speaker's arrival as she emerged from the room to my left, the doors sliding open, revealing a library beyond.

She was tall and lithe but lacked the lines that indicated strength. The glowing eyes gave her away as Fae, however, so I doubted she was weak. But after seeing nothing but large, muscular men, it was quite a change. She was almost elfin in nature, except she had to be close to six feet tall.

"I'm Fahll'ok," she said, lifting a slim hand in greeting.

My attention momentarily reverted away from the library as I took her greeting. "Mila," I said with a shrug. "So, you're the reason Korr'ok left this place?"

Fahll'ok sighed. "He's been so angry ever since learning his brother was alive. I guess I shouldn't be surprised he's trotted that back out."

"I don't get it. Can you explain?" I asked. "Are you and Korr'ok …"

"*Were*," Fahll'ok said sternly. "We *were* a thing. A long, long time ago."

"What happened?"

"I made a really bad decision," she said.

"Kraw'ok."

The Fae nodded, long brown hair shimmering with the movement, reflecting the torchlight, turning her locks amber. "Yes. I chose him. A terrible mistake, and one I'm constantly paying for all this time later."

I tried to comprehend why she would stay with someone for two hundred years if it were a mistake.

"Why?" I whispered. "Why stay? Why have I never heard about you?"

"Korr'ok was hurt," she said. "Not that I can blame him. I was young and capricious back then. I … don't know what I was thinking."

"I see." I tried to hide the uncertainty in my voice.

If Korr'ok came for me and found his old flame as well … what would he do? Would he still want to take me with him? Or would a full-blooded Fae be more to his liking?

"You wonder why I haven't left," Fahll'ok said, misinterpreting my body language.

"Well, yes. That's one thing I'm wondering."

"At first, it was my family. He took my sister and infant brother and threatened to kill them if I left his side."

"Bastard," I snarled, fury renewed at Korr'ok's piece-of-shit brother.

"But then he got a child on me," she whispered. "I can't leave. Not until I have my son with me. So, I stay."

The misery Fahll'ok was suffering couldn't be ignored.

"Hopefully, you won't have to stay for much longer," I said, trying to keep the resignation from my voice.

"What do you mean?"

"Korr'ok is coming," I said.

"What? Are you sure?"

"Yes."

What remained to be seen, what was currently throwing everything I thought I was figuring out for a loop, was which one of us would be leaving with him.

Soon enough, I would find just how he *really* felt about me.

I wasn't sure I was going to like the answer.

CHAPTER FORTY-TWO

Korr'ok

By the time I arrived outside the gates of House Duloke, I had gathered quite a crowd. Word had spread during my walk up the long, sloped hill that rose to the seat of all power in Duloke. People emerged from their houses to line the street. None spoke, but all eyes watched me as I went past, shoulders straight, head held high. They stared, and in their eyes, I read an eagerness. They knew why I was there. There could only be one reason to approach like that in the open. And they looked forward to it.

I didn't. It wasn't what I wanted, not at all. I would have been more than content to take Mila from Lady Mirgave and leave Faerie behind forever. But now, returning to the place that had long been my home and seeing the hope on their faces, I knew there was no way I could turn back.

Not from them ...

And not from Mila.

That blue-eyed, half-Fae firecracker who never strayed far from my mind. Her death had hurt me, and in that pain and the realization of her true nature, I'd sought anger. A place I'd sought refuge many times before. My fury protected me from many things, but it couldn't protect me from her. By being angry at her, I had only hurt myself.

She deserved more. Deserved everything I could ever give and more. I just had to hope it would be enough to win her back.

The gargoyle-topped walls of House Duloke loomed large over me, a reminder of the obstacle in my way. There was a step I had to take before I could, hopefully, take Mila as my own. Not just her forgiveness either. No, first, I had to do something I'd sworn to myself for ages I didn't want. Something I *still* didn't have any desire for.

The crowd peeled back as I stepped up and wrapped my hands around the Faerie steel, the cool metal set into the stone walls on either side, blocking the path of any who tried to enter. For as long as I'd lived there, the gates had stayed open. My father had been willing to meet with anyone to offer a favor.

Duloke had been a good place to live under his rule, and as a power, we'd grown into the strongest House in all Faerie. Lord of lords, my father had been. A Fae, no less, unafraid to rule with an iron fist, to trample his enemies beneath his feet, and the best trickster that lived. Always able to turn the wording of any agreement in his favor.

Living in Fae was not an *idyllic* place by any means. But we had lived *good*. There was food aplenty, and the only enemies were the Fae around you. War was not a threat.

Now, looking through the gates, the entire House seemed to sag under the soft violet light that illuminated all of Faerie. It looked worn and old. Vulnerable.

Kraw'ok was scared, and the building reflected it.

"Coward," I growled, reaching up to take hold of the gates. The wards cast upon them unloaded their magic into me. I threw my head back and howled as red magic cascaded down into my arms, etching lines into my arms and down my back. The energy built and built, coalescing into a glowing ball of incandescent red energy half a yard across in front of me. All around, the air turned an opaque red, hiding me from external eyes.

The pain was nigh intolerable, and my body took a pounding from the magical assault, but I hung on, bellowing my defiance back at the gates while shunting every ounce of power I could into the ball.

Slowly, the air cleared, and an audible gasp went up from the crowd as they realized I was still standing. The gates were dull and listless now. Stripped of their power.

"My turn," I smiled and unleashed the ball of energy I'd been holding. It flew forward, blasting open the gates and heading up the cobblestones to the front of the house, where it exploded outward, shattering every window and announcing my presence with a shriek.

The shockwave ripped out in every direction, pulling at my hair and clothes, but I leaned forward, absorbing the impact and stepping through the ruined gates onto the property.

"Let the Lord of House Duloke come forth!" I bellowed, wondering if my brother would recognize the true reason I'd come.

I doubted it.

My arrival was loud enough that it didn't take long for a response, which came in the form of the entrance opening wide, spitting out two columns of Fae warriors in full battle regalia. They came marching at the double toward me but slowed far enough away that they weren't coming to fight. Not yet at least.

Then, with the entrance glowing blue to hide him in shadow until he had exited the house, my brother strode forth, flanked on either side by women who clearly would have preferred to be anywhere *but* at Kraw'ok's side.

"Come for something?" he called, stopping shy of the line of guards, though they had opened a space for him and his entourage.

"Yes," I replied stonily, ignoring the taunting call behind his words.

Beside him, Mila shifted slightly, her eyes looking at me, then away, then back to me. She was looking at Fahll'ok, I noted, curious as to why she kept looking at the other woman.

As for Fahll'ok, she looked much the same as two centuries earlier. Tall, lithe, beautiful ... and no longer interesting at all. She looked worried and concerned, but her attention wasn't on Kraw'ok, or even me. It was behind her. Within the House? I glanced back at the open doorway. What was my brother up to in there?

"You don't honestly think that I'm going to just give them up, do you?" Kraw'ok replied, trying to sound confident. I could see how his eyes darted past me at the crowd, eyeing the large group of Fae.

I laughed, the sound ringing loud and clear. "You misunderstand ... *brother*," I said, the last word a snarl that produced audible silence from all parties. "I'm not here for the women."

Mila's face fell at that, but I didn't let it distract me. I couldn't. After all, the recognition was just forming on Kraw'ok's face as I laughed my denial.

"That's right," I said, speaking clearly now, so

there would be no doubt. "I'm here for *you*! I name you traitor and usurper of a throne that rightfully belongs to me. Here, now, in front of the people of our House, I challenge *you*."

Mila's head snapped up at that, eyes wide. I gave her a wink. Hopefully, she would take it the way I intended. That I intended to fight my brother for the right to rule House Duloke. And that when I won, the first thing I intended to do was—

"*I accept*," Kraw'ok hissed, suddenly flying at me with outstretched arms, propelled by a wave of magic.

I should have seen the poor faith but technically legal attack coming. He *had* accepted the challenge before coming at me. By a millisecond. Technicalities were all that mattered to the Fae, however, and as he slammed into my midsection, I was forced to remember that.

We went down, Kraw'ok raining blows on me as I fought to get my arms around to protect my face. His surprise allowed him to strike first, and he made the most of it. By the time I threw him aside, my face and forearms were streaming thick blood from a number of cuts. None debilitating, however.

I summoned a circular shield of magic as my brother returned, delivering a thunderous blow to my protection, courtesy of the sword he'd taken from one of his attending guards.

With a snarl, I flung out a hand, magic yanking a second sword free of its sheath and sending it flying toward me. I gripped the hilt just in time to block another strike, my forearms ringing from the blow.

"I'm going to kill you, just like I killed them," Kraw'ok growled, just loud enough for me to hear.

My foot swept out, scything through his legs in response, sending him falling to the ground. I leaped to my feet and stabbed down with the sword, but he swatted it away, using his other hand to throw more magic at me. I batted it aside, but the movement forced me back several steps, giving him time to get to his feet and set himself.

"Give it up," I said. "And I'll let you live."

And I would. The Fae didn't lie. I just never said for how *long*.

Kraw'ok, of course, knew this, which was why he didn't bother with a reply, just swept in with lightning-fast strikes, the sword blurring as he attacked. The speed and fury were expected, but his skill was not something I was ready for. He drove me back, step after step, toward the remnants of the front gate.

Clearly, he'd been practicing.

His mouth pulled back in a sneer as we crossed

through the gates into the city that sprawled down the hill around the massive house.

"You're going to lose," he taunted as our blades clashed, sparks flying. With a shove, he pushed me backward. "All of this for nothing. What a waste."

I kept silent, waiting for him to come at me. Predictably, my silence goaded him on. We fought back down the hill I'd climbed, the people of our House silent around us, watching from either side.

"She's going to be mine," Kraw'ok said, a hint of frustration in his voice as the fight continued and I didn't speak. "I'll get her with child. Born of my seed, deep in her body."

If he expected that to make me mad, he was right. But I harnessed that anger and poured it into the speed of my blade. Snarling, I went on the offensive for the first time, driving him back.

Up the hill we went, my sword darting left and right, striking like lightning. I sent magic surging into the blade, the edge peeling a sliver straight out of his blade as I struck downward from overhead, forcing my brother to backpedal and turn his sword over to present the unspoiled edge.

"There's something you need to know," I stated as I drove him back through the gates, muscles bunched with fury. "Something I want everyone to hear. So that there is no confusion, now or going forward."

Kraw'ok tried to use magic, but I attacked faster, preventing him from focusing enough to release it.

"I say this now," I called loudly, my voice carrying to the soldiers and the crowd beyond the gates. "So that all will know and understand the consequence. Let it be clear."

"Just *die* already!" Kraw'ok jeered, interrupting me. "Then I will take my prize."

I swatted the sword out to the side and planted a boot in his chest, sending him hurtling backward through a stone sculpture in the middle of a nearby garden.

"SHE IS MINE!" I howled at the top of my lungs, pointing at Mila.

My magic surged out, snatching her from where she was and yanking her over to me. I met her, my free arm holding her clear of the ground as I kissed her long and hard, bending her over to dip her. Her arms wrapped around my neck, and she held on tight.

With a roar, Kraw'ok came at me, sword held high.

I brought my blade up to block the mighty strike.

And our blades shattered on impact, pieces scattering everywhere. Behind me, Mila hissed in surprise.

My brother reacted first, chopping down on my wrist, sending the hilt and a few inches of blade flying off. I backed up, but his magic caught my heel and tripped me. It was such a simple move, so casual and basic. I never saw it coming. I went down, and he was on me in a flash, the six inches or so that remained of his blade slicing down toward my throat.

I grabbed his wrists and held on, trying to push him back. We stayed locked in combat, my strength against his leverage. I was bigger, but he had the better position.

Slowly but surely, the blade dropped toward my neck, ready to slice it open to my spine. Kraw'ok knew it, and he grinned.

"I have you now," he spat.

"Almost," I said. "But you forgot one thing."

"What's that?" he asked.

"*He's mine*," Mila snarled just as she drove my sword through his chest from behind, the very tip of the shortened blade emerging from the other side, blood pouring down its jagged edge and onto me.

CHAPTER FORTY-THREE

Mila

Kraw'ok had a moment to gasp, his body going stiff. Then a blade of pure energy extended from Korr'ok's forearm, and he took the head from his brother's body in one sharp motion.

Grunting, he tossed the body aside and stood rapidly to tower over me, leaning down and examining my face.

"Are you okay?" he asked quietly, not entirely able to keep composed, worry slipping through.

I covered a smile under the guise of touching the wound on my forehead, well aware it was bleeding profusely. I tore a piece off half his shirt and pressed it to the wound, holding it firm.

"I'll be fine," I assured him, somehow stirred by the sight of his firm stomach under the ragged hem of his shirt, despite the blood streaming down my right side. "Just a piece of the blade."

"Are you sure? Did he hurt you? Touch you somehow? Anything?"

"I'm fine," I repeated, my body on fire, and not all of it from the shard that had cut me wide. When I'd gone flying across the battlefield, only to be kissed like that in front of everyone, Korr'ok had awoken something in me that wasn't about to go away anytime soon.

But it wasn't just my body. In my mind, something had *clicked*. A realization, perhaps, one I hadn't realized I was waiting for.

"I'm glad you're okay," he said. "When he showed up at House Mirgave like that, I worried I might not see you again."

"Quite the change from the Korr'ok of a few hours before," I said, unable to keep my voice even.

"I thought you had lied to me," I said. "The idea that you could go through your entire life unaware that you were different seemed impossible."

"There's a big difference between knowing on some level that you're different and realizing you're a half-breed between humans and Fae," I countered, crossing my arms. I felt a bit silly with his shirt half-adhered to my forehead, but I knew we needed to get this out and over with. "I spent most of my life being beaten up. I thought that, and the fact I healed quickly, was what made me different. Not ... this."

I gestured around me for emphasis.

"I believe you now," he said. "And I'm going to spend a long, *long* time making it up to you so that you believe me."

"Are you now?" I said with a wry smile.

"Oh, yes," he said.

"And what makes you think I'm going to let you?" I teased, my lips moving upward in a smile, my tone light.

"Because you want to live," he said deadpan.

"Excuse me?" I blinked rapidly, licking my lips. "Are you going to kill me if I don't?"

"Of course not," he said. "I would die defending you. But I promised the Dark Lady of Mirgave that, in exchange for not pressing any charges against me for striking her guards and letting me go, I would take you as my wife and rid her of a thorn in her side."

Now my jaw really did hit the ground. "So, you ... just offered me up as your bride to some random lady?"

"To myself," he said firmly. "I didn't offer you to anyone. I *claimed* you. You're mine, Mila. And that is the way I intend it to *always* be."

I stared at him. He stared back. Red eyes into blue.

"Can we even do that?" I asked, recalling those differences. "I'm part of a different house. Are we able to just … marry?"

He grinned.

"What?"

"You're asking if it's possible," he said. "Which means you've already accepted the idea of being my wife. You just have doubts that it's allowed. Not that you don't want me."

"Well, um, uh, I mean, I just …" I fell silent.

Shit. He was right. I *had* done that.

"I'm glad it's settled, then," he said.

"It is *not* settled," I said defiantly, my mind suddenly engaging again. "There are two problems here."

"There are?"

"Yes," I said, tapping my breastbone. "First, you take this thing out of me. I am *not* going to be controlled like that by anyone ever again. I am going to be *free*."

"Of course," he said instantly. "Once you're healed, we will undo the marking. Now that I am Lord of Duloke, even Dannorax won't challenge that. It's over. What is the second thing?"

"Secondly," I said, crossing my arms, "I'm not going to marry someone unless they love each other."

"Love," he repeated.

"I'm not into arranged marriages. You had better figure it out, mister. I'm not sure if Fae have a concept of it, but I am half human, and to me, it means a lot."

"What does it mean to you?" he asked softly.

"My definition is my own," I told him. "It's different for everyone."

He thought about it, then nodded. "I have claimed you, Mila. On several occasions. I want you as mine. Nobody else's but mine. The idea of us not being together, of you not being with me, is repulsive. The thought of you being with another man drives me berserk with rage. You don't belong there. You belong with me."

"Great," I said, fighting down the insane lust that surged through me every time he claimed me as his like that. It was tough to hate when such a powerful, hulking person stated something so unequivocally like that.

But it wasn't what I wanted to hear.

"That wasn't the right response," he said, confused. "Was it?"

I shrugged. "It wasn't wrong. I believe you when you say all that. I feel it. And I'm okay with it, Korr'ok. But it's only *half*."

His brow furrowed.

"Also," I said, "can we finish this somewhere else? Maybe where the guards, half the city, and your brother's headless body aren't watching?"

That snapped him out of it. He started barking orders at the guards, then called to the people of the city, asking for volunteers to come into the House and begin work on restoring it.

Dozens came without hesitation. I watched as he effortlessly slid into the position of Lord of House Duloke.

He might have never wanted the responsibility, but there was no denying it. He was born to it.

"Come," he said, taking my hand and leading me over to Fahll'ok, who was standing around uncertainly, waiting to be told what to do.

A wave of nerves tightened my shoulders as we drew close. Despite what Korr'ok had told me, I couldn't help but feel like he wanted to choose her. The woman of his past. The *true* Fae, not a half-breed like me.

"You're free," he told her. "You may go."

I touched his bicep. "She has a son," I said quietly. "Your brother was holding him hostage."

The snarl that exploded from Korr'ok sent both of us women back a step. "Of course he did. Come, let us get your child. I would have you never set foot in the House again unless it is your desire, Fahll'ok. You've been punished enough."

Then he took *my* arm and led me into the House.

It wasn't how I expected a human to handle

such things, but as I had to keep reminding myself, I wasn't among humans anymore. I was living with Fae, and they were very, very different.

CHAPTER FORTY-FOUR

Mila

"Have you had more time to think about what I said?" I asked as Fahll'ok and her son exited the throne room, excited to start a new life somewhere far from the seat of power.

All my worries had proven to be fruitless. I should have known it was just Kraw'ok trying to be a dick by showing her to me. Another way he'd sought to undermine his brother.

"I have," he said thoughtfully.

"What did you come up with?" I asked, curious about where his mind was leading him. Would he understand what I needed him to say? What I had to hear before I could truly let myself be with him?

"You said I was only saying half of what I had to say. And that threw me for a loop at first," I rumbled slowly, "because I was saying everything. I was telling you that I wanted you to be mine. I claimed you in front of everyone."

I stiffened as worry built that he hadn't understood what I'd meant.

"It wasn't until I saw Fahll'ok and her son together that it came into perspective." He stood, turning to face me on the chair I sat in on his right, a much smaller, less ornate version of his throne. "You are mine, Mila. I will claim you in front of anyone, challenge anyone for you. And I do so because I want you. Because *I* care about *you*. Those are my feelings. I long for you. Every minute we're apart, my body aches for you. My mind misses you. My soul misses you. The very core of what makes me a Faerie is *better* with you around."

A smile blossomed on my face. He *had* understood.

"That is why I want you to be my wife," he said, dropping to one knee. "My lady. The half-human, half-Fae woman that I *love*."

I stared.

"Perhaps my definition of it isn't perfect," he added hurriedly. "But it's *my* definition of it. I love you, Mila."

I shuddered.

"I love you," I whispered. "In some strange way, throughout all this, I have managed to fall in love with you."

He reached for me and placed a hand on my chest. I stayed perfectly still, watching his face as warmth built under his palm, turning to heat. My skin started to crawl, but I fought through it, my eyes locked on his. The pain grew as the heat burned me.

I didn't cry out.

Red and gold light swirled around his fingers, catching my eyes, but I couldn't tear them away from him. Not yet. Irritation turned to agony. I gritted my teeth, breathing sharply as he pulled the bond from my chest.

As it tore free, I cried out.

The pain receded swiftly, and my white-knuckled grip on the chair's arms eased, blood returning to the digits. I breathed, refocusing my gaze on Korr'ok, who still had a hand on my chest.

"Hi," he said softly.

I smiled. "Hi." I took stock. "I don't feel any different."

"Nor should you. It was only active when I used it. Why? What did you expect?"

I blushed a little. "I figured that this ... uh, *feeling* inside me would calm. That I wouldn't be quite as, um, well, you know ..."

The tips of his fingers slid slowly past my collarbone while he grinned. "Oh, so you thought this wasn't natural? That the way I make your body react was something I made you feel?"

"Well, not entirely," I whispered as he stole my voice. "But perhaps amplified."

"Nope," he chuckled. "That's *all* you."

"Oh," I said.

He placed a hand on my inner thigh, causing all sorts of chemical reactions in my brain.

"*Oh.*"

"Come with me," he said, standing abruptly.

"Where are we going?"

"Somewhere private," he rumbled. "So I can fuck your brains out until that feeling fades."

"Uh-huh," I managed, stumbling down the steps of the throne after him. "Yeah. That sounds good."

Korr'ok swept me up from the third-last step into his arms, holding me close.

"And then," he said, carrying me from the throne room pressed hard against his powerful chest, his equally bulging arms wrapped entirely around my tiny body, "you're going to give me what you owe me."

"What's that?" I asked, suddenly nervous.

"A second date," he said, reminding me that I'd only ever ended up going on one with him.

CHAPTER FORTY-FIVE

Mila

"Well, that's that," I said as the stone door closed behind us, sealing off Irrt'ok's corpse. "Any other loose ends we need to handle?"

It had taken us two days to get around to dealing with him. In the flurry of activity that had followed the fall of Kraw'ok, he had sort of slipped my mind for a bit.

"Just one," he said.

"What's that?" I asked, curious.

"Actually, two, now that I think about it. First, we must get married," he said, smiling at me. "I don't want to put that off for too long."

"So, we should get to planning?" I bit my lip at the flutter of my heart.

"Oh, yes. There's lots of planning that must be done. I'm Lord of House Duloke now. I have to plan for the here and now and the future."

"The future?"

He grinned. "Oh, yes."

"And what future are you referring to?" I asked cautiously.

"The one that keeps my House firmly under control."

I frowned at him, letting him guide us up the stairs. We went up past the main level of the House and continued ascending.

"What are you planning?" I asked. "What will keep your House, or *our* House, under control?"

Korr'ok kept smiling like a madman, leading me out onto the roof, its flat surface bathed in the strange purple glow that was the light in Fae.

"An heir," he growled, lifting me and pushing me back into the nearest wall.

My legs wrapped around him, my hands settling down his back. "An heir?" I echoed once I'd found my voice again. "You want an heir?"

He growled, kissing my neck. "As soon as you let me, I will put a baby in you."

My body did all sorts of strange things then.

Growing up the way I had, living the life I'd lived, I'd never expected that children would be in my future. I could never have justified bringing them into a world like that.

But now, my world was different.

"A baby," I whispered, momentarily distracted from everything else.

Korr'ok took a pause, pulling his mouth away from my neck. "Or two," he rumbled suggestively. "Or three."

He wanted a big family. I bit my lip, but there was no sense in trying to stop the grin from fading. It was a dream come true.

"We can have kids," I said. "But under one condition."

"Name it."

"They have to be brought up with knowledge of their human heritage. I want them to know where their mother came from and what belongs to them."

Korr'ok winced. "My love, you cannot step foot on Earth for ten years, and I will not go without you. Must we wait that long?"

Right. I'd forgotten that little detail. I also didn't want to wait that long for kids. My human side wanted them sooner.

I pressed a finger into his sternum. "Then the day I can return, we will go. *Promise me this*, Korr'ok."

He stared straight into my eyes, the red glow extra bright. "I swear it. On that day, I will take you."

"Okay," I whispered, satisfied with the vow. "Now, today, right here, right now, you take me another way. Got it?"

With a growl, the fingers of his left hand grabbed the collar of my shirt and ripped it away. I gasped.

"Now, how am I supposed to walk around when we're done?" I pointed out.

Korr'ok pulled my pants off the same way, leaving me in my underwear. "What makes you think you're going to be able to walk?" he rumbled, taking his shirt off and laying it on the floor as a makeshift blanket.

"What are you going to do? Break my legs?" I joked.

He rolled his eyes, and I continued letting him guide me down on my back.

We could worry about clothes later.

As he leaned over me, I noticed something dangling from his neck. It was a medallion. My eyes narrowed as I focused on it. I'd seen it before. It was the one he'd hidden in the drawer.

"You're wearing it now," I whispered as he kissed my neck, my hands running up the back of his head, grabbing his horns and pulling him into me.

"Yes."

"Why?"

He paused, arching an eyebrow as he looked

up, his face telling me he had more important things to focus on. "Because it is the symbol of my House. I have come home. It's now appropriate to wear it again."

"Oh," I said.

"Now, can I continue?" he asked, kissing his way down my body, leaving me a squirming mess well before his tongue rolled across my clit for the first time, sending spikes of beautiful agony deep into my body, a teaser of what was to come.

"Yeah, okay, you can keep going," I moaned, my back arching as he inserted a finger, touching all the right buttons to make me tremble.

"Glad to hear it," he said from between my thighs, moments before filling me with a second finger, curling them both up as they moved deeper inside me, touching my most sensitive areas.

I gasped, clutching his shirt, desperate for something to hold onto. Without speaking, he grabbed my hand and placed it on the back of his head. Eagerly, I latched on with both, pulling him in tight, pushing my sopping cunt into his greedy mouth. I wanted his tongue, needed it, craved it ...

The answering growl vibrated through my pussy, simply adding to the wonderous sensations he was inflicting upon me, driving me closer to the edge without slowing. One by one, the muscles of my body tensed, starting from my toes and the back of my neck and moving inward and between my legs, until I was all but frozen, gasping, on the cusp of—

"Ffffuuckkkkk," I moaned as I shook violently, unable to control the throbbing sensation as it flooded my body, pummeling my mind into mush while endorphins rode my bloodstream like surfers, filling me from the tips of my fingers to my toes with their warm.

But there was no time to recover. Korr'ok kept licking, his tongue not stopping, his fingers sliding in and out, brushing my g-spot every time. My face closed down, eyes glued shut, and the only thing I could focus on was the absolute hammer wave of pressure on my clit.

"I don't think—oh, god." My tune changed in an instant as my body warned me it would come *again*, a second time, without a cooldown.

Which was precisely when he added a third finger, slipping it in, stretching me ever so slightly more.

I twitched so hard my pussy bounced off his chin. At the moment, I didn't care, but I was sure we'd laugh about it later.

This time, Korr'ok slowed himself as I shuddered down from the highs of a mind-blowing orgasm, all but melting into the roof. He and his tongue brought me down to rest, where I lay for a minute—or maybe more. I had no idea.

All I knew was that I was breathing and a warm smile was fixed on my face. Even if I'd wanted to, I didn't have the energy to make it go away.

Then hands were lifting me into the air, holding me against a body carved from stone as Korr'ok lay flat, taking his time to settle, leaving me straddling him, his cock flat to his stomach, the shaft pressing up between my lips. Idly, I ground my hips against it, enjoying the shivers it produced in both of us.

Wordlessly, I knew it was time when we were both no longer satisfied with the tease and needed *more*. I slid my hips a hair forward, reaching behind to grab his thick cock and guide it into my entrance.

The angle meant he slid the entire tip in at once, drawing a gasp from my lips. Hands gripped my hips and lifted me, easing the pressure on my insides until I'd begun to adapt.

We locked eyes, Korr'ok's gaze brightening as my face tightened with every inch that all but impaled me as I was settled onto him. My pussy ached deliciously as I took him deep, filling me in a way no other man had.

Or would.

That was it, I realized with a start, my eyes flying open to stare down at Korr'ok, my fingers digging deep into his chest as I lifted and sank deep once more.

That was the last man I would be with forever. There would be nobody else for the rest of my life besides Korr'ok. He was *it*.

My forever.

"I love you," I whispered, grinding a little faster. "Now and forever."

His eyes widened, and he pushed his hips up a little, making me moan at the unexpected extra length inside me.

"As I've said all along," he growled, his hands sliding up my sides to play with my breasts, teasing my nipples. "You are *mine!*"

There was no more talking after that. My hips moved faster. His hands controlled the rest of my body. He had them on my breasts, my waist, and at one point, he wrapped a thick, meaty hand around my neck. I held onto his wrist, using it as leverage as I rode him wildly, shuddering with ecstasy at his power and dominance over me even while I had him on his back.

And then he exploded inside me, filling me with his cum, the blisteringly hot sensation shooting me over the edge, my walls clamping down around him, milking him greedily of every last drop. Then I collapsed onto his broad chest, rising and falling with his every breath as I recovered one gasp at a time.

"As I said," Korr'ok grunted, brushing loose strands out of my face. "*Mine.*"

EPILOGUE

Dannorax the Dragon

I stared down my snout at the speaker who had disturbed my peace. "You're sure about this?"

The being looking up at me stared crossly. "Do I really look like the type to make this sort of fucking bullshit up?"

Smoke curled up from my nostrils at his arrogance. The being calmed, but that was his only concession to my subtle display of anger.

"And what would you like me to do about it?"

The red-skinned monster with yellow eyes trembled with fury, his long fur-covered tail twitching around, the pointed tip eager to find a target to sink its razor-sharp edges into. "I want her brought in and punished. *Nobody* tries to bind me as a mate! It's against the law. You know this as well as I do. Do your job!"

I rose on four monstrous legs as the giant chamber darkened everywhere but my eyes. The being stiffened, resisting the downward pressure I was exerting with my mind.

"Do not presume to tell me what to do. You forget your place in my Court."

The demon struggled and fought. Truly the most stubborn of creatures. The more powerful they became, the more irritating they were to have around. It was no wonder they had been banished. He, however, had proven himself useful on more than one occasion.

I eased up on him, the lesson having sunk in. The demon straightened but said no more, showing he wouldn't engage in a contest of wills or more.

"I take it she did not succeed?"

The demon snorted. "Of course not. She's a nothing, a nobody. I got a look into her mind to get a picture of her and a name. I don't know who taught her to cast spells, but we need to find out. We can't have just anyone hand out this sort of magic to normals."

A rumble filled my belly. He had a point.

"Very well. Give me a description, a name, and where to send the Gray Knights to pick her up. Then we'll bring her to the Court for questioning and punishment," I said, a wicked grin spreading across my face.

It pleased me to no end to see them be punished. I looked forward indeed to the woman being brought in and tasting her fear as she was claimed. Perhaps even by the very same member of the Jury whom she'd tried to bind. Now that would be some delicious irony, indeed!

The demon Beliel spoke. "Her name is Lilith, and she runs a bakery on the edge of downtown."

>>>Click here to read about Mila and Korr'ok's first trip back to Earth with their family!<<<

Want more of the Twisted Court?

Click to get "The Demon Prince's Accidental Bride" (The Twisted Court Book 2)

OTHER BOOKS BY RILEY STORM

Thanks for checking out my other books!

Below you can find all my novels, divided up by series. The brackets indicate which of my worlds the series is written in. So dig in!

You can also go to my website for the full reading list and order:

Get the Reading Order

4 Princes

Prince of Fire

Prince of Storms

Prince of Iron

Prince of Tides

Soulbound Shifters (Soulbound Shifters #1)

The Wild Moon

As Darkness Falls

Fate Unbound

Blood & Fangs (Soulbound Shifters #2)

Soulbitten

Blood Letter

Queen of Darkness

Shattered Wolf (Soulbound Shifters #3)

Under a Cursed Moon

The 'Ex'-Mate Hunt

Bond of Fate

Dragons of Mount Aterna (Five Peaks #1)

The Complete Box Set - Link

Includes:

A Mate to Treasure

A Mate to Believe In

A Mate to Protect

A Mate to Embrace

Dragons of Mount Teres (Five Peaks #2)

The Complete Box Set - Link

Includes:

In a Dragon's Mind
In a Dragon's Heart
In a Dragon's Dream
In a Dragon's Soul

Dragons of Mount Valen (Five Peaks #3)

Her Dragon Guardian
Her Dragon Lord
Her Dragon Soulmate
Her Dragon Outcast

Dragons of Mount Atrox (Five Peaks #4)

Dragon's True Mate
Dragons' Second Chance Romance
Dragon's Fake Wedding Date
Dragon's Devotion

Dragons of Mount Rixa (Five Peaks #5)

Dragon Claimed
Dragon Loved

RILEY STORM

Dragon Bound
Dragon Savior

Storm Dragons (Winterspell Academy)

The Complete Box Set - Link

Includes:

Stolen by the Dragon
Trapped by the Dragon
Dragon's Chosen Mate

High House Ursa (Plymouth Falls #1)

Get the Complete Shifters of Plymouth Falls 15-Book Box Set

OR

Get the Five Book Bundle (Click Here)

Includes:

Bearing Secrets
Furever Loyal

Mated to the Enemy
Shifting Alliances
Blood Bearon

High House Canis (Plymouth Falls #2)

Get the Complete Shifters of Plymouth Falls 15-Book Box Set

OR

Get the Five Book Bundle (Click Here)

Includes:

Savage Love
Blood Mate
Moonlight Bride
Shadow's Howl
Royal Alpha

High House Draconis (Plymouth Falls #3)

Get the Complete Shifters of Plymouth Falls 15-Book Box Set

OR

Get the Five Book Bundle (Click Here)

Includes:

Fire Dragons Bride
Mated to the Water Dragon
Ice Dragon's Caress
Earth Dragon's Kiss
Claimed by the Dragon King

About the Author

Riley Storm

Riley is one of those early morning people you love to hate, because she swears she doesn't need caffeine, even though the coffee-maker is connected to her smartphone. She lives in a three-story townhouse by the good graces of a tabby cat who rules the house, the couch, the table, well, basically everywhere. When she's not groveling for forgiveness for neglecting to pet her kitty enough, Riley is strapped into her writing chair coming up with crazy worlds where she can make her own decisions of when feeding time is and how much coffee can be drunk without her friends—of which she has three—holding yet another intervention that they threaten to post on the internet.

Find her on:

Website: www.highhousepress.com
Facebook: Riley Storm Author
Email: riley@highhousepress.com

Printed in Great Britain
by Amazon